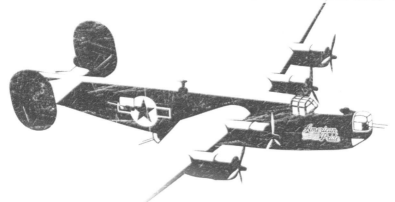

★ ★ A WORLD WAR II NOVEL ★ ★
GUNNER'S RUN
★ ★ ★ RICK BARRY ★ ★ ★

journeyforth®

Greenville, South Carolina

Library of Congress Cataloging-in-Publication Data

Barry, Rick (Richard C.), [date]
Gunner's run / Rick Barry.
    p. cm.
    Summary: In 1943, nineteen-year-old Jim Yoder serves as a waist gunner
aboard a B-24 in the United States Army Air Corps, but through a strange
chain of events, is trapped behind enemy lines in Hitler's Europe, alone, on
foot, and on the run, and finds himself returning to his family's staunchly
pacifist Mennonite roots.
    ISBN-13: 978-1-59166-761-2 (perfect bound pbk. : alk. paper) [1.
Soldiers—Fiction. 2. World War, 1939-1945—France—Fiction. 3.
Christian life—Fiction. 4. Pacifism—Fiction. 5. Mennonites—Fiction.
6. France—History—German occupation, 1940-1945—Fiction.] I. Title.
    PZ7.B28038Gun 2007
    [Fic]—dc22
                                                          2007002965

Cover photos: iStockphoto.com © Andrey Krasnov (wings), © Jo Ann Snover
(gunner's station), © Carl Stone (bullets); National Archives (B-24 Liberator)

All Scripture is quoted from the Authorized King James Version unless otherwise
noted.

Mack Gordon: From "Chattanooga Choo Choo." Lyrics by Mack Gordon
© 1941 Twentieth Century Music Corporation.

William E. Henley: From "Invictus" by William Earnest Henley, 1875.

Gunner's Run
Rick Barry

Design by Craig Oesterling
Page layout by Kelley Moore

© 2007 BJU Press
Greenville, South Carolina 29609
JourneyForth Books is a division of BJU Press.

ISBN 978-1-59166-761-2
eISBN 978-1-60682-413-9

15 14 13 12 11 10 9 8 7 6 5

Dedicated to those who
never returned

CONTENTS

Acknowledgments

Some novels may be the result of one individual's efforts, but this story is not one of them. In addition to weeks of researching on the Internet and in the Elkhart, Indiana, Public Library, I benefited from the critiques, memories, and encouragement of a number of friends.

My first thanks goes to my wife, Pam, who is my number one supporter and first reader in my writing projects. Others who scrutinized the manuscript and offered valuable suggestions are Ray Barry, Charles Howell, Brandt Dodson, Randall Dunn, Mary Hunter, Nick Harrison, and of course my editor, Nancy Lohr.

Additional thanks goes to several WW II veterans. Gerald (Jerry) Folsom, a former B-24 copilot and past president of the 44th Bomb Group Veterans Association, contributed his expertise by correcting several errors. Mike Billey, a radio operator of the 452nd Bomb Group, shared his memories of being under fire in a B-17, bailing out over hostile territory, and trusting in God during dreary months as a POW and on a forced march that cost the lives of many Allied soldiers. A former ball-turret gunner with the 94th Bomb Group, Don Kiser shared memories that were as fascinating as helpful. Like many veterans of WW II, the men mentioned above would not take a million dollars in exchange for the friendships and camaraderie that they gained during the war. At the same time, though, they would not take a million dollars to do it all over again. Sincere thanks to them and to many others just like them.

"Pilot to gunners. Keep your eyes open. We're almost to target. By now every German fighter in the area knows where to find us."

I pressed the intercom button to respond to Lt. Conover. "Bring 'em on. We're ready."

Manning the B-24's right-waist position, I could force my voice to sound confident, but the sharp claws of dread were digging deeper into my stomach. Inside thick gloves, my hands were clammy with perspiration despite the frigid wind whipping through the bomber's interior.

Once more I checked the machine gun mounted in the window of the Liberator's right side. Although I had test-fired it over the English Channel, I wanted to be certain everything was ready. I studied the ammunition feeding belt. At an altitude of twenty thousand feet, guns could freeze up in the -40° temperature. But everything seemed in order, ready for action.

Except me. I felt like vomiting.

Who knows? I thought. *Maybe we won't see any fighters. I wouldn't mind a milk run for once.*

I turned to see Dan Carlson, the gunner manning the left-waist window. Dan caught my eye and winked. He held up a gloved hand and curled his thumb and forefinger into the "okay" sign. Despite the green oxygen mask covering the lower half of Dan's face, I could tell that my pal was, as always, chomping a wad of chewing gum. Dan never went anywhere without a pack of Juicy Fruit.

I turned back to my own window. A visual sweep of the skies revealed no enemy fighters in sight. Against my will, my eyes strayed six feet to the left, to the only shiny patch in the bomber's olive-drab interior. Although the ground crew had riveted in this new piece of aluminum to repair the damage, my heart thumped harder when I recalled the Messerschmitt 109 whose 20-millimeter cannon had blasted a hole there just a week earlier.

So close that time. Gotta stick to my gun and shoot first. Can't let them get that close . . .

I didn't really need Lt. Conover's warning to keep my eyes open. Ever since our formation had crossed the English Channel and headed over German-occupied France, my eyes had roved back and forth, up and down, straining to pick out the dark specks that could signal Luftwaffe fighters. I squinted into the sun. Nothing.

No matter how hard I willed my muscles to relax, my shoulders ached from tension.

Involuntarily I glanced again at the spot where the Messerschmitt cannon had blown a gash in the Liberator's fuselage. I recalled the ear-splitting chaos of blasted metal. I could still feel the fragments pelting my flak vest and the sudden blast of icy air gushing into the aircraft.

For just an instant, I squeezed my eyes shut, as if that would stem the flow of memories.

So close that time . . .

The B-24 had suffered a serious wound on that mission. I knew the feeling. For a long while I had carried an invisible wound in my soul. Unlike me, though, bombers can be repaired to fly again. I knew of no patch that could heal the hurt inside of me.

Unexpectedly, it occurred to me that I should thank God for sparing my life. However, just as quickly as it had come, I brushed the notion aside.

If He had anything to do with sparing my life . . . well, He owed me.

Chapter 1

Back in Indiana Dad would be praying for my survival. Margo would be praying too. In her letters she had promised to pray. If those two only knew how close I had come to proving their prayers a waste of time . . .

"Hey, bandits at two o'clock high!" Eddie Pulaski shouted over the intercom. He was manning the twin Browning machine guns in the upper turret.

Instinctively, I swung my gun up to the two o'clock high position. I could see nothing but blue sky and scattered wisps of clouds. Off in the distance, sky and ground blurred together, making it impossible to distinguish the horizon.

How can Eddie do that? He always spots them first.

After repeatedly straining my eyes, I finally made out what Pulaski had seen—a dozen specks, ahead of us to the right, and rapidly closing from a higher altitude.

"Yup! They're Jerries, all right. Messerschmitts!" came Eddie's voice again.

Because of our combined airspeeds, the fighters closed the distance incredibly fast. In no time, they tilted their wings and began a dive toward our formation.

"Ready, Yoder?" Eddie called over the intercom, his voice rising in pitch.

"You bet!"

"Cut the chatter," Lt. Conover called over the intercom. "Shoot your guns, not your mouths."

We weren't supposed to use the intercom more than necessary. But in moments like this, it was natural for a gunner to forget and blurt something to a buddy.

Flashes appeared on the leading edges of the Me-109s' wings. For the moment, none of the enemies were shooting at our craft, which we had dubbed *American Pride*. But over the heavy drone of the Liberator's four engines, I heard Pulaski's twin machine guns come alive up in the top turret. *Thump—thump. Thump—thump.*

I picked out an enemy fighter, aimed, and squeezed off a burst of my own. Pause. Another burst. The glowing tracer rounds interspersed with .50-caliber shells showed clear misses.

"No good, Yoder," I muttered inside my oxygen mask. All I did was pepper the air. "Shoot ahead. Let them fly into your rounds!"

However, that advice wasn't so simple. Our bombers flew level and straight, but the swift and agile fighters twisted, turned, and dodged every which way as they closed on us, fired, then zoomed away to circle around for another pass from a new angle.

I instinctively swung my fifty this way and that, spewing lead at any German plane that ventured close enough for a shot. No thinking now. Just aim—shoot. Aim—shoot. Aim—shoot.

A red-nosed Focke-Wulf 190 banked tightly and dove—straight at *American Pride*. I hadn't even realized that these new combatants had entered the fight. Of course, I understood that the enemy pilot was just trying to take out any bomber and didn't care about me personally. But the angle of attack gave the appearance that this guy was singling me out for his personal attention!

I yanked my gun up, framed the cross hairs of my Sperry gun sight on the Focke-Wulf, and fired burst after burst as quickly as the feeding arm would pull the shells into the gun. Flashes from the wings of the FW-190 verified he was firing right back.

I didn't hate the Germans. I never even called them "Jerries," "Krauts," or the other slang our gunners used for them. And right now, I wasn't trying to kill the German pilot who seemed bent on ending my life. As my machine gun spat out the rounds, my only goal was to survive this duel by knocking that killing machine out of commission. In the next few seconds, the loser would be either him or me.

Abruptly, the left wing of the FW-190 sheared away from the fuselage. I inhaled to shout an exultant "Yes!" But the word died in my throat. Instead of falling away, the crippled fighter cartwheeled, twisting around like a wounded boomerang as it careened straight toward *American Pride*—and me.

With a shout, I dropped my gun and flung myself backward, expecting impact any second . . .

The next day, I sat on my bunk in the Quonset hut. This was a rare moment, because out of twelve gunners who lived there, I was the only person in the hut for the moment. The radio was tuned into Calais, a German-run station, which was currently playing swing music. For news, we gunners often tuned in to the BBC or the Armed Forces Network, but for popular music the German stations offered the best variety. Of course, Nazi propaganda came interspersed with the music, but we always ignored that.

In my hand I held a pen, but the sheet of paper in front of me was practically blank. So far, the only words I had managed to squeeze out of my brain were

Dear Margo,
  How are you and your folks getting along?

After that opening line, I simply didn't know what else to say. Not that the life of an airman on a B-24 bomber was boring. The mission of the day before had certainly proven that. Even though I had arrived in England only a few months earlier, I had already experienced more than my share of nerve-wracking experiences. But could I describe all that to Margo?

"Nah," I whispered to myself. "Even if the censor didn't chop that stuff out, I shouldn't frighten her by describing what it's really like up there."

I closed my eyes and pressed my fingertips to them. Immediately the near disaster from the previous day sprang onto the screen of my mind: The FW-190 boring straight toward *American Pride* with its guns spitting death. The wing of my target shearing off. The crippled fighter spinning around and around, directly toward us . . .

Next I recalled the deafening scream George Baker had let loose. Suspended beneath the Liberator, George had swung his ball turret around just in time to see the 190's wing break off with the plane spinning out of control toward us. I had instinctively thrown myself backward against the fuselage, but down in the cramped ball turret George had nowhere to jump. I didn't even need the intercom to hear the shout that he let loose.

Seconds later, George had transformed from terrified to fuming. "For crying out loud, Yoder, or Pulaski, or whoever smeared that 109! Good shooting, but try to knock 'em down a little farther away, will ya? That last one barely missed us. If I'd had a broom, I could've dusted off that guy's cockpit as he passed under me!"

Recalling George's words made me smile. I pictured my gunner friend reaching down from the ball turret to swat the German plane with a broom. Of course, it was impossible, like something you might see in a newspaper cartoon. But George had to crack some kind of joke to recover from his panic. That's the same reason that I had replied, "Why, I did that on purpose, George. I was hoping you would snap off a piece of that fighter's tail for a souvenir."

The one bright spot in the incident was that I knew I hadn't killed the pilot. George saw his white parachute blossom several thousand feet below, and that was all right by me. I just wanted to stop Hitler, to knock those planes down so they couldn't take out any more of our guys.

Back in the present, though, I stared at my nearly blank page. *So what else should I write to Margo?*

The truth was, every man aboard those bombers, from the nose gunner up front to the tail gunner in the rear, would have preferred to be safely back in the States rather than imitating a duck in a carnival shooting gallery. But none of us were quitters. As our radio operator, David Rose, liked to phrase it, "We've got a job to do. It's a lousy job, and it's a dangerous job, but somebody's gotta do it, and that somebody is us!"

I lowered my pen to the sheet of paper and continued my letter.

You asked me to describe what it's like to serve aboard a bomber, but putting it in a letter is hard. You sort of have to be here to get the full effect. We usually have plenty to do, with flying, plane recognition classes, and classes on ditching procedure. I'm glad you're not here. I mean, I'd love to see you, but it's just too dangerous to be in England these days.

I paused. That last part could come across like I was bragging about flying over the war zone, but I hoped she wouldn't take it that way. I searched for a way to continue the letter without actually describing the hair-raising sensation that accompanied almost every mission. I didn't care to mention the bloodstained bodies that were pulled from shot-up planes. I also wasn't about to describe the bombers that fell victim to flak and exploded in midair. Of course, Margo wasn't naïve. She knew that bombers got shot down.

I decided to skip the war talk and just mention other things.

It's funny, but British people don't always speak the same English language we do. Over here they call a radio a "wireless." A truck isn't a truck; it's a "lorry." And a flashlight is an "electric torch." Here in Europe, men even cross their legs differently. We American guys cross our legs with one ankle over the opposite knee. But the European men cross their legs with one knee over the other. The British say they can tell us "Yanks" just by how we sit.

I've never described our living quarters for you. They call it a Quonset hut. It's a half-tube of corrugated tin with a door in each end. The bunks are metal, with metal springs underneath, which aren't so bad. But instead of mattresses they give us "biscuits," which are big, square canvas cushions crammed with stuffing. We're supposed to arrange these over the bedsprings, but mine never fit the bed. Charlie Barnes says these biscuits are wonderfully comfortable—but only when compared to sleeping on concrete! Me, I think the Nazis invented them to keep us awake.

We had some excitement in the barracks a couple nights ago. Remember how I wrote that Eddie Pulaski is always pulling crazy stunts? Well, there's this potbellied stove in our hut for heat. Sometime after midnight, Pulaski tiptoed over to it and dropped in a couple of .45 bullets from his pistol. You should have seen the guys diving under their bunks when those things started shooting off inside the stove! I still have a bruise on my chin from where I banged into the cement floor. And in the middle of all this commotion, Pulaski was roaring with laughter. He's really a great guy, but just then we all felt like strangling him.

One nice thing about our little Quonset hut is that only one of us gunners here smokes. The larger huts have a constant haze from all the cigarettes.

Thanks for being such a good letter-writer, Margo. I mean, I write to my dad too, but he never was much for writing letters. (Which is funny, since he's a mailman and delivers them all the time.) If it weren't for you, I'm not sure who I'd write to.

I squinted at that last sentence. Even though I had passed twelfth-grade English just the year before, I wasn't positive whether the word "who" was correct, or if it should have been "whom" instead. Then I noticed the last word in the sentence and was positive old Mrs. Baxter would frown and cluck, "Tsk, tsk," if she caught me ending a sentence with a preposition. In the end, I just shrugged and left the sentence. After all, I figured that a nineteen-year-old guy aboard a United States Army Air Force bomber in 1943 had more important things to worry about than grammar rules.

Staring at the curved wall of the Quonset hut, I relived that week in spring when I met Margo. The 1942 school year had ended on Thursday, June 4, and I finally had my diploma. For a long time Dad had objected to my enlisting in the army. Our branch of the Yoder clan came from a staunchly pacifist Mennonite background. Even though Dad had attended the nondenominational

Jordan Memorial Tabernacle since marrying Mom, the pacifist roots still ran deep in him.

"Think what you would be doing," he would argue. "Every time you shoot an enemy soldier, you'll be sending his soul straight to hell."

"Maybe," I would counter, "but those Nazis are slaughtering innocent people in Poland, Czechoslovakia, France . . . Who's going to stop them if Americans don't step in?"

Dad wouldn't budge. "Poland . . . Czechoslovakia . . . Let them handle their own problems. America should take care of America."

If anything, his arguments only hardened my resolve to enlist. To avoid these debates in those final days before reporting for basic training, I took my Indian Scout 101 motorcycle out for long rides in the countryside surrounding Elkhart.

Despite President Roosevelt's pleas that Americans save precious rubber by not taking pleasure drives, those rides were important for me. Partly they were my way of saying good-bye to home, since I had no idea when I would see the Hoosier state again. Partly my jaunts around the county were a chance to mourn. Instead of high school graduation being joyful as it was supposed to be, it had turned into a time of sadness. Just hours before the evening commencement service on Rice football field, my friend and fellow senior Jack Fields had drowned while trying to swim across White's Gravel Pit on the west side of town. Four more hours, and he would have received his diploma. Suddenly his life was over.

Of course, a final reason for my rides was that I had worked hard at W.W. Wilt's grocery store to buy that Indian Scout. I wanted to feel the wind whipping through my hair and clothing a few more times before storing it in the garage.

Then came the glorious day when I had turned my motorcycle toward the hills of Bristol, a smaller town just east of Elkhart. I had already zipped past a roadside fruit stand before the smiling image of the girl with chestnut-colored hair fully registered. She had been handing a paper bag to an older woman. Even though I was shy around pretty girls, I instantly decided that this would be a great day to sample some fresh strawberries. I did a U-turn and buzzed back to the fruit stand. That's how I had met Margaret, who preferred to be called Margo, just ten days before I boarded the train that carried me away for basic training.

I imagine I sounded totally tongue-tied when I tried to strike up a conversation with her. All I could come up with was the profound remark, "I don't think I've seen you around here before."

But she seemed not to notice my ineptness. With a playful twinkle in her eyes, she had replied, "A lot of people haven't seen me around here before. We're from Dayton. My parents bought this fruit farm from my Uncle Amos during the winter. These strawberries are our first crop."

From there the conversation nearly faltered until I mentioned that one of my cousins also lived in Bristol. When I asked if she knew Sally Ann Yoder, the new girl's face lit up.

"Sally Ann is one of the first girls I met in school! She is so sweet. And you're her cousin?"

Bingo. I had found a conversation starter. As Margo and I talked that day, I was smitten by her beauty. But this girl had an attractiveness that was definitely more than skin deep. I found Margo's endearing personality, her easy giggle, and her sense of humor as enchanting as those deep, green eyes of hers. Margo had a natural knack for conversation that immediately put me at ease. In no time she seemed like a long-time friend . . .

Suddenly a door in one end of the Quonset hut banged open, jerking my thoughts from Indiana back to Shipdham, England. In waltzed Pulaski, Baker, and our tail gunner, Charlie Barnes. In his hands Pulaski carried a bushel basket filled with straw.

"Hey, Jimmy boy!" Pulaski called to me. "You should have gone to town with us. Your eyes are going to pop out of their sockets when you see what we found!"

I tossed my unfinished letter and pen onto my cot and stood up, eyeing the basket suspiciously. After Pulaski's caper with the bullets in the stove, I wasn't going to step any closer until I was positive this wasn't some sort of gag.

I looked at the basket. "Looks like all you found is a bushel of moldy straw. Are you going to spin straw into gold for us, Eddie? Or should I say, 'Rumplestiltskin'?"

"What we got here is worth its weight in gold," Charlie Barnes drawled in his Tennessee accent. "At least during war time it is!"

George dug a hand into the straw and, grinning triumphantly, fished out a chicken egg. "Feast your eyes on this beauty, Jim! And there's more where that one came from. We got a whole basket of 'em!"

My suspicions vanished as I rushed to pluck another egg from under the straw. "Eggs! Real ones! And they're clean—not even stamped for rationing. Where in the world did you 'find' these?"

Among the guys in our hut, the word "find" often meant, "steal," and I didn't want to get in trouble for eating some general's breakfast.

"Now, don't go gettin' all suspicious," Barnes drawled. "It's not what yer thinkin'. What we found was a poor-lookin' farmer standin' along the road with a wheelbarrow and this here basket in it. We couldn't believe it when he hollered, 'Would you Yanks be interested in some fresh eggs?' But sure enough, that's what he had!"

"How much did they cost?" I wanted to know.

"Twenty cents apiece," Baker replied. "That would be highway robbery back home, but over here . . . Well, just tell me when was the last time you saw anybody selling eggs that weren't rationed?"

I let out a whistle. "Twenty cents apiece! That really is robbery. But how are we going to cook them? All we've got is the pot belly."

"We've got more than that," George replied. "Take a gander." From beneath his jacket he pulled out an iron frying pan. "He also had this for sale. I guess Churchill's scrap-iron collectors haven't melted down all the skillets in England after all."

I shook my head in amazement. "You guys are a wonder."

"Shucks, y'all, what are we waitin' fer?" Charlie asked. "Let's get cookin'!"

By the time the other gunners of our hut straggled in, Charlie and George were hard at work over the stove. The first batch ended up scrambled, because neither of them had much experience cracking eggs, and they kept breaking the yolks. But by the third skillet full, Charlie was developing a knack for it. Like me, the other gunners licked their lips and eagerly lined up for their share of the eggs. We all chipped in to help pay for them, and we rolled our eyes as we relished the flavor. After this treat, it was going to be tough going back to the powdered eggs in the mess hut.

It went without saying that no one would mention a word of this to the officers, which were Lt. Conover, our pilot; Lt. Peterson, copilot; Lt. Curt Cochran, the bombardier; and our navigator, Lt. "Mac" Hardwick. After all, officers already received better treatment than the rest of us. Even though our crew worked as a tight-knit group on missions, George spoke for the rest of us when he said, "Let the officers find their own eggs!"

We had just finished cleaning up the evidence of our feast when a gunner from one of the other planes entered the hut. Because the newcomer was from Alabama, Charlie Barnes had struck up a friendship with his fellow Southerner.

"Say, y'all heard the news yet?" the new arrival asked.

"What news?" Charlie drawled back.

"Our squadron is on alert. There's a rumor goin' around. I don't know if it's true, but if it is, we're in for a big one tomorrow!"

May 14, 1943, had not dawned yet. When we were awakened at 3:00 a.m., the so-called morning was still as black as the inside of an ink bottle. After we had eaten as much breakfast as our jittery stomachs could hold in the mess hall, we trudged over for mission briefing.

It was always the same before each bomb run: we sat down for briefing, and some officer from intelligence would pull the curtains on a huge map of Europe and describe our mission for the day. On the map would be a line of red tape stretching from our base in Shipdham to whatever our assigned target for that day would be.

Our planes never flew directly to the target. Instead, in order to keep the Germans guessing, the entire formation would first fly in the direction of one or two diversionary points. But when we reached a spot called the Initial Point, or I.P. for short, the navigator in the lead plane would guide us into a turn that would head the formation straight toward the real destination for the day. That way, the Germans had to keep their fighters spread thin and ready to defend a lot of different targets at once.

After the mission, all planes that hadn't been shot down would turn their noses back to England. After we landed, the crews would head back to the same building where we had been briefed and undergo post-mission interrogation.

In darkness my fellow gunners and I sauntered into the briefing/interrogation hut. Because attack from enemy planes was always a real possibility, not a single light bulb gleamed in the predawn gloom. Out on the hardstands—the circles of concrete surrounded by soft soil—fueling teams and ordnance men worked by feel as they topped off the B-24s' gas tanks and loaded them with ammunition and whatever kind of bombs the mission planners had chosen for today's raid.

The men in the briefing room made nervous small talk while we waited to learn our route for the day's mission.

"Hey, maybe it'll be the Big B this time," one man from another plane said. "I've been waiting a long time to give *der Führer* a taste of his own medicine!"

That comment sparked a round of agreement, such as "That's right" and "Me too!" Despite the bravado, though, all of us realized that a mission to the Big B—Berlin—would involve murderous flak and a heavy loss of planes—and friends. So far in this war, no Allied bombs had dropped on Hitler's capital, and in my opinion it was too soon to try. As much as we would love to carry the war to Hitler's doorstep, no one ever complained when the High Command ordered us out on a milk run that involved no concentrated flak zones and veered clear of known fighter bases.

"Men," began a major from intelligence, "just last fall, British airmen were calling General Eaker's Eighth Army Air Force 'Eaker's amateurs.' They thought we were insane for attempting daylight precision bombing. But you're successfully doing what the British declared couldn't be done. And even though the newspaper correspondents don't give the Liberator groups the credit you deserve, you have been doing an excellent job. The entire Eighth Army Air Force has been slowing down Hitler's war production, and as members of the 44th Bombardment Group, you have had a share in that success. We're still a long way from the end of the war, but Col. Johnson asked me to say he is proud of each and every one of you."

Some of the listeners grinned. I saw Eddie Pulaski pat himself on the shoulder. Most, however, held their peace as they waited to hear the bottom line.

Of course, we appreciated the message from Col. Leon Johnson, who had become the Commanding Officer of the 44th back in January. He was right. The 44th Bomb Group had suffered a lot of enemy flak and lost so many planes that some people said the 44th was jinxed. Adding to our sour feelings, news reporters spotlighted the glamor boys, as we called them—the guys who flew the B-17s. It didn't matter that our Liberators could fly farther, faster, and carry a heavier bomb load. Maybe there was just something romantic about a sleek aircraft named a "Flying Fortress" that naturally sparked interest.

"I hear that some of you have been grumbling that the Flying Eightballs are being used for diversionary tactics. Well, let me promise you—today's raid is no diversion. You're going to get as big a slice of the action as you'll ever want."

At the major's signal, the curtains were pulled back. This morning the red tape stretched northeast from Shipdham to end at Kiel, on the coast of the Baltic Sea. At this sight, whistles and low groans filled the briefing room.

"I won't kid you," the major continued. "This mission won't be a milk run. Kiel will be well defended. It's the site of a major German shipyard, and we've got to take their ships and submarines out of action."

As he talked, I took in the general picture, but as a gunner I didn't memorize all the little details. Mostly I was interested in which enemy fighter bases we might pass along the way. One city I always dreaded going near was Abbeville, France. We had nicknamed the German pilots based there the Abbeville kids, but those guys were crack pilots and knew how to shoot. They had shot down scores of British RAF planes and American ones too, including some from our 44th BG. I was glad to see that our course for the day took us nowhere near Abbeville.

I also wanted to know what kind of flak to expect. Fighters I could stand. At least I could see them and shoot back. But flak—it just zings up unexpectedly from gun batteries on the ground and fills the sky with exploding shrapnel. I hated it. The city of St. Nazaire was so well defended that we called it Flak City. This raid on Kiel wouldn't take us near there, but intelligence promised plenty of flak around Kiel.

Oh, well. Every mission gets us closer to the end of the war. As soon as we finish our quota, we'll get rotated back to the States.

Still, I was glad I had finally finished my letter to Margo and handed it to Lt. Conover to be censored and mailed.

Later, when all of us had boarded our planes with our gear, the pilots and copilots ran through their preflight checklist. Around 7:30 a.m. *American Pride* pulled away from its concrete hardstand and lumbered out to join the other planes on the perimeter track to head for the take-off runway. The line of B-24s looked like a gaggle of gigantic aluminum geese waddling one after another. Finally, thirty seconds apart, bomber after bomber roared down the runway and soared skyward.

American Pride's four powerful Pratt and Whitney Twin Wasp radial engines were straining as our wheels left the ground. All together we carried ten crewmen—which was normal—plus about eight thousand pounds of incendiary bombs. After the hundred or so Flying Fortresses leading our formation dropped three hundred tons of high explosives on the shipyards and submarine works at Kiel, our 44th Group was to follow up with incendiaries that would set fire to the rubble and, hopefully, halt construction.

This first part of a mission didn't bother me. Rising over the English countryside and circling while more planes rose and formed into squadrons and groups took time. It was relaxing just circling, circling as the planes slowly gained altitude under their heavy loads.

More than once I wished I had brought along the Eastman Brownie camera that I had bought with $3.60 of my graduation money. A photograph of our airborne squadron out my waist window would look pretty inspiring, I thought. I also figured that a picture of me with my machine gun would be impressive to send to Margo. Unfortunately, the camera was tucked safely in my dresser drawer back in Elkhart. Peaceful Indiana seemed a million miles away.

I glanced at Dan Carlson, my fellow waist gunner. Chewing his ever-present wad of gum like a cow with its cud, Dan was sitting on an ammunition box and browsing a dog-eared copy of *Reader's Digest.*

George Baker always waited until we were over the English Channel before crawling into the cramped ball turret. At the moment he was sitting farther up the fuselage. George was reading too. He hunched over a tattered booklet called *Captain America*

Comics #1, whose cover showed the red, white, and blue hero delivering a roundhouse punch to Adolf Hitler's jaw. George had reread that first issue so many times that the pages were all wrinkled and working loose from the staples.

Eddie Pulaski was up in his turret, and I never knew what he did up there at times like this. But one fact that I could bank on was that he wasn't reading. As far as I could tell, this particular son of Polish immigrants had never read anything more complicated than the dipstick of his car back in Detroit.

To pass the time while the planes climbed and assembled, I pulled out my wallet. For security reasons, we airmen didn't carry any identification other than our dog tags, which hung around our necks twenty-four hours a day. Diaries, too, were forbidden. The brass at Bomber Command didn't want any information falling into enemy hands if we "went down," as the gunners put it. But my wallet did hold the only photograph of Margo that I owned. Plus, I had received a letter from her the previous day, and any news from home was worth rereading two or three times—especially when the sender was as gorgeous as Margo. With the light of the early morning sun gleaming through my waist window, I began to read:

> *Dear Jim,*
>
> *I promised to write regularly, but I'm afraid there's nothing exciting happening in Bristol, or anywhere else in Elkhart County. At least, not exciting compared to what you're doing in the USAAF. I've never been in an airplane, so I can only imagine what it must be like to look down and see the tops of clouds.*
>
> *When I read the newspaper, it seems like "victory" is now the most popular word in the language. Maxwell's Butcher Shop is advertising "victory pats," a salon is styling hair into "victory cuts," and the ad for Firestone tires says they offer "victory values." And, of course, everyone is planting "victory gardens" to stretch America's food supply. Except for the gardens, I don't see how all those things will help beat the Nazis. But these reminders about the war do make me think of you.*
>
> *Yesterday I was listening to the "Gospel Sunshine Hour" on WTRC radio. They had a sermon about praying for others,*

*and naturally that brought you to mind. My parents and Clint
and I pray for you every day, Jim, at suppertime.*
   *Well, I better close this letter. It's my turn to cook supper,
and I haven't even started yet. Wish you could be here to join
us!*
   Sincerely,
   Margo Lace

I pondered that closing. One part of me wished that she had
signed it "Love," instead of just "Sincerely." In the last several of
my own letters I had gone out on a limb and signed with the "L"
word, but she wasn't following my lead. My sensible side understood that she couldn't. Margo and I had known each other for
only ten days before I headed off to basic. Even though we had
corresponded regularly since then, we still didn't have enough
of a relationship to label it "love"—even if I was falling for this
minister's daughter.

The church thing was another obstacle. Margo was clearly
dedicated in her faith, and I had pretty much turned my back on
God. Of course, I tried to act wholesome around her folks. But
even without saying so outright, I knew that Margo would never
let herself fall in love with—or marry—any guy who wasn't as serious about living for God as she was. In every letter she included
some tidbit about praying or Bible reading, or radio sermons.
Of course, I had listened to WTRC too, but never the "Gospel
Sunshine Hour." I hadn't heard that program since Mom's funeral. My favorite broadcast was "Let's Talk Sports," the evening
show hosted by Bill Frink.

I folded the letter and tucked it back into my wallet. All in
all, I simply didn't know where I stood with Margo. Was she dating other guys—church types—while I was over here with Nazi
fanatics taking pot shots at me? Just imagining it made me jeal-
ous. But then again, I had no real claim on Margo. After all, we
weren't engaged. She wasn't even my girlfriend, although I wished
that she were.

Once our formation was over the English Channel, the time
for relaxing was past. George squeezed into the ball turret, and we
gunners test-fired our weapons.

Around ten thousand feet or so, Lt. Conover's voice sounded in our headphones. "Pilot to crew. Oxygen time. We're getting up there."

Reluctantly I fastened the rubber oxygen mask over the lower half of my face and inhaled deeply. It was working fine. Even though the oxygen mask was dark green and not yellow, somehow its cold rubber made me think of a duck's clammy foot slapped over my mouth and nose. The comparison was absurd, I knew, so I never mentioned it to the other gunners.

To avoid as much flak as possible, our formation headed northeast, out to the North Sea. Today, though, shortly after we flew over the Frisian Islands off the coast of occupied Holland, things started to happen. The intercom clicked, and I heard Lt. Peterson up in the cockpit, "Copilot to crew. Welcoming committee just arrived. Bandits at 12:00, high."

In the air war, enemy aircraft could approach from literally any direction, and they might attack us from above or below. To describe a fighter's position quickly, we imagined the round face of a clock lying flat, with the 12 at the plane's nose and the 6 on the tail. A plane approaching from the right would be at 3:00 high, low, or level. An attack from behind would be at 6:00. These planes were now approaching from head-on, the 12:00 position, and high above our own altitude.

From my waist window, I couldn't see fighters approaching at 12:00. But before long I heard Eddie Pulaski's twin .50s begin pounding up above, and in the nose turret Curtis Cochran was firing his guns too. When we got into the thick of the fighting, I saw both Focke-Wulfs and Messerschmitts, lots of them, buzzing around like angry hornets.

We droned on toward Kiel, shooting at fighters when we could, but being careful not to blast any of our fellow bombers. Another danger was shooting our own plane. More than once a waist gunner got so excited that he stitched a line of shells through his own plane's wingtip as he tracked a fighter. I was determined not to repeat the error.

As we approached the shipyards that housed U-boats and surface ships, enemy antiaircraft guns down below spewed a murderous spray of exploding shells into the sky all around the formation. Here, German fighter pilots stayed clear to avoid getting struck by their own flak gunners. Because of that, I had time to watch the puffs of black and gray smoke mushrooming into an umbrella over the area. These "instant clouds" were fascinating to watch and almost mesmerizing. But they held death and destruction for any plane caught too close to them. This was one of those days when the guys described the flak as "so thick you could get out and walk on it."

Up ahead the leading B-17s were dropping their bomb loads. From my side window, I could glimpse billows of oily smoke rising from Kiel.

Suddenly another Liberator in our 506th squadron caught a shell that exploded right in the nose of the plane, blowing the cockpit apart. It was the *Dixie Doodle*, named as a compromise when half the crew wanted to call it *Yankee Doodle* and the Southerners voted to call it *Dixie*. In horror, I watched as *Dixie Doodle*—now pilotless but with all engines running—slowly tipped and rolled out of formation.

"Jump!" I shouted instinctively even though the crew of the plane couldn't hear me. But with the pilot and copilot dead, no one was left to punch the alarm to bail out. The men in the back of the plane had no clue what was happening.

Dixie Doodle's number one engine on the left wing overlapped and then gouged into the wing of another Lib, just like a buzz saw grinding into a wooden plank. The orange and black explosion that erupted was straight from a hellish nightmare. Both planes were immediately obliterated into millions of shards of scrap metal. Against all hope I strained to spot parachutes opening, but not one was to be seen. Twenty men had just perished. That wasn't just a number either. These were guys I knew. They had eaten breakfast with me that morning.

Down in the ball turret, George was keeping count of our casualties. "That's three Libs down. No, four! The Jerries just got one more!"

The intercom clicked. "Bombardier to pilot. Bomb bay doors open."

I had been so entranced by the scenario unfolding around us that I didn't realize we were now on our bomb run.

"Five!" shouted George from below. "They got five Liberators, and we ain't even dropped our bombs yet!"

Suddenly a new voice broke over the intercom. It was David Rose, at the radio man's table. "I'm hit! I'm hit!"

When the copilot, Lt. Peterson, asked Rose how bad it was, the radio operator replied, "A chunk of flak smashed through and gashed my thigh. Didn't go deep, but it's bleeding fast. I think it'll be okay if I wrap it up tight."

"Hey! What are those lame brains doing?" It was Pulaski in the upper turret. Over the intercom he launched into a string of curses that would have made a drill sergeant blush.

Like Pulaski, I couldn't believe my eyes. Several thousand feet above us, a squadron of Fortresses had drifted out of position on the bomb run. They were releasing their bombs right through our formation! Just when I had thought I couldn't be more scared, our own planes were dropping bombs to the left and right of us!

The two-hundred-fifty-pound M-67 multi-purpose bombs flashed past my waist window so closely that I could clearly distinguish their yellow noses and tail fins against the olive drab of their casings. Fortunately, the bombs passed between our planes on the downward plummet to Kiel, but the sight of those near misses had my heart pounding.

Incredulous, I shook my head. *What a way to fight a war!*

Meanwhile antiaircraft shells from the ground were still bursting all around us. These shells didn't need to strike a plane to score a kill. Their fuses were preset to explode the instant they reached our altitude. In anger I shot a few bursts of fifty-caliber shells streaming earthward. The odds of hitting somebody manning an 88-millimeter gun had to be a few million to one, but I did it anyway. How I despised flak.

Come on, come on! I urged the bombardier. *Drop those eggs, so we can get out of this inferno!* After sweating for a seeming eternity, I finally heard the magic phrase.

"Bombardier to pilot. Bombs away."

Now the bombardier could close the bomb bay doors and reduce the arctic blast howling through the plane's rear section.

"Hey, wait!" came Dan Carlson's voice over the intercom. "Don't shut the bomb bay yet. We've got one hung up in the rack!"

I turned and stared up the fuselage to where the open bomb doors left a gaping chasm in the belly of *American Pride*. Sure enough, one of our magnesium cluster bombs had refused to fall and was stuck there. Normally it was the radioman's job to make sure the bombs had released properly. Quick-thinking Dan had realized that David Rose, wounded as he was, couldn't manage it.

Unfortunately, stuck bombs weren't uncommon. It sometimes happened on both B-17s and B-24s. The engineers and ordnance men never figured out a way to make the bomb racks foolproof for a quick release. Another gunner once told me about a B-17 that tried to land with a stuck bomb. As soon as its wheels bumped against the tarmac, the thing broke loose and exploded right under the plane. No survivors.

A click, and Lt. Conover's voice responded over the intercom. "One of you guys back there get that thing out of here. Drop it anywhere. Make it snappy."

My eyes locked with Dan's. In them I could see the same thing that I was sure he saw in mine—fear. We didn't want to admit it out loud, but neither of us wanted to monkey around with a bomb while hanging on for dear life over a yawning hole twenty-eight thousand feet above the ground, and with enemy 88's shooting up at us the whole time.

I broke the silence. "Well, Dan, this is a job that calls for a real man. You're older than I am. I say we let you handle it."

"Whaddya mean, I'm older than you are? We're both nineteen!" He was furiously chomping his wad of gum as he talked.

"Sure, but I was born in November. Your birthday is in September. So you're at least two months older than I am. It's all yours, chum."

"Hey, you can't saddle me with this job. Didn't I ever tell you?"

"Tell me what?"

"I'm afraid of heights."

"You're afraid of . . . ?" I burst into laughter despite the tension of our predicament. People with phobias about altitude simply didn't serve in the U.S. Army Air Force—except as ground personnel. But the laugh helped to lighten the mood.

"You Yankees need me to crawl up there and show y'all how to do it?" drawled a voice over the intercom.

The last thing I needed was Charlie Barnes making us look foolish. "Just stay where you are, Charlie, and don't let any Messerschmitts plug us in the tail."

"Don't y'all worry about me," the Southerner replied. "Them Jerries couldn't hit the broad side of a Barnes!" This was Charlie Barnes's favorite punch line, and he was always looking for a chance to repeat it.

Lt. Conover's voice sounded again, and he was losing patience. "Cut the chatter! As soon as we're clear of flak, fighters will be waiting to pounce on us. When they do, I want every gunner at his post. I don't care who nudges that thing loose; just dump it!"

Dan pulled down his oxygen mask so he could speak without using the intercom. No humor was in his eyes. "Look," he said above the engines' roar, "I had to work a bomb loose once when I pulled a mission on *Kentucky Derby*. It gave me the willies. I'll feel better about this if you take a turn at it."

I couldn't think of a reply. Somebody certainly had to do it. Suddenly I was elected.

"Right waist to pilot," I said. "I'll do it. Just hold this bird level and steady." My words were flat. I wasn't playing hero.

Each of us airmen was tethered to his position by three lines: an oxygen line to breathe at high altitude, a cord to power our electrically heated flight suits, and the intercom line for communication. I unhooked from the plane's main oxygen and attached my line to a portable canister of oxygen. Next I unplugged my electric line and the intercom, cutting me off from voice contact with fellow crew members.

Swallowing hard, I worked my way forward, holding on to the inside of the fuselage for balance as I stepped along the catwalk. Only about eight inches wide, the catwalk was, at best, a precarious perch for this kind of maneuver.

"Sure, he'll feel a lot better if I do it," I grumbled to myself. "But what about how I'll feel?"

The bomb bay doors on a B-24 don't open downward on hinges like those on a B-17. Instead, they roll up from both sides, similar to the action of a roll-top desk, only upside down. This reduces air drag during a bomb run, and after the bombs are away, the doors roll back down until they meet in the belly of the plane.

I tucked the green oxygen canister snugly into my fleece-lined jacket to free up both hands. Inching my way along the catwalk toward those open doors, I tried not to look down. However, in my peripheral vision I could see that we were passing over houses, streets, and patches of farmland as we left the suburbs of Kiel in our wake. I had never stood so close to those doors when they were open. The 200-mile-per-hour wind gushing around me made it feel like I was in a bouncing wind tunnel. My knees felt weak.

What I wouldn't give for a safety rope!

I glanced back at Carlson. He had stopped chewing—definitely a rare moment—and above the dark green of his oxygen mask his eyes followed my every move. He nodded and circled his gloved thumb and forefinger into his usual "okay" sign.

Gripping an aluminum rib of the fuselage with one hand, I leaned over and examined the bomb. We carried different types for different raids, depending on the target. As a gunner, I didn't usually pay attention to such details. This bomb, however, was different. It was a one hundred-pound incendiary, a type that the 44th hadn't used since before our 506th squadron arrived as replacements. Instead of TNT packed into a steel casing with fins on the back, this bomb resembled a bundle of a hundred or so sticks, each about three feet long, with the whole cluster banded together. The idea was that once released, the "sticks" would break loose and scatter under the force of our propellers' turbulent prop wash and ignite multiple fires on the ground.

I wasn't familiar with incendiaries. Could a burst of flak detonate it right in the rack? If so, *American Pride* carried enough high-octane fuel to light up the sky.

Stop thinking so much, I chided myself. *Just do the job!*

From where I stood, I couldn't understand why the bomb hadn't fallen. With my free hand I wiggled the rack. Nothing. I jiggled it harder. The bomb refused to budge. Inching still closer and leaning over the open hole, I pushed down on the bundle, expecting it to drop away. Still the thing defied gravity. What could I do?

I felt a tap on my shoulder and turned to see Dan, stretching out a hand holding a screwdriver. With this I could trigger the release mechanism manually. I accepted the screwdriver and turned back to my task.

Whomp!

An explosion and puff of black smoke directly below signaled that another battery of flak gunners was opening up on our squadron. No time to waste now! My imagination running wild, I could already picture one of their shells whizzing straight up *American Pride's* open belly at three thousand feet per second, with me still leaning over that abyss. The metal skin of a bomber is thin and doesn't offer much protection, but it was certainly better than nothing.

Whomp! Whomp! More shells were bursting around us. The enemy gunners were getting a fix on our altitude.

Holding on tightly, I leaned over and looked for the right spot to insert the screwdriver. Dan had said that he got the willies from doing this job once. That was a world-class understatement for how I felt in that moment.

A tremendous explosion—*Ka-whomp!*

American Pride took a direct hit. The plane lurched as if some giant, invisible foot had just kicked her from below. Even before I applied pressure to the screwdriver, the violent shudder freed the troublesome bomb, which dropped out the plane's belly.

But the upward lurch threw me off balance. My gloved hand wrenched loose. In the next instant, I tumbled in the same direction the bomb had gone.

For a fleeting instant my hands shot out, and I wildly grappled for something—anything—to stop my fall. I almost got a grip on the bottom section of the bomb rack, and a blur in the corner of my eye might have been Dan leaping forward to grab me. But with my body dangling out the belly of the plane from the chest down, I didn't have a chance. The rushing wind seized me and literally ripped my grasp from the last support that could have kept me in the plane. I was falling!

Cruising at 200 miles per hour, a B-24 creates a powerful slipstream. Caught in that blast of air, I felt like an autumn leaf trapped in a tornado. I was tossing every direction at once as I tumbled head over heels. In rapid succession glimpses of clouds, ground, and my own rapidly shrinking plane flashed past my eyes. The oxygen bottle whirled away, yanking my mask off with it.

Sheer terror shot through my mind. I was hurtling earthward. None of my friends could save me now.

My parachute!

Because we weren't paratroopers, bomber crewmen received parachutes, but no training jumps to go with them. All we had ever received was a description of how to use them, along with the instructor's smiling promise, "If you ever need one, you won't worry about not getting a practice jump. You'll use it just fine."

Although most of us didn't wear our bulky parachutes throughout a whole flight, I made it a point never to take mine off over enemy territory. We wore harnesses, with the chest-pack parachute snapped to the harness with metal clips.

Now I had stopped tumbling and was plummeting face up, my back rushing toward the earth. Whether from fright or because of my gloves, I don't know, but my fingers couldn't feel the metal D-ring of my ripcord. Even though I was still a long way up and in no immediate danger, I panicked. I yanked off my gloves and flung them away. At last I located the D-ring and wrenched it hard with both hands. Billowing white silk spilled out and rippled upward. When the canopy popped open like a giant white mushroom, the force jerked me so roughly that it rattled my teeth.

My heart was still pounding crazily, but at least now I floated safely, suspended between sky and earth. In contrast to the hours of the enormous Pratt and Whitney engines' ear-numbing droning, the only audible sounds now were the delicate rustle of air through my shroud lines, plus the far-off *whomps* as flak bursts sought out targets high overhead. Even these were growing fainter as I descended.

Feels just like soaring on my own private cloud, I mused when my mind cleared a little.

I looked up and watched *American Pride* winging westward, along with the rest of the 506th squadron. The number three engine, the inboard one on the right wing, was smoking. The detonation that slammed me overboard must have also damaged the engine. By now Lt. Conover would have feathered the propeller blades on that one, turning the blades sideways so they would slice into the wind edgewise and reduce drag.

As I watched, it looked like the bomber's wings waggled up and down. Perhaps it was Lt. Conover's way of waving good-bye to me. Or maybe he was just struggling to keep the old girl steady. I couldn't be sure.

Whenever a plane went down, we looked for parachutes and breathed a sigh of relief when we saw them. From his position in the ball turret, George Baker would have spotted mine and would be wishing me good luck right now.

There's no such thing as luck, Jim. There's just God, and He's the One you should depend on.

The thought came to me unbidden. That was one of those sayings my mom had often repeated while I was growing up. It was just one more of her teachings that I had cast to the wind after her funeral.

But now I had no more time for idle gazing at the sky. My friends were heading back to Shipdham in Norfolk, England, and I was descending toward the one spot on the entire globe that I didn't want to be in—Hitler's Third Reich. About that time I noticed that my right hand still clutched the now-useless D-ring, which had a foot-long wire trailing from it. I opened my fingers, letting it race to the ground ahead of me.

Now that I was getting used to the sensation, I didn't mind floating without the safety of an airplane around me. But now I was worrying about how to land without breaking anything useful, like an ankle or a leg.

I had heard about paratroopers coming down on top of power lines or bouncing off rooftops, and these thoughts weren't pleasant. However, my worries were wasted, for the wind was guiding me toward an open field with a paved road alongside it. Cows grazed nearby, and the scene would have looked fairly tranquil if not for the military vehicles screeching to a halt and the uniformed figures dashing toward my landing site.

While still high up, the sensation was that I was barely moving under my canopy. Now, though, as I neared the earth, the ground seemed to be rising quickly toward me. Moments after I drew my feet together, I thudded into plowed soil and toppled onto my side. My feet stung the same way they had the time I jumped off the roof of our house back on Beardsley Avenue when I was fifteen.

I tried to stand, but the wind was still wrestling with the parachute. Lying on the ground, I unclipped the lines from my harness and finally struggled to my feet.

Shouting men in uniforms closed around me. Some carried rifles; one pointed a pistol. A civilian ran up huffing too. He squinted at me and waved a pitchfork in my direction. I wondered what he was planning to do with that thing. I also wondered if the soldiers would let him.

Suddenly my guts felt like stewed cabbage. Over a hilltop, dark smoke curled upward, and I hoped that last incendiary bomb hadn't landed on anybody these guys knew personally. But I wasn't about to let my enemies see fear in my eyes. Instead I fell back on defiant American humor.

"Hi there. I'm from the United States of America and just thought I'd drop by. President Roosevelt wants to know if you guys are ready to knock off all this foolishness and surrender? If so, I'll be happy to collect all your weapons right now." I extended my arms as if I expected them to stack their rifles on them.

"*Hebe die Hände hoch!*" a gruff voice barked.

Another soldier sneered something that ended with the word *Luftgangster.*

Although I studied French in high school and even got pretty good at it with the help of a neighbor lady who was born in France, I didn't speak German. At least not more than a handful of phrases I had picked up in the army. I had no inkling of what the first fellow had said. But I did recognize *Luft* as their word for air, and the word *gangster* was easy enough to translate, despite the accent. They were arresting me as an "air gangster."

Finding myself looking up the business ends of several rifles, I decided that this might not be the best time for jokes. I reached for the sky, just like they do in cowboy movies.

As soon as my hands were up, one of them snatched my Colt .45 from its holster. Until he did, I had forgotten that I even had it on me. He seemed more eager to seize the pistol as a souvenir than to disarm me.

An officer with a scar on his left cheek kept shouting guttural commands, which I understood about as well as I understand ancient Chinese. When I stared blankly, another soldier angrily pantomimed undressing, and they made me remove my outer flight gear and boots.

When they had searched all the pockets, they slapped me around and frisked me. I carried no other real weapons, but they confiscated the Buck knife I always carried. I was supposed to have an escape kit with me if I ever bailed out, but under the circumstances I didn't have even that.

Satisfied, they tossed my fleece-lined jacket and flying boots back to me. I suppose they figured my flying days were over. That's how it looked to me too.

I slipped my boots on. A rifle muzzle boring into my back and repeated shouts of *"Schnell!"* encouraged me to start toward a waiting truck.

As I trudged along, I thought, *Well, if there's no such thing as luck, what is this? Seems like the dumbest kind of bad luck, if you ask me.*

As soon as I thought this, another idea popped into my mind. I don't believe in ghosts or anything like that, but I could almost hear Mom's voice replying, *It could be worse, Jim. What if your parachute hadn't opened? What if you had been hit by flak? What if the whole crew had been blown from the sky? You still have things to thank God for.*

If Mom had been there, she certainly would have said something like that. She had always been firm in her faith and constantly looked on "the bright side," as she called it, even when she was dying from leukemia.

Okay, God, I thought. *It's true. Things could be worse. I should be glad I'm still breathing and didn't break any bones. But if You're really watching out for me, I'm going to need a lot more help before I get out of this mess.*

Just then my right hand bumped against my hip pocket.

My wallet. It's gone! Maybe it popped out when I bounced on the ground?

I stopped in my tracks and turned around, scanning the earth. The wallet didn't have much money in it—just a couple of English pound notes—but it did contain that photograph of Margo that she gave me at the train station, plus the last letter I received from her. I had no intention of leaving those treasures behind, especially if I was in for a long stay at a POW camp.

Officer "Scarface" shouted something and jabbed a finger toward the road.

"My wallet," I said slowly and clearly. "I lost my wallet. Let me go back and look for it."

"Nicht!" Scarface blurted, and even I understood that to mean "No."

"Hold your horses, buddy. This will only take a second," I replied. I took a step toward the spot where I had hit the ground.

In the same instant I glimpsed a shadow on the ground rushing me from behind. Pain shot through my skull, and I saw stars. My world went black.

As the fog in my mind gradually lifted, I became conscious of riding in some kind of truck. I was sprawled face down where the soldiers had dumped me. The right side of my face bumped against the gritty truck bed every time the vehicle bounced over a pothole.

A throbbing from the back of my head told me that someone had clubbed me. Other aches on my body gave clues that I had been dumped onto the truck bed without any particular tenderness.

I opened my eyes and lifted myself onto one elbow. Two soldiers of the Wehrmacht sat on a wooden bench and regarded me with steely eyes.

"Where are we headed?" I asked. Just speaking made the ache in my skull hurt worse.

They observed me in silence.

Slowly, I eased myself into a sitting position. My bootlaces were flopping, so I tied them while waiting for the cobwebs to clear from my brain. That done, I inched backwards.

Another bench was on this side of the vehicle, and I eased myself onto it. I wasn't convinced that the two ogres watching me wouldn't kick me for sitting up without permission, so I moved slowly, just to make sure I didn't startle them.

"Hey, Smiley," I said to the surlier-looking of the two. "I could go for a bite to eat. How about a sandwich or something?"

Still no reply.

"You know. Food? Chow? Vittles? I don't expect anything fancy. Even peanut butter and jelly would be okay."

The two exchanged glances but remained stone-faced.

"Aw, forget it. I bet people in this country never even heard of peanut butter."

I closed my eyes and rode in silence. The knot on the back of my head still throbbed, but closing my eyes relieved a little of the pain.

After about two hours of jolting along, the vehicle slowed and ground to a halt. A pause, and then someone outside swung open the tailgate.

One of my traveling companions growled, *"Raus!"* which I assumed meant "Get out!" or "Move it!" or something similar.

I climbed down, my two guardians following me with rifles held at the ready. I found myself standing on a cobblestone street in a small town.

Two local soldiers led me through a metal gate in a brick wall and into a large, two-story building of ruddy-brown brick. I couldn't guess what the structure had been used for in past days, but on entering I understood that this was to be my temporary jail. Led by the two locals and followed by the two from the truck, I was marched down a corridor and shoved into a makeshift cell. The heavy door thumped shut behind me.

A key clanked loudly in the lock, and suddenly I was left alone in the little room. The heavy tread of boots echoed back up the hallway, but I dropped to my knees and peered through the gap beneath the door anyway. I was pleasantly surprised to see that they hadn't stationed a guard on the other side.

Quickly I surveyed the room for anything that might provide a means of escape. Time was crucial, and I knew it. Within an hour, perhaps less, the Germans could be back for me to complete the trip to whatever stalag they were taking me. If I wanted to escape, better to try now, before barbed wire and guard towers hemmed me in.

The chamber was roughly twenty feet by twenty feet, and it was depressingly void of anything that looked like it could help me. There was one small window—heavily barred. My only furniture was a rickety wooden chair in the center of the room. In one corner was a foul-smelling bucket, probably for toilet purposes. Littering the wooden floor were a few miscellaneous nuts and bolts, some of them quite rusty. Judging by the look of these and some oily stains on the scuffed floor boards, I assumed that this room had once contained machinery. I examined everything on the floor carefully, hoping to discover some overlooked key, a hacksaw blade, anything useful . . .

While scouring every square inch of flooring, the yellow paint spots on my fingertips caught my eye. I knew how they got there. Eddie Pulaski had showed up with a can of yellow oil-base paint that he "found" in an ordnance building. It was the same bright yellow they painted on the bomb fins of lead aircraft with their pinpoint accuracy Norden bombsights. When the brightly painted bombs of the lead plane dropped, all the following bombardiers would likewise toggle their switches to release their payloads. Imitating countless other gunners, Eddie suggested that our crew paint a miniature yellow bomb on the left chest of our flight jackets to represent each mission we had flown. Twenty-five missions was the magic number that would end our tour of operations and rotate us back to the States.

Looking at those yellow spots on my fingertips, I grunted. "Life sure can change in a hurry. Less than twenty-four hours ago I was happily painting little bombs on flight jackets. Today I'm getting kicked around like yesterday's garbage by a gang of thugs in uniform."

Out of all the nutty memories that could have popped into my mind came the words to a poem. Shortly after Mom had died of leukemia, I had to memorize a poem for a speech class. In the library I discovered "Invictus" by the British poet William E. Henley and chose this one for two reasons: first, because I wasn't a big fan of poetry, and this one was fairly short. Second, in my anger against God for letting Mom die, I adopted the same independent attitude Henley expressed in his closing stanza:

> *It matters not how strait the gate,*
> *How charged with punishments the scroll,*
> *I am the master of my fate:*
> *I am the captain of my soul.*

Burning those lines into my memory, I had vowed to make them my life's motto. Never again, I had told myself, would I entrust my fate to God. I was going to seize the reins of my destiny and do whatever I wanted, whenever I wanted, and however I wanted.

Stepping to the barred window, I watched German townsfolk going about their business in the streets. Some looked weary and depressed. Despite their sober countenances, however, even the most straight-faced citizen out there looked cheerful compared to how I felt in captivity.

"Some master of my fate I turned out to be," I grumbled. "More like a stray mutt at the dog pound."

I turned and delivered the wooden chair a savage kick with my boot. It skittered across the cell and bounced off the wall, toppling onto its side.

Three years of accumulated bitterness and frustration had been like an anchor, dragging my soul deeper and deeper into a dark abyss. Basic training and the war had distracted me for a time. So did Margo, the one bright spot in my recent life. Now it might be years before I saw her again. I was at the end of myself and had no idea how to face the future.

Or did I? There was one thing I could do. It was something I hadn't done seriously since before Mom died. I could pray.

I scoffed at the idea. *I don't remember how to pray.*

At least, that's what I told myself. Even though I had continued attending Jordan Memorial Tabernacle in Elkhart with Dad, it had been a long time since I paid attention during sermons. Instead of listening, I would purposely daydream. Sometimes I even sneaked in pocket-sized books that I would lay open between me and the end of the pew. Observers might have assumed that my eyes were lowered to help me soak in the pastor's morning message. Far from it, my thoughts were miles away. I would be reading James Fenimore Cooper's *Last of the Mohicans* or other adventures. After all, I figured, if God had refused to do me any favors, why should I do any for Him?

The way I saw it, God could have kept Mom alive when she was in Elkhart General Hospital. But He didn't. He just let her waste away from the leukemia that wracked her body until she had no strength to fight anymore. She died right before my eyes.

Margo finally pried these feelings out of me the evening before I left Elkhart, and she had urged me to let go of my anger.

"Bitterness is like a cancer, Jim," she had said to me. "If you don't let it go, it will eat you up on the inside. I can't explain why heartbreaks happen to wonderful people. But I do know that God is more concerned with what happens to our eternal souls than what happens to our temporary bodies. From what you say, your mom understood that. She must be in paradise with the Lord right now."

Those unexpected words had shined a narrow shaft of light into my gloomy life when Margo spoke them. Now I considered them more seriously. However, I'd been angry at God for so long, it was difficult knowing how to "get right" with Him. Part of me wanted to do it, but another part of me resisted. The ache in my head wasn't helping me to think clearly either.

I paced my cell like a panther at the zoo. *Should I pray, or shouldn't I?*

I despised hypocrites, and I wasn't going to ask God to help me if I didn't mean business with Him, once and for all.

Mom had faith in God. Dad had faith in God. Margo and her folks had faith in Him. So why was this so hard for me? I tried to analyze faith scientifically, but soon realized that science had nothing to do with it. Either there's a God, or there isn't. If there is—and I believed this even when I shunned Him—what was my relationship with the Creator going to be? That was the million-dollar question.

Should I, or no?

As I contemplated my bleak jail cell and my future as a long-term "guest" of the Nazis, I finally concluded that a more appropriate moment was never going to come along. If I was ever going to pray again, it might as well be now.

Haltingly, I stepped over to the rickety chair and set it back on its legs. Sinking beside it onto my knees, I propped my elbows on the chair's scuffed-up seat.

You don't have to do this, a bodiless voice in my mind seemed to whisper. *Forget about God. You don't need Him.* The voice didn't speak in words as such, but I definitely felt the impression of that message.

I hesitated. Finally I broke through the anger and doubt and decided to talk to God and get this over with. Taking a deep breath, I clasped my hands and closed my eyes.

"God," I prayed quietly. "You know that I haven't talked to You in a long time. I don't know why You let Mom die so young, and I admit I've been pretty mad about that. But somewhere deep down inside I believe that, no matter what happens, You're still running the universe, and You care about us dumb people. Maybe You arranged my accident to teach me a lesson. Or maybe it was a brainless mistake. I don't know. But I do know that there's a lot I can't do in my own strength. Maybe I deserved to get captured after the way I turned my back on You. But now I'm asking You to forgive me for everything wrong I've ever done. From now on, I'm putting my trust in You, not in me. Amen."

Instead of opening my eyes, I still hesitated. I wanted to make one more request but wasn't sure how many petitions I was allowed to squeeze into one prayer. And this request was a biggie. Finally I added, "God, there is one more thing. I've been taught that it's my duty as a serviceman to escape if I can. Humanly speaking, I don't see any way out of this mess. But if there's anything I'm overlooking, any way out of here, I'm asking that You'll show it to me."

When I stood up, I heard no chorus of angelic voices. No fireworks exploded; no trumpets blew. I was still a prisoner. Had anything happened? Yes, I felt that something had happened. But what? The jail cell was the same, but something inside me was different. If nothing else, I no longer felt bitter toward God.

I'm a prisoner on the outside, but in a strange way I feel free on the inside.

I recalled a phrase that I was pretty sure Jesus once said: "Ye shall know the truth, and the truth shall make you free." Was that what I was experiencing?

The heavy clumping of boots echoed down the hall. The lock clicked, and two new guards entered, apparently curious to see the American prisoner from the way they gaped at me. One of them growled the word "Luftgangster" along with some other German sentences that contained a threatening tone. His pal carried a wooden board, which served as a tray. He placed my meal on the chair. After they exchanged a few phrases, they left, re-securing the door behind them.

I sighed. "Why couldn't I have studied German in high school?" I lamented. "My French isn't doing me a bit of good."

On the makeshift tray were a hunk of dark bread and a mug of steaming dark liquid. It looked like coffee but smelled more like boiled acorns or something equally peculiar.

Probably imitation coffee for wartime, I concluded. But I was famished and, after giving thanks to the Lord for this provision, I devoured the skimpy meal.

My stomach pacified, I sat on my only chair and allowed my eyes to wander around the makeshift jail cell. I still contemplated escape, but could see no way out. As a boy I had read a lot about Harry Houdini, the magician who specialized in escaping from boxes, cages, and even strait jackets. Of course, there was never any real magic involved. Houdini relied on hidden keys or illusions that made his feats appear supernatural.

"I don't know," I sighed. "I don't see how to fake even an illusion of escape. Maybe it's hopeless."

Then I spotted something I hadn't noticed before. In a crack between two floorboards were wedged two sturdy eyebolts—bolts whose tops ended, not in an octagon like regular bolts, but in a curved loop, or "eye." Screwed into a hoist or sturdy beam, such thick bolts would allow someone to run a rope or chain through the eyes to suspend heavy machinery or other weights.

Gradually an inspiration began to materialize in my mind. I studied the ceiling, then looked back at the bolts jammed into the crack.

Wait a minute! I thought. *Wait just a minute, Jimbo. That's a crazy idea. But it's so nutty that Houdini himself would try it! It just might work!*

Clawing at the bolts with my fingernails, I tried to pry them loose from the crack where they were embedded between the floorboards. No luck—they stuck fast. Poring over the floor, I located a stray wood screw. Manipulating the screw as a miniature pry bar, I managed to dislodge the bolts, which I pocketed.

Next I dragged the rickety chair to the door. I stepped onto it, balancing carefully on my shaky platform. Examining the wooden ceiling above the door, I couldn't help but smile. About five feet apart above the door were two crevices. I picked two points in the cracks and began to file with the screw, trying to enlarge two spots into which I could screw the bolts. Up and down, up and down I filed with the screw, as I created rounded holes.

I wiped my sweaty forehead against a sleeve. My fingertips were becoming raw from working the screw. My arms ached from holding them straight up for so long. At last I picked up the bolts and fitted them to the holes I had widened, listening all the while for the soldiers that I knew would soon return for me. But the holes were still not wide enough for the bolts. Returning to the screw, I worked it in and out, in and out, so feverishly that the screw felt warm from friction.

Once again I pulled the eyebolts from my pocket and twisted them up into the holes as tightly as I could, but that wasn't very far. Flesh and bone fingers aren't much competition against oak. I pulled off my flight jacket, wrapped part of a sleeve around the bolts, and managed to tighten them a few extra turns.

Still not in far enough to trust my full weight to them. But how can I tighten them without a wrench or pliers?

Glancing downward, I got another inspiration. I hopped down and wrapped my flight jacket around one wooden rung between the chair legs. Leaning on the jacket, lightly at first, and then with all my weight, I heard a muffled snap.

I picked up the twelve-inch rung, remounted the chair, and slid the rung halfway through the eye of one bolt. Then twisting the rung with both hands as if I were turning a crank, I was able to tighten both bolts deep into the ceiling, much deeper than I could have with bare fingers.

Now I searched the floor for a piece of stray rope or twine—none. Several oily rags lay crumpled in one corner. I picked them up and knotted the rags together until I had a loop of cloth, which I hung from one eyebolt.

Next I slipped the chair rung through the remaining eyebolt. Holding on to each side of the rung like a trapeze bar, I slowly pulled down with all my weight. It held! Now I did a chin-up off of the chair. Just as I hoped, the bolt showed no sign of budging from the ceiling.

As I worked, my hands trembled from excitement—or was it from fear of trying to pull this off? I prepared for the next step of my experiment. Still gripping the wooden rung as a trapeze, I swung my legs up and tried to insert one foot in the cloth loop dangling from the other eyebolt. I missed on both the first and second attempts, but the third try paid off—my right foot caught in the loop, and then I shoved the other through as well. Above the locked door, I was hanging parallel to the ceiling, and just inches below it. I was like a human fly hugging the ceiling above the entrance.

I craned my head to look down. The plan just might work, but only if the guards weren't too observant.

However, the effort of holding my chest pulled up to the wooden bar was straining my arm muscles. I prided myself on my physical condition, but this was an unusual position for muscles to hold for very long.

I'll never be able to hang like this for a long time. Maybe it wasn't such a brilliant plan after all.

Besides, I had left my flight jacket on the floor.

I was about to slip my feet out of the loop holding them up when I heard boots clumping down the corridor once more. My heart lurched. Should I hurry and climb down, or go through with this? My mind racing, I weighed the situation, then decided to try it. I jerked myself back into my horizontal position above the door and froze in place.

The now-familiar sound of the key clicked in the lock. I twisted my head sideways just in time to see the door swing outward toward the corridor.

"Raus!" a voice barked.

I held my position and breathed slowly, silently, through clenched teeth. My heart was thumping so loudly in my ears that I was afraid it would betray me. My arm muscles, too, were beginning to ache from the strain.

"Raus! Raus!" This time the voice was both commanding and irritated.

Some other German word was angrily uttered in the corridor, then I glimpsed the top of a helmet as the impatient soldier stepped into the room, directly below where I was performing my human-fly trick.

The helmet whipped left and right as the guard looked for me. But I wasn't in sight. Logically, he wasn't looking straight up!

Suddenly the man turned and exclaimed, *"Er ist nicht hier!"* The top of a second helmet popped into view as a second soldier pushed inside and looked left and right.

Don't look up. Please don't look up!

The two guards exchanged a couple more incomprehensible words, and then both turned and pounded back up the hallway. Their shouts were loud enough to be heard halfway across the Fatherland.

I could hardly believe it. *It worked! These specimens of the "master race" never suspected that their prisoner was dangling right above their thick skulls the whole time.* And best of all, they dashed off and left the door standing open.

No sooner had I dropped to the floor than the whole building erupted into a mass of shouting voices, slamming doors, and running boots. The search was in full swing for the American Luftgangster—who was still in his cell, massaging aching arms.

For a fleeting moment I considered remounting my little trapeze in case someone thought to double-check the cell, but I quickly rejected the idea.

My muscles can't do that a second time.

I crouched in the corner of the cell as I pondered my next move. I hadn't had time to plan ahead, and I had half expected the goons to look up and spot me immediately. The inside of the building was now silent, but the shouting continued outside. I was tempted to sprint down the hallway and make a dash for freedom, but at the same time I knew my flying coveralls would betray me instantly. A quick recapture was inevitable.

What should I do?

After a few more minutes of crouching and listening, I stood and peered through the bottom of my barred window. Outside, German soldiers were frantically running up and down the streets, popping in and out of shop doorways, and screaming back and forth to each other. What a hornets' nest my stunt had stirred up! Had I committed a huge blunder in letting them think I had escaped? In their present frame of mind, it was hard to say what one of them might do if I was recaptured. Who would blame them if they shot first and asked questions later?

I pushed my fears to the back of my mind, knowing that fear and doubt could only hurt my chances of escape.

Well, God, I guess I'm going to try this. Be with me now!

Gingerly I stepped out the doorway and into the corridor. Apparently every soldier in the place had rushed outside to join in the manhunt. I walked slowly down the hall, trembling with fear of discovery. At about the midpoint in the corridor I came to a door that had been left ajar during the occupants' frenzy to leave.

Taking no chances, I peeked into the room before passing, just in case someone remained inside. The room contained none of the enemy, but I nearly let out a whoop of joy at what I did find—six bunks for sleeping and German uniforms hanging from wooden pegs. Judging by the wrinkles, I assumed that these had been cast off and awaited laundering.

Excited and nervous at the same time, I hastily picked up the closest uniform and held it next to myself. Too small! My arms would stick out those pygmy sleeves by five inches. No good!

The next uniform appeared to be almost my size. I pulled it over my own clothes, not daring to waste time changing, nor to leave my own clothing behind as a clue. Lastly I kicked off the insulated flying boots and pulled on a spare pair of *Wehrmacht* boots that I found in the bottom of a locker. They were about one size too large, but they would have to do.

Lifting the mattress on one bunk, I stuffed my boots beneath it. They would be discovered, of course, but not right away.

The transformation was complete. I stepped to the door, and then paused to look around the room one last time. No weapons in sight. Not even a pistol.

No matter. Somewhere in the Bible it says something like, 'If God be for us, who can be against us?' I won't worry about weapons.

Trying to act as "German" as possible, I hustled out of the building and into the bright sunshine of the street. I struck a fast pace down the road, pretending to be looking left and right for an escaped American. No one paid any special attention to me, but I felt as conspicuous as an elephant. Soldiers were even halting automobiles and trucks to challenge drivers for their papers.

Just then I realized that I had left my fleece-lined jacket in the cell.

I hate to lose it, but now I'm committed. I'd be a fool to turn back just for a jacket.

Suddenly someone directly behind me shouted something in German. I felt a sudden temptation to flee, but I fought back the urge and looked.

An officer—I wasn't sure what rank—stood in the middle of the street and glared at me. Now I was sure that this was the person who had shouted, and he had definitely been addressing me. I had no idea what the man had said, so I put a hand to my ear and cocked my head, pretending that I simply hadn't heard. Actually, this would have been quite likely with all the noise and confusion of soldiers running about and civilians scrambling to get out of their way.

The officer yelled something else and pointed to a narrow alley. I couldn't understand a single word, but I thought I caught the man's meaning. He wanted me to search up the alley.

I gave a quick nod of the head and obediently dashed into the alley, all while wondering if instead of the nod I should have replied, *"Jawohl!"* or given the Nazi salute or something. No matter, a glance over my shoulder showed that no one was following.

I emerged from the far end of the alley and continued up the next street, still jogging at a good clip. I had been on the Blue Blazer track team back at Elkhart High School, so running was one thing I was used to. I just hoped no one would notice that I had no rifle like the other searchers who crossed my path. However, everyone seemed intent on finding a man who looked like an American airman, not a German soldier.

I trotted down streets and around corners until, finally, I neared the outskirts of town. Peering down one street, I could see that a roadblock was hastily being set up in that direction.

With another furtive look backward, I made sure no one was following and then ducked behind a house. Here I found a well-tended garden, beyond which was a stone wall about shoulder height. I scrambled over the wall and found that I was practically out of the town. Nearby was a road, and beyond that were more plots of tilled earth, but no other houses.

Still trying to maintain the pretense of a search, I set off across a grassy meadow until I came to a stand of birch trees. Relieved to find some cover, I plunged into the woods. Stopping to lean against an ancient elm tree, I gasped for air.

As soon as I began breathing easier, I wondered what my next course of action should be.

Hide here and rest? Impossible—soon the entire countryside will be swarming with troops. Right now, the main thing is to put more distance between me and them—and the sooner the better!

I pushed deeper into the woods. Fallen trees and prickly undergrowth hampered my speed, but after a while I came across a path. As I jogged along, I gazed up at the fading sun's rays, which still tinged the treetops with gold light. I had no idea where the trail would lead, or even the name of the town I had just escaped from, for that matter. And in that precise moment, I didn't care. I was free!

Still looking upward, I murmured an audible, "Thank You."

But I'm still trapped behind enemy lines. Where do I go from here?

I was making good time as I jogged along the path. Half of me wanted to stay on the trail in order to put as much distance between me and my pursuers as possible. My other half kept nagging, "This path is dangerous. Animals didn't make it; people did."

In the end, I resolved to stay on the path as long as the light lasted. After that I stepped off it and cut cross country by moonlight, which was sometimes difficult with the canopy of leaves overhead. I moved warily. This was no time to sprain an ankle by tripping over a rotting log.

I was no stranger to walking through woods by night. Back home in Indiana, Dad had always added to the family food supply by deer hunting. Much of the countryside around Elkhart was open farmland and off limits to hunters. But we also had plenty of wooded areas where deer roamed at will. As soon as I was old enough, Dad took me with him on these expeditions. When you spend hours at a time quietly sitting in the woods and listening for movement, your sense of hearing grows keener. Now, as I hurried along, I would occasionally pause and listen, alert for any sound that might be man-made. This time, I wasn't the hunter in the woods—I was the hunted.

At one point I came across a spot where the trees abruptly ended, and a paved road crossed my path. I looked left and right.

No sign of life. I longed to get out of the woods, and this road was a real temptation.

No. They'll be watching all the roads. A nice, wide road seems like the easy way, but it will lead you right into destruction.

Where had those words come from? Sure, they were my own thoughts, but they reminded me of something else. As I peeked out from my leafy concealment, I wondered why that thought struck me as so familiar.

With another glance left and right, I stepped out and hustled across the road. Maybe later I could travel by roads, but for now I would stick to the woods.

On the far side, I hadn't marched more than fifty feet into the trees when I heard the sound of a motor. I slipped behind a tree trunk and peered back the way I had come. I didn't have to wait long. The bright beam of a spotlight cruised down the road.

You guys are going kind of slow, I thought. *I bet you're looking for something.*

I grinned grimly despite the hunger gnawing my stomach.

Well, you're not going to find me that easy. Not if I can help it!

I turned and stealthily pressed farther into the safety of the woods. I was glad that a recent rain had left the carpet of leaves underfoot soft and moldering. Instead of crunching noisily under my boots, the leaves made a barely audible *shump, shump* sound. Unfortunately, no wonderful plan of action was developing in my mind. How to get out of Germany?

As an aid to downed Allied fliers, the army had printed maps of Europe on rectangles of silk that could survive multiple folding and could pass through water with no harm done. Each map went into escape kits that we carried on the planes. Unfortunately, due to the unorthodox way that I exited *American Pride,* my escape kit didn't come with me. Of course, now I sincerely wished that I had the map, compass, chocolate bars, and other items in the kit.

A year earlier, I couldn't have described the location of Holland, Belgium, Luxembourg, or most of Europe to save my life. Happily, after staring at the wall map during so many briefing sessions, by now I had a pretty good picture of the continent emblazoned in my mind. Switzerland bordered Germany on the south, and that was neutral, but it was also hundreds of miles away. I couldn't imagine hiking so far without being discovered.

France should lay roughly southwest of my position, and that was much closer. In France, underground partisans were a thorn in the Nazis' side, and I knew that they sometimes aided downed Allied airmen. But virtually all of Europe had fallen under the shadow of the swastika, and that included France. How could I contact the Resistance without advertising my presence and risking recapture?

You're looking too far down the road! Just do the next right thing. Take this one step at a time.

I began to wish that I had been trained as a pilot instead of being sent to gunnery school. A pilot might have been able to locate a Luftwaffe airfield and steal an airplane, which would be the quickest ticket home—if Allied planes didn't shoot me down first.

In the end, I decided to set my sights on France. Besides, England also lay in that direction.

The warmth of the afternoon sun was long gone, and chill dew settled over the woods. Shivering, I missed my flight jacket more than ever. I had considered throwing away the German uniform, but now I decided to keep it through the night for warmth. Another blessing was that I still had on the long underwear that we gunners wore. So I continued stumbling through the woods as fatigue dragged at my eyelids.

"What I wouldn't give right now for a hot serving of English fish and chips and just one of those wool blankets on my bunk back in Shipdham!"

Of course, dreaming about food when you're cold and miserable only makes the situation bleaker. In the dark woods I couldn't find any sort of shelter. While in school, I had checked out every Edgar Rice Burroughs book on Tarzan, the ape man, from the school library. More than once in Burroughs's tales he described how the savage hero would sleep, not on the ground, but up in a tree, where he would wedge his body in the V where a trunk divided. Looking up, I did spot some divided trunks high overhead, but couldn't imagine sleeping that way even with a rope to hold me in place.

So much for fiction stories!

As a last resort, I huddled under the low boughs of a pine tree. A mattress of dry needles kept me off the dank ground, but my sleep was fitful, partly from the chill and partly from fear of waking to discover a rifle barrel jabbing me in the face.

When birds began twittering before dawn, I stood and stamped my feet to get the blood circulating in them. Now that I had escaped, I decided that I didn't need the helmet anymore, so I jammed it between thick pine boughs to conceal it, and then pressed on.

"I've got to find some food!" I muttered under my breath.

Even as a newcomer to the business of escaping and evading, I understood that a starving man would be more likely to make stupid mistakes or even surrender. I didn't want to fall into that trap. As I stumbled along, I searched for anything edible growing in the forest. I did find a few mushrooms that I knew were edible, but those did little to quell my stomach's demands.

"Even if I stumbled across an apple orchard, nothing would be ripe in May!" I complained to myself. "Why couldn't I have fallen overboard in the summertime?"

I also wondered when all this woodland would end. Hitler had claimed that the citizens of the Third Reich needed *lebensraum,* room for people.

"I'd say this country is lousy with lebensraum!"

Later that day I paused to give my body a five-minute rest. As I sat on a fallen log and looked around, something struck me as odd. When you spend a lot of time in the woods, you get familiar with nature. Now, though, something in the forest seemed not quite right. A stone's throw from my resting place was a low mound covered with leaves and twigs. Of course, leaves and twigs decorated the entire forest floor, but in this one spot they seemed—what? Placed there on purpose? And why was that the only spot where no small saplings, ferns, or other plants grew?

Curious, I walked over and examined the mound. Placing one boot on it, I pressed down and felt something hard beneath a layer of soft earth. The impression was of a rock or a log buried just under the surface. When I scraped aside some leaves, the edge of an olive-drab tarpaulin appeared.

What would anybody hide under a tarp so deep in the forest?

Halfway expecting to find a pile of military supplies, I lifted the tarp. Instead of military gear, however, I found what looked like the entrance to a homemade shelter of some sort.

I considered fleeing, as someone obviously knew about this place and wanted to keep it hidden. But my survival instincts told me this discovery might yield something to eat. Coming to a snap decision, I pulled the tarp back farther and crawled through the entrance.

The light was poor, and my body blocked the morning light filtering through from behind me. But immediately my hand encountered a shape I couldn't mistake. It was a flashlight. Flicking it on, I shined the beam around the little chamber.

Clearly somebody had lived here. Maybe they still did. I was relieved to see no signs of military equipment at all, so this wasn't an army bunker. Instead I found blankets, an axe, kerosene lanterns, wooden crates, water cans, clothing, and a variety of miscellaneous items.

Could this be a primitive hunter's lodge?

I poked through a pile of clothing atop a blanket and was astonished to see that it included a woolen skirt.

What sort of woman lives underground in the woods?

I considered the possibility of partisans. "But this is still Germany," I argued with myself. "No partisans operate in Germany. France, sure. Holland, sure. But not inside the Third Reich!"

No matter who lived here, I concluded that my best course of action would be to search for food and then clear out, pronto. I unscrewed the cap to one of the water cans and took a long swig. I hadn't had a drink since the imitation coffee in my cell the previous afternoon.

Next I lifted the lid of a wooden crate. Inside were unmarked tins of various sizes. I opened one and nearly shouted "Hallelujah!" Inside were apples. They were yellowed, and some were slightly bruised, but I was in no position to complain. I stuffed two into the pockets of my German uniform pants and took a bite out of a third.

I opened another tin and to my great delight discovered it was filled with biscuits. I stuffed a couple of these into my already bulging pockets and took another bite of apple. The crate contained a half dozen other tins of various sizes, and beside it stood two more crates. Suddenly I felt like a thief who has found more treasure than he bargained for and isn't sure how to make off with all his loot.

Curious about the second crate, I tried to lift the lid. It was nailed shut. I moved to the third and tried it as well. This time the lid yielded with a slight squeak. However, before I could pick up the flashlight to peer inside it, my ears detected a shuffling sound behind me. I froze.

In the next instant another flashlight flicked on, catching me fully in its beam. When I turned, the glare from the second light prevented me from seeing clearly, but I could discern three silhouettes near the entrance. I mentally criticized myself for getting so excited that I forgot to remain alert.

A person never knows what bizarre thought will come to him in just such a moment. I amazed myself by remembering the childhood bedtime story about three bears who catch Goldilocks eating their food while they were out.

The thought of food reminded me of the bite of apple still in my mouth. I swallowed it. Then, for the second time in two days, I slowly raised my hands until they touched the log roof.

"Okay, boys," I said, "looks like you've caught me fair and square. But can I at least enjoy a last meal before you shoot me?"

For a long, tense moment the three newcomers remained as motionless as I did. A male voice whispered something to another in German, and once again I wished I knew more than a smattering of this language. The beam from their flashlight was still in my eyes.

"Can you at least lower the light?" I asked, not knowing if my captors would understand my request.

Again there was a whispered consultation. This time, though, I did catch one word that I understood: *Englisch*. The German word is so similar to ours that it's unmistakable.

"I'm not English," I said slowly. "I'm American."

Making an obvious show that my hands were empty, I slowly lowered them and unbuttoned the German tunic to reveal my own USAAF clothing beneath. I was no expert in the rules of warfare, but I knew that in my own uniform I would be treated as a POW. Running around Nazi Germany in a Wehrmacht uniform would most likely earn me a bullet as a spy.

Again the three whispered among themselves. I caught the sound of a woman's voice.

What's going on here?

At last the third silhouette, the woman, spoke in stilted English that held a touch of British accent. "You are really American?"

"You got that right. And I wish I were back in the USA right now."

"Who told you where to find us?" she asked.

I shook my head. "Nobody. Look, I don't have any idea who you are, or even where I am. Yesterday I was flying on an American airplane. We dropped bombs on Kiel. There was an accident, and I ended up floating down to Germany by parachute. I escaped and ran away until I accidentally found this place."

The woman translated all this to her male companions. Then one of them asked a question, which she translated.

"Are you alone? No other American flyers are with you?"

"Nobody else. Just me."

After the three consulted, the woman said, "Step outside, please." The three slipped out the doorway and out from under the tarp.

They don't want any blood inside, so they're going to shoot me in the woods.

However, when I reached the open air, I discovered that my "captors" weren't military at all. These were dark-haired civilians, and judging by their soiled clothing, they had been living in the underground shelter for some time. They didn't even carry weapons, just the flashlight.

Are these Gypsies?

The taller of the two men spoke, and the woman interpreted. "Because of your German uniform, we at first thought you came to arrest us. By coming here, you have put us in danger. We are not free people. We are Jews, but Jewish people are no longer welcome in Germany. We had no money to leave. We had no Gentile friends to hide us. So we created this place. We live here. We hide and hope for happier days."

At last I understood. Even back in my humble home town, the *Elkhart Truth* had carried news stories of brutality against Jews. My crew's radio operator, David Rose, was Jewish, and more than once he had vowed that he would throw away his dog tags if he ever had to bail out over the Fatherland. Each dog tag included a letter, which signified the bearer's religion. The "H" on Rose's would immediately peg him as "Hebrew."

"You cannot remain here," the woman said, interpreting again. "If you escaped, they are searching for you. If they find only us, it will be bad. But if they find you here with us, it will mean instant death for sheltering you. You cannot remain."

I shook my head. "I don't want to remain, as you put it. I want to go to France, so I can get back to England. Can you tell me exactly where I am and which direction to go?"

The woman put this to the leader, who seemed to be her husband. He smiled for the first time and relayed a question through the woman.

"You truly do not know where you are?"

"No. I'm lost. I don't have a map."

"That is good," the woman interpreted. "In that case we will give you some food and send you on your way. But we cannot tell you where you are. If they capture you, you might—what is your expression?—'spill the peas' about us. But if you do not know where we are, you cannot tell anyone how to come here."

I saw the point. "Thanks a lot. By the way, my name is Jim. Jim Yoder." Foolishly, I reached out a hand and expected them to introduce themselves. The woman let me know that wasn't going to happen.

"There is no reason for you to learn our names. We must be strangers. Even we cannot remain here now. The soldiers who search for you may find us instead. We must move to a second place, not so good as this one. All we can do is give you some food and send you away."

"It's a deal." I pointed to my pants pockets, which bulged conspicuously. "I've already taken some of your food. I hope that's okay. If you could give me one more drink of water, I'll scram and forget that I ever saw any of you."

The woman looked puzzled. "What is 'scram'?"

"It's American lingo. It means I'll get out of your hair and won't come back."

"Get out of my hair?"

"Leave quickly."

Hearing this, the two men nodded. They weren't unfriendly, but obviously wanted me gone, the sooner the better. The shorter, silent man slipped into the shelter and returned with a small metal flask, plus a loaf of dark bread with the beginnings of mold growing on one end. He handed these to me.

"We do not have much to spare," the woman interpreted again in her clipped accent. "We must stay in hiding for a long time. But we will give you these."

I accepted the items offered. "May the God of Abraham, of Isaac, and of Jacob bless you for your kindness."

The woman blinked in surprised to hear such words.

"You are an unusual person," the woman said on her own. "A foreign Gentile who speaks like a Jew."

"I believe in the same God you do," I replied. Because I hadn't seriously read the Bible for some years, I wasn't sure what else to say, but felt I should add something. "He makes me feel like Jews are relatives of mine."

She rendered my words into her native tongue. Her husband's face couldn't have looked more surprised if I had announced that I was born on the planet Mars. He spoke quickly, with gruffness in his tone.

"In our country," she relayed, "the government claims God is on its side. Every soldier of the Wehrmacht wears a buckle that says, 'God with us.' But we do not know Gentiles who speak like you, about feeling related to Jews."

Growing impatient, the taller man spoke rapidly.

"My husband will . . ." The woman searched her mind for a word that she didn't know, then started over. "He will put a piece of cloth over your eyes and guide you through the forest. It will be safer for us if you do not see how to return."

I didn't appreciate the idea of being blindfolded, but what could I say? These three were frightened. Every minute I lingered made them jumpier. Each of them constantly glanced around, searching the undergrowth with their eyes as if they expected soldiers to sprout out of the earth itself.

"All right," I agreed. "First let me get rid of these Wehrmacht pants. Maybe you can use the cloth to make something." I pulled them off over my boots and transferred the food to my own pockets. "Ready."

A black rag went over my face, blocking all light. Someone took my left hand, and we started forward. No more words were exchanged, but by the sound of our footsteps, I realized that there were only three of us.

The woman probably stayed behind. Perhaps to pack their gear.

As they led me through the woods, whoever held my hand led me skillfully, and only once did I stub my boot against a tree root. After nearly an hour we came to a place where a fraction of light filtered through the cloth over my eyes. The rag whipped off, and I found myself blinking in full sunshine beside a railroad track. Beyond the track were rolling hills with clusters of trees on them. Occasional farmhouses dotted the distant landscape.

The younger of my two guides broke his silence for the first time. He pointed down the railroad track and uttered one phrase in English: "Go to there."

I assume that was the limit of his foreign-language skills. He pointed again to emphasize the direction I should take. Then the two turned and faded back into the woods.

I started walking down the center of the tracks, but didn't feel safe. Here I was, sauntering along in full daylight dressed in USAAF clothing with a loaf of bread in my hand as if I were heading to a picnic in the Norfolk countryside. But what if someone saw me? The alarm would go out, and I would be chased down like a criminal. Earlier I had wished that I could get out of the woods, but now I yearned for their protective cover.

This is no good. It doesn't feel right. I can't expect to get very far without somebody spotting me. All it will take is one schoolboy, one farmer in his field, and they'll be after me with pitchforks.

What could I do? Go back to the Jewish hideout and plead for civilian clothes? No, I might wander all over the forest without stumbling across it a second time. Even if I did locate it, the three Jews hiding there would be terrified and angry to see me again. I would not put them at risk.

Even though I enjoyed basking in the warm sunshine after my chilly night under the pine, I stepped off the tracks and into a clump of birch saplings. Sitting down, I figured I was out of sight and could think through my predicament while I had a bite to eat. I pinched the green spots off my bread, then broke off a piece and popped it into my mouth.

The bread was dry and stiff, but grew moist from saliva as I chewed. Suddenly I recalled that Jesus always offered thanks before breaking bread. I swallowed my morsel and bowed my head.

"Thank You for providing this daily bread in such an unexpected way. Amen."

As I broke off a second bite, I tried to dredge up recollections about what the Bible says about praying. In the back of my mind I halfway recalled a passage about God knowing what things people need even before they ask, but that He wants them to come to Him with their needs anyway.

"Well, Lord," I said quietly, "I'm still a long way from real freedom, but thanks for helping me this far. Thanks for letting me stumble into those folks' hiding place, and for the food they gave me. Protect them, and help me to stay close to You, no matter what happens . . ."

I continued munching on the loaf.

Sure wish I had some civilian clothes. But even if I did, somebody might wonder why a guy my age is hiking along the railroad instead of in the army. Boy, do I wish Dan or Pulaski or one of the other guys was here!

I always figured that if I ever had to bail out, all the other guys would bail out with me. Not in any dream had I foreseen being on the run, alone, in Nazi Germany.

No, not totally alone. God is with me.

By the time a fourth of the bread was eaten, I resolved to stay hidden among the saplings and to rest while the sun was shining. That evening, I would continue my journey toward France under cover of darkness.

I wonder . . . I know I'm heading southwest, but depending on how far the soldiers drove me when I was knocked out, I might not be heading toward France at all. If I'm still close to the coast, I'll hit Holland or Belgium before I reach France . . .

The idea of multiple border crossings weighed on my mind. Borders would be guarded, especially during wartime. My heart sank at the possibility of sneaking into eastern Belgium, only to face another border on the western side.

I sighed.

I wonder how long it will take for Dad to get a telegram that I'm missing in action? He only met Margo once, that night we went to hear the Elkhart Municipal Band in Studebaker Park. Will he think to call her and tell her what happened?

56

Even though Margo wasn't officially my girlfriend, in less than two weeks I had grown closer to her than I had to any of the girls from my own school. Normally I got tongue-tied around girls—the cute ones anyway. Or I ended up tripping over my feet in front of them and feeling foolish. But right from that first meeting at her father's fruit stand, Margo's lighthearted giggle and warm, green eyes had somehow put me at ease. Also, she had a way of asking just the right questions that helped to keep a conversation flowing naturally. With her I never worried about running out of things to say. It would have been a comfort to have her smiling photo with me.

If only those goons had let me go back for my wallet.

As the afternoon wore on, I reviewed in my mind the things Margo and I had done together in the days before I left for basic training. Of course, when I first invited her out to Judd's Drug Store to enjoy a sundae—"made with Furnas ice cream," as the sign in the soda fountain boasted—I hadn't realized such a simple outing would be out of the question.

"My father is more than just a fruit farmer," Margo had told me with a twinkle in her green eyes. "He's also the new pastor of Bristol Chapel. If any boy wants to invite me out, first he has to come to the house and spend some time with our family and let Daddy get to know him."

Those two revelations had nearly driven me away right there. Me, date a pastor's daughter? And the whole scenario of asking permission from "Daddy" had seemed totally old-fashioned. But something about Margo made me go through with it. So that evening I found myself eating meatloaf and mashed potatoes with the Lace family, and undergoing a cordial grilling from her father. Reverend Lace was pleased to learn that I regularly attended Jordan Memorial Tabernacle. What I hadn't mentioned was that I only attended out of obligation to my father.

Making a good impression on Margo's younger brother, Clint, was much simpler. A blond, tousle-haired seventh-grader, Clint was fascinated by motors, whether they were on boats, cars, aircraft, or motorcycles. Just one glimpse of me pulling into the driveway on my Indian motorcycle was enough to convince Clint that I was okay.

After supper, however, when Margo and I were alone on the porch swing, she intuitively sensed that I wasn't on the same spiritual level that she was. In the following days she pieced together the story of how Mom died and about my bitterness toward God. I was afraid she would reject me then and there. But she surprised me.

"Jim," she said, "I believe it was God who led you to our fruit stand. I think He wanted you to meet my family. We can pray for you, and maybe help you find your way back to Him."

At the time I had thought, *Nope! It was that dazzling smile of yours that stopped my motorcycle.* But of course I didn't voice that opinion. Looking back, I wondered if maybe Margo had been right all along. I knew she was praying for me. Dad had been praying even longer. But in my rebellion, I hadn't wanted anything to do with God or anybody who goes to church.

Funny how life can suddenly turn upside down, I mused. *Or better yet, right side up.*

I closed my eyes and managed to catch some brief naps while the sun's warmth eased the pain from my bruises. After the emotional strain since my tumble from the plane and the escape, it felt good just to relax and doze—while I had the chance.

I awoke to a tickling sensation on my cheek. A breeze had sprung up, brushing a tall blade of grass back and forth across my face. I sat up.

Clouds had overrun the sky, and dusk was setting in. I was glad for the overcast. A cloudy night holds more of the day's warmth than clear skies. Saving the apples and biscuits in my pockets for later, I nibbled some more from the loaf, then washed it down with a few swallows from my flask.

Time to hit the road.

I left my hiding spot and began hiking along the railroad tracks.

This is more like it, I thought, noticing the deepening gloom with satisfaction. *I can make out the tracks well enough to walk easily, but no troublemakers will get a good look at me.*

I walked for about an hour before the first train came barreling down the tracks. It approached from behind, but even before it appeared from around a bend, I detected the sound of it vibrating through the steel rails beside me. With plenty of time to spare, I hopped down the elevated rail bed and hid in a thicket until it thundered past.

I resumed my plodding. Occasionally my boot would catch on an uneven tie, but all in all I was making much better progress than I had been while wandering through woods and stumbling over rotten tree trunks. The pace was faster, and following an established course gave the impression of going the right way, even though I was uncertain of where I was.

Hour after hour I trudged, sometimes stepping behind a tree to let a train pass, and then continuing on my way.

Not even somebody to talk to. I never realized what real loneliness is.

Back home I sometimes whistled when I was alone. Now, of course, that would be foolhardy. I needed to pad along quieter than cat. Sometimes I talked to God a little in my thoughts, but I tried to keep my ears alert for any hint of danger.

The woods were far behind me now, and I was passing tilled fields. Whether anything had yet been planted I didn't know. But in mid-May nothing would be growing.

As the night grew old, I began to worry. Where would I hide when the sun rose? I didn't dare to get caught out in the open. I had just begun to consider sheltering in a barn when it occurred to me that farmers begin their day earlier than other folks. If I had any hopes of sneaking into a barn unseen, I should do it right away.

As soon as the next likely looking farmhouse loomed into view, I left the railroad line and cut across a field toward it. Even before I reached the yard, a ferocious barking split the night. I had no way of knowing whether the farmer's dog was tied up, nor if it would back up its bark with teeth, but I turned and sprinted back the way I had come. Breaking into a cold sweat, I sped down the tracks with the hound's howling receding behind me. Perhaps the homeowner would blame the ruckus on a fox. I hoped so.

I passed two more farms before I mustered the courage to try again. This time I gave the house a wide berth and circled around to approach the barn from the opposite direction. When my hands at last touched the weathered wood of the barn's rear wall, I felt like a spy skulking through the night. Peering around the corner, I saw no one. Every nerve alert, I slipped open the barn door and quickly pulled it shut behind me.

When my eyes adjusted to the deeper gloom inside, I realized that this barn held neither cows nor horses, as I had expected. There were stalls, but these were void of life.

Maybe all the livestock has gone toward war the effort.
I inhaled deeply. My grandparents and many school friends lived on farms. I relished the wholesome scent of hay. All barns must have in common the same earthy smells that conjure up images of a simple life lived close to the land.

When my eyes had adjusted to the deeper darkness inside, I found an old-fashioned plow. From pegs on the wall hung a myriad of other farm implements: sickles; pulleys; pitchforks and shovels; buckets; kerosene lanterns; a bow saw; plus blinders, bridles, bits, and horseshoes for the absent animals.

I came to a rough workbench on which I found an oilcan, a wooden mallet, snippers, a pair of pliers, and a couple other tools that I couldn't identify. Nothing, though, struck me as helpful in my flight from the Nazis.

There was no tractor, and I momentarily wondered if Europeans still did all their plowing with oxen. A quick check of the first two stalls revealed them to be bare and swept clean. The third stall contained heavy burlap sacks. I opened one.

Potatoes! Thank You, Lord!

Despite the fact that I was in enemy territory, I felt a little guilty for removing half a dozen potatoes from the top sack. When I was twelve, my boyhood friend Roy Thompson and I got caught stealing a watermelon from his neighbor's field. Old Mr. Bontrager put us to work scrubbing windows and shoveling horse manure as punishment. Even though he let us keep the watermelon when we finished, I had never dared to take anything that wasn't mine again. Until now.

You're not really stealing, I told myself. *This is war. You're just depleting the enemy's food supply. Besides, it's your duty to escape by whatever means possible.*

The fourth and fifth stalls were heaped with hay, despite the fact that no cattle were in sight.

I climbed a wooden ladder to the loft, but it was empty, except for some old spindle-legged chairs and a table gathering dust. In the loft, there wasn't so much as a horse blanket to hide under. In the end, I descended the ladder once more and burrowed into the hay until I reached the back of the fifth stall in the rear corner of the barn. Once there, I thanked the Lord for the potatoes, wiped the dirt from one, and bit into it.

The tang of raw potato on my tongue brought back memories of Mom. When I was young, she would slice potatoes to fry them in a black iron skillet. Sometimes she would hand me a slice, which I sprinkled with salt and ate uncooked. I hadn't experienced that flavor in ages . . .

The sudden creak of door hinges jerked me back to the present. Under the hay, I instantly froze. Somebody's shoes were scuffling across the dirt floor. Next I heard metallic clunking and banging as the visitor retrieved whatever bucket or tools he had come for. Within five minutes the door creaked again, leaving the barn in silence. I exhaled a sigh of relief and continued gnawing my potato.

That day stretched on and on. Nestled in my sweet-smelling hiding place, I did manage to catnap on and off. But my nerves were on edge, as I never knew when the farmer might enter and start clunking around again. In addition, hay was poking in my eyes and up my nose and scratching the back of my neck. It's one thing to play in hay as a kid, but quite another to lay under it stiff with fear of moving and discovery.

As I lay hidden, I periodically heard light scratching and the scurry of miniature feet.

Field mice. I hope they don't decide to squirm their way into the hay with me!

I also wondered about lice. Could a person get them from hiding under hay? As soon as I thought that, I could almost feel the nasty creatures burrowing into my hair and crawling up my sleeves.

You think too much! Knock it off!

Still, I resolved to scrub my hair and scalp as often as opportunities allowed.

During the afternoon, I heard the sound of aircraft engines droning far off in the distance. Positive they must be B-17s, I felt like rushing outside to see fellow Americans, even if they were high overhead. Instead, I stayed put and nibbled some more of my bread until the sound faded and disappeared.

At long last darkness seeped back into the barn, and through a knothole in the wall behind me I saw blessed twilight settling over the farmyard. I waited until full night had arrived before I ventured to the door. Despite blackout conditions, a faint glow shone in the window of the house. Hardly breathing, I eased the barn door open just enough to squeeze out and then retraced my steps back to the railroad tracks.

I didn't feel fully rested, but so far I had beaten the odds. I was still free—at least for now.

That first experience of sneaking into a farmer's barn turned out to be one of many in the following days. I didn't always spend an entire day hiding in a barn. When I could find a suitable haystack in a field, I preferred to wriggle into that or into a clump of bushes rather than spend my days cooped up in a barn and fearing detection. Unless I found a lot of hay or straw or something else in a barn to conceal me, I just scrounged for potatoes or carrots or anything else that looked useful and kept moving.

One night, though, a sudden downpour caught me out in the open. The only shelter I could find was beneath a railroad trestle. If I had had a raincoat, I would have continued walking. Since I didn't, I spent half the night and all the next day huddled under the trestle, feeling wretched and waiting for the weather to clear.

Some nights I covered a fair distance. Other nights, though, I barely progressed at all, especially near towns and villages. When the tracks approached any population center, I feared to stay on them. Towns meant curious eyes, police, and soldiers. So I would leave the tracks and make my way across country clear around the town until I could relocate the rails on the far side. These side trips resulted in barking dogs and heart-pounding minutes spent crouching in ditches or behind tree trunks.

I had assumed that staying hidden would be my main challenge. Not so. Instead, my continuing crisis was finding sufficient food and water to keep me going. Not every barn contained vegetables for the taking, and I didn't dare to drink from the ponds and lakes I saw by moonlight. Diarrhea or some worse illness could bring my escape to an abrupt halt.

Out in the country, I discovered that some homes still used outside wells, the kind with buckets lowered on a chain or rope by a hand crank. When thirst drove me to them, I learned what a lesson in patience it is to lower a bucket slowly, inch by agonizing inch to minimize squeaking, and then to draw it up again at the same snail's pace. And all the time I was cranking, I would scrutinize the farmhouse and hope no one inside was staring back at me from those darkened windows.

One miserable and frightening experience was the time hunger drove me to risk exploring a shed just before dawn. The shed was behind a house, and its back side was actually cut into the side of a low hill. Inside I found coping saws, chisels, wood planes, hand drills, clamps, and similar tools. Evidently someone used the shed as a carpentry shop. But it was also a storage shed, and in the twilight I found two barrels against the back wall.

I lifted the lid of one barrel and found it empty. Inside it, however, the pungent scent of pickle brine lingered strongly. Excited, I shook the second barrel. Judging by the weight and sloshing sound, it was nearly full.

Pickles! That will be a nice change from potatoes and brown apples!

However, no sooner did I begin hunting for a pry bar than I heard voices approaching from outside. I was trapped! Yanking up the lid of the empty barrel, I stuffed my frame inside it. I had barely settled the lid over my head when I heard footsteps scuffing the wooden floor.

Two voices were carrying on a conversation. Listening, I concluded that this was an elderly man and a young boy, possibly a grandson. What they were creating, I don't know, but I spent hours in that barrel, my knees pressed to my chin, listening to the sound of sawing wood, filing, and a running discussion in a language I couldn't follow. Meanwhile, the sickeningly strong odor of pickle juice permeated my nostrils, my mouth, and every breath that filled my lungs.

Even my hopes for escape during a lunch break were dashed. Around midday an elderly sounding matron arrived with a meal. I was forced to listen to these three munching and slurping and chatting happily while the daggers of hunger—plus the ever-present smell of pickles—was driving me insane! My one consolation was that I hadn't drunk much water the night before and didn't feel nature's demand for an outhouse.

Finally, late in the afternoon, the man and the boy closed up shop and exited. I waited a while longer to make sure they were really gone before emerging from my cramped prison. I could hardly get myself out. The hours of being pickled in a barrel made my knees and ankles feel like I was a hundred-year-old man suffering from arthritis. Once free, I perched on a three-legged stool and peeked out the shed door as I massaged my leg muscles until evening.

However, the delay did reap one dividend: on the table sat a pot of very weak tea, long gone cold. I drank my fill, and then poured the remainder into my flask. Also, a partial loaf of dark bread had been forgotten, along with a jar of homemade peach marmalade. Rejoicing, I placed these in the burlap sack I had picked up on a previous expedition. By this time, however, the mere thought of crunching my teeth into a pickle made me nauseous. The second barrel remained untouched as I slipped into the night.

No more risks! I chided. *Even if you don't make a single mile of progress, it's better to be patient and safe than to take one risk and get caught.*

Another dilemma arose over the simple matter of washing. In May the waterways of Germany were far too brisk for bathing, at least by my standards. But after a week on the run, I couldn't tolerate my own odor. I began washing by moonlight whenever I happened across a suitable stream or lake. Using one wet rag and one dry one, I would scrub one portion of my body, dry it off, and proceed to wash another part of myself.

My feet were the tricky part. Because I was constantly ready to break into a dash at the first cry of alarm, in that first week I never removed my boots or socks. And how could I rinse out my one pair of socks when I needed them dry for walking?

"I say, old boy," I told myself in a mock British accent, "you can't keep those boots on day and night until you reach England. You're liable to catch trench foot or some such dreadful thing."

So I devised a system. I would stop at a stream or puddle to bathe my feet and wash my stockings. Then, to keep the leather boots from chafing as I walked, I would stuff them with tender leaves and grass before pulling them on. That done, I would wring out my socks and dangle them from two sticks protruding from my hip pockets to air dry while I walked. It was a primitive laundry system, but it was the best I could manage under the circumstances.

I don't think I'll ever take socks for granted again, I mused as I trudged down the tracks one night.

More than once rabbits startled me. I'd be walking along and suddenly hear a flurry of noise over dry leaves. Of course, my heart would leap from my chest even before I spotted the rabbit zigzagging away in a pattern of fast hops. Each time this happened, I vowed it would be the last. And it was—until the next time.

In my solitude, I increasingly talked to God as I endlessly set one foot in front of the other. It wasn't formal praying, filled with a lot of *Thee's* and *Thou's*. Instead, I just plodded along and talked to Him in my thoughts. I asked for my daily bread—or potatoes, or whatever else I could eat—but I said more than that.

It occurred to me that my dad back in Elkhart would be pretty unhappy if the only time I talked to him was when I wanted a few dollars or the keys to the car. Spending time together and talking is part of being a family. So I figured that maybe the Heavenly Father felt the same way. As I plodded, I told Him my feelings, my worries, and my questions about the future. Back home, I had planned on going to trade school and becoming a mechanic, working on cars, trucks, or motorcycles. After all, engine work came to me pretty naturally. Now, though, I wasn't so sure about that plan. Home seemed impossibly far away, and I could hardly imagine being back there. The war was dragging on . . .

I also tried to recall verses from the Bible. As an airman, I had received a small Bible with a metal plate in the front. It included a picture of President Roosevelt and his good wishes for protection and success. But past that point I had never bothered to read it. So

I dredged my memory, trying to piece together ancient Scriptures I once ignored, but which now contained new insights.

Sometimes I just let my mind roam to thoughts about friends and fun times. I chuckled when I recalled the conversation on the hardstand the morning we took off for Kiel. David Rose had sighed and said how much he missed the bagels his family had in Brooklyn. Unexpectedly, Charlie Barnes from Tennessee had loudly agreed.

"Ah know just what ya mean. Our family used to raise 'em back in Hartsville."

Then, when everyone in earshot turned questioning eyes on Charlie, he added, "Now we don't got no more bagels. Just a couple hound dogs."

Charlie never did figure out why everyone burst into laughter.

Of course, I didn't dare to hum songs aloud, but I did let them "play" in my mind. In Shipdham I had memorized the most popular songs from Radio Calais and Breslau. As I plodded, my surroundings often reminded me of these tunes. For instance, one melody that I especially enjoyed was "Moonlight Serenade," and the crescent moon overhead soon brought it to mind. The night sky also made me think of "Deep in the Heart of Texas" because of its line about the stars at night being "big and bright" in the Lone Star State.

Naturally, walking the rails as I was, it was only a matter of time before Glenn Miller's popular "Chattanooga Choo Choo" surfaced in my thoughts. When I got to the line, "Can you afford to board the Chattanooga Choo Choo?" I inwardly laughed.

I wish I could. Then maybe I could stop tramping along these tracks!

Immediately I stopped. A switch had clicked inside my brain. As if seeing them for the first time, I stared at the twin ribbons of silver stretching ahead in the moonlight.

Why didn't I think of that before? What a numbskull! Instead of cowering in the bushes every time a train roars along, I should be figuring out how to hop aboard one! That would save both time and shoe leather!

Obviously, a seat in a passenger car was out of the question. I had no civilian clothing, no papers, nor the language skills to fake being a citizen of the Reich. Worse, I hadn't shaved for at least ten days by that time. Even though my whiskers didn't grow as fast as Eddie Pulaski's, the bristly stubble on my chin would undoubtedly draw attention to me as a hobo—or an escaping Allied soldier.

But what about a freight car? If I could sneak into a boxcar headed south or southwest, the locomotive could do the hauling, while I could do the snoozing!

I continued walking, but now my mind was turning this plan over and examining it from all angles. Was it possible?

I can't run fast enough to jump aboard a train at full speed. It would be foolhardy to try. But what about when a train is slowing to stop somewhere? Or maybe on the other side of a town, when it's slowly beginning to chug away?

In my mind, I traveled back to Elkhart. Railroad tracks run through the middle of town, and trains frequently halted traffic on Main Street. Some of the boxcars rolled past the crossing with their doors open. Clambering into one might not be difficult at slower speeds. On the other hand, only empty cars had open doors. That meant nothing to hide behind if a railroad employee were to glance inside.

No, I told myself. *If you're going to try this, you better get a car hauling cargo. You need some cover.*

I spent the rest of that night walking, but with no opportunity to put my plan into action. Although I passed a couple villages, I doubted that a train would bother to stop for these, so I didn't either.

Toward dawn I happened across a deserted, tumbledown shell that must have once been a homestead. Whatever it had been, no one had lived there for a long while. I descended to the cellar. Fallen stones, broken planks, and decaying lumber littered the earthen floor. I piled the stones to form a hiding place. It was no bigger than a coffin—just large enough to stretch out and rest. For concealment, I pulled broken planks over the top.

"What a life," I sighed as I slid the final board into place to cover my head. "Hiding and sleeping when the sun is up, and out prowling the countryside under cover of darkness. I'm becoming a creature of the night."

I had never actually read the novel about Count Dracula, but I knew a little bit about the main character. Except for the part about biting victims' necks, my existence seemed to be just as dreary. One comfort, however, was that the weather was finally turning warmer. Plus, my new hiding place was fairly comfortable . . . and away from prying eyes.

How many days had I been on the run? My weary brain couldn't recall. Days and nights were melding together in my memory. Lack of sleep and the ceaseless tension were wearing me down. I couldn't remember ever being so exhausted.

I'd have to be dead to have less energy. Must look like a walking corpse.

But now, at last, I had found a shelter where I felt I could sleep as deeply as I wanted for as long as my body needed it.

So tired of being tired. But I can sleep here. No one will ever find me in this little "tomb."

Immediately fatigue swallowed up my thoughts. Like a stone sinking into black waters, I sank into deep slumber.

Into my stupor gradually crept the sound of voices. As a person slowly drifting back from drugged sleep, I became aware that I was lying flat on my back. But rather than a soft mattress beneath my body, something hard and unyielding was there. I wanted to shift my position, to lie on my side, but I couldn't will my body to respond. It was almost as if my mind were no longer connected to my limbs.

The voices from my dreams grew louder now, and closer. Vaguely understanding that I had been sleeping, I ignored the voices. After all, they made no sense. They were only jumbled syllables without meaning, the stuff of dreams.

Be quiet. Let me sleep! Let me rest a little longer . . .

However, bit by bit the misty veils shrouding my brain thinned and lifted. Then a question formed: *Where am I?*

I recalled that I was somewhere in Nazi Germany. The running, the hiding, the foraging for food all came back to me, even if the details were fuzzy. But where was I at this precise instant? Lying on something that felt like hard-packed dirt? Had I been buried alive somehow? Perhaps a bomb blast?

Still the voices murmured, sometimes almost in unison, then one at a time. But now I realized that these weren't just any voices. They were German voices!

With that realization, my body stiffened, and my eyes snapped open. But opening my eyes made scant difference. Totally disoriented, I was still unable to focus on a dark mass that seemed just inches above my nose.

Where in the world am I?

Then, out of the corner of my right eye, I perceived a flicker of yellowish light.

Tilting my head, I found myself gazing between two cracked stones at the glimmer of a lone candle. Around the candle sat several boys, about eleven or twelve years of age.

At last I realized where I was. *Of course! The little tomb I made out of debris in the broken-down cellar! But what are these boys doing here?*

Peering out from my hiding place, I watched as the boys talked animatedly. To my American ears, the foreign tongue was pure gibberish, but the hand gestures and the *ak-ak-ak-ak-ak* sound one of them was making were perfectly clear. He was describing an air battle, possibly a German fighter that he had personally witnessed. Back in Shipdham, we gunners sometimes waved our hands the same way as we retold combat experiences around the potbelly in our Quonset hut.

Must be some kind of boys' club. I should have realized that anywhere there's a deserted building or a house under construction, boys will come to explore.

One of the youths passed a long object to another, and I caught a glint of reflected candlelight. It was a sausage, followed by a knife. One at a time they were passing these around, cutting off a slice, and snacking on the sausage. I licked my lips.

Meat. Real meat. I had no idea how long it had been since I tasted meat. I wasn't even sure what time of day it was, although the gray light in the cellar suggested I had slept all day—or could it be two days?

Thank goodness I don't snore. They would have discovered me before I knew they were here.

The youngsters' conversation dragged on and on. I wanted to be on my way, but they seemed in no hurry whatsoever.

Here I go again. Trapped until these kids go home. Well, at least I'm lying flat this time, and I don't have to endure pickles.

Chapter 11

Still there was the tantalizing image of that sausage making the rounds. Maybe I couldn't smell it, but I wanted to. Like a gunner tracking a Focke-Wulf through his Sperry gun sight, my eyes followed that sausage from hand to hand. My tongue moistened my lips once more.

What I wouldn't give for just a couple slices!

When my stomach growled the first time, I felt it more than heard it. I slid my left hand to the spot and pressed down hard, hoping to stifle any further noises. It was not to be. The sight of that sausage and my merciless hunger conspired against me. Every other minute my stomach would rumble, and no amount of hand pressure or will power would silence it. To the contrary, the noise was becoming louder.

At first the boys didn't notice. Suddenly, though, one of them raised a finger and shushed his pals. He stood and climbed halfway up the broken steps as he searched for the source of the sound.

My stomach growled again, louder than ever. Now all the boys were on their feet and searching the floor. Maybe they thought a sick puppy had crawled into the cellar. When the tallest one picked up the candle and began walking around, I was afraid of what might happen next.

I shut my eyes and faked death as one of them lifted the broken plank that covered my face. A gasp, a long hush, and then a soft babble of voices tinged with both fear and awe.

Don't touch me, I thought. *If they touch me, they'll feel my skin is warm, and they'll know I'm not dead. Just go home and let me get out of here!*

Even though I might have been able to overpower them, I wasn't going to attack a bunch of innocent kids. Sure, I was a soldier, but they weren't, even if they did live in the Fatherland.

Just go away.

Fingers pressed against my cheek before being jerked away. A youthful voice blurted an exclamation. The game was over.

I opened my eyes and looked into four terrified faces. *"Guten Abend,"* I said, using one of my few German phrases.

Count Dracula himself rising from a coffin couldn't have ignited more sheer terror. Hysterical shrieks erupted. The candle flew to the floor and snuffed out. Each boy pushed and shoved his comrades as all of them fought to be first up the rickety steps.

"Hey, wait! I won't bite your necks!" I leapt from my hiding place, scattering rubble and cracked planks as I did.

They weren't listening. All they wanted was to flee that cellar as fast as their feet would carry them. By the time I reached the top step, they were already scrambling down a path across a meadow that must have been a plowed field in earlier years. They were shouting loud enough to wake real corpses.

No time to waste! Get out of here!

I had no way to guess how long it would take before those boys reached home, nor how long before some adults returned to investigate. I stumbled back down the steps just long enough to snatch up my burlap sack. To my great bliss, I also found the remains of the sausage in the dirt beside the now-extinguished candle. The last boy holding it must have dropped it out of fright.

Thank You, Lord! Thank You for some meat!

Even though my hands trembled with fear of discovery, I bit off a hunk before sprinting in the opposite direction the boys had gone. It tasted heavenly!

Running for the Blue Blazers had never pumped me with so much adrenalin. Like twin pistons, my legs sprinted faster than ever. When I reached the railroad tracks, I slowed, but only to a trot. I wanted to put as many miles as possible between me and any pursuers.

Just don't let them have dogs.

In the fading light of dusk, I might evade human eyes, but a trained dog can detect a scent long after his quarry has vanished. Did Germans use hound dogs like the police in America? I wasn't sure. My one hope was to find and board a train that would carry me away from this district—and fast!

The farther my legs carried me from the site of the close call, the more rationally I was able to think. As I race-walked along the tracks, I reviewed the incident with the boys in my mind.

I did blurt some words in English, but by then the boys were hollering and running for their lives. I doubt if they heard anything past Guten Abend.

How would parents react if their breathless son ran home jabbering that a man who had been buried in a tumble-down building had sat up and uttered, "Good evening"? It was possible that they would assume a vagrant had been sheltering there. Or perhaps they would scold their son for trespassing on someone else's property in the first place. On the other hand, if the boys detected my American accent, the authorities might launch a manhunt to capture the suspicious fugitive.

It was impossible to say how this situation might pan out. I maintained a brisk pace. An occasional bite of sausage or a swig from my flask fortified me for the effort. Now my mind was clear, sharper than it had been for days.

When the railroad tracks crossed a narrow river, I paused and considered: might it be possible to lie on a log and simply let the current carry me downstream?

Not a smart idea. That water will have your teeth chattering in no time. And where would you find dry clothes to wear after you wade back ashore?

I did make my way down the mossy embankment and pulled my boots and socks off. Just in case someone did decide to trail me with dogs, I walked downstream along the bank a good distance before stepping into the current and wading back to the trestle. Then, with boots and stockings dangling around my neck by the laces, I carefully crossed the river beam by beam on the underside of the trestle, instead of on top.

Well, if anyone uses tracking dogs, that might confuse them a little, I thought when I reached the far side. Maybe not, but I was trying any trick I could. Pulling my footwear back on, I continued down the tracks. My maneuver had cost some time, but in my opinion it was worth the effort for peace of mind, if nothing else.

I hadn't traveled far before I once more heard the distant rumble that was now becoming so familiar. I hopped off the tracks and scooted down the gravelly embankment. No trees were near enough to offer cover, so I stretched out, stomach down, among some weeds. I didn't harbor any serious expectation of jumping onto a fast-moving boxcar out here in the middle of nowhere. I had watched enough cowboy movies in the State Theater on Main Street to know that would be a challenge even while riding a horse at full gallop. Right now, I just wanted to study the German trains. What kind of handholds could I expect? Was there any way to hide and ride in the undercarriage of a car, if not on top?

When the train actually appeared, however, it didn't come from behind me, as I at first expected. Instead the locomotive puffed into view from around the bend in front of me. In this case, even if it had been traveling in slow motion, I would not have hopped aboard. This one would have taken me in the wrong direction, back the way that I had just come.

Still, the experience proved educational. Following the locomotive and the coal carrier, the first cars rumbling past were for passengers. After those came a string of flatcars bearing some kind of machinery or military hardware covered by tarpaulins. Lastly came a series of boxcars, none of which had open doors. When the final car rattled past, the rush of noise and wind quickly diminished until the chirping of crickets was the only sound to disturb the night. I continued my journey. As I walked, I reviewed the train in my mind, wondering if there were any bits of information there to aid me.

By midnight, I still hadn't heard any shouts or barking dogs, nor was there any sign whatsoever of pursuit.

Eventually the single track I had been following converged with another.

Okay, so do I keep going the way I have been, or should I head up this new line?

I plodded forward, hoping that the double tracks meant that I was coming to some place worth being in.

Another hour passed before the next train approached. This time it was on the new track, and it was heading in my direction. I observed from behind a tree as the locomotive thundered past my position. Watching its metal wheels rolling along, I resolved definitely to find a way onto one of those cars at the first opportunity.

It must have been close to 3:00 a.m. when I noticed that houses to the left and right of me were growing more frequent and closer together. At first I gave little thought to this, probably because it was the time of night when brains grow sluggish.

As I proceeded, however, I also plodded past factories and warehouses. Clearly, I was on the outskirts of a town, or perhaps even a city. Thanks to Britain's Royal Air Force and its campaign of nighttime bombing, no lights were shining to reveal the town's presence or size, but I could discern silhouettes even though clouds now obscured the setting moon.

And where there's a town, there will be at least a train depot!

The thought excited me, but also made me nervous. I was already bending if not breaking my "No risks" policy by approaching a population center. I sat down on a rail to rest my feet and to consider my next decision. This could be a critical juncture. I didn't dare rush ahead too confidently. Like Dad said when I bought my Indian Scout 101, "A little confidence is good. Too much confidence can land you in a hospital—or a cemetery."

There's still a lot of darkness left, I told myself. *I could walk a little farther to check out the situation and still have time to hurry back, if there aren't any good hiding places.*

I decided to try it.

Okay, Lord, I can't do this alone. Don't let me blunder into a trap.

My senses were all on alert as I proceeded forward. A fog was creeping in, limiting my vision even more and muffling the night sounds I was used to hearing. Now a third track appeared out of the mist and converged on the two I was already following. Obviously, I was getting somewhere, even if I didn't know where that might be.

Echoing in the night ahead were metallic squeals and bangs. But it wasn't the banging of artillery. I had heard similar sounds back home. There, such noises reverberated from the rail yard where train cars were shoved back and forth as they were coupled and uncoupled from each other. I tried not to get excited, but hope welled inside my chest like balloon. I walked faster.

As far as I know, I never passed a fence or anything to mark the perimeter of the marshalling yard, but eventually I realized that I was already inside it. Enhanced by the fog, darkness reigned. However, despite the gloom, I recognized the hulking shapes of freight cars and multiple sets of tracks paralleling each other. Here and there in the night swayed the soft glow of covered lanterns where workmen examined the linkage between cars, inspected the wheels, and checked the brakes and whatever else railroad employees examine.

Somewhere out there was a metallic chinking sound, which made me picture someone poking around with a steel bar. I trashed all notions of hiding in the undercarriage of a car.

Workers might spot me in the undercarriage as they went about their work.

For a fleeting second I toyed with the idea of sabotaging one or two cars, just to prove to myself that I was still in the war. Maybe it would be possible to drop handfuls of dirt or pebbles into the axle bearings? But then saner reasoning prevailed.

Don't go playing hero now. You've survived this long by keeping your head down and leaving no sign of your passing. Just get yourself aboard a train headed the right way!

Giving a wide berth to the circles of light around the lanterns, I stealthily penetrated deeper into the marshalling yard. The first boxcars I came to were standing on side rails by themselves. I could have climbed aboard easily, but didn't bother. Because these cars weren't coupled to a locomotive, they weren't guaranteed to move anytime soon. I pressed onward.

Now I was creeping furtively under cars and flitting into darker shadows whenever voices or lights headed in my direction. In the foggy darkness, I was afraid of tripping over a rail and sprawling in a noisy heap. I stepped gingerly, breathing through lips that were ever so slightly parted. My heart thumped inside my rib cage, but I forced myself to edge along as silently as a seasoned burglar.

"Karl, *komm hier!*"

The voice was so near and so loud that the speaker sounded nearly on top of me. I ducked and crawled underneath the nearest car, cracking my skull on something iron in the process. Stupidly, I had assumed that all of the workers were carrying lanterns. But whoever owned the shoes that crunched past my position certainly wasn't carrying one. I figured he must know his way around pretty well.

Praise God for this fog!

Moments later, two pairs of feet came into view. This time, though, a halo of light warned of their approach even before I heard them. I shrank backward behind a metal wheel to prevent "Karl" and his buddy from discovering me by accident.

After the pair had gone, I berated myself for the near-fatal incident. *Not so eager, Yoder. Go slow. Full alert! You can't bail out if you mess up now.*

When I slunk from under the car, I noticed a paleness streaking the eastern sky. Dawn was approaching. I needed to find a hiding place, and soon.

Proceeding forward, I came across a series of flatcars covered with netting. However, the camouflage material did little to disguise the hardware underneath: army tanks. These confirmed my hope that this train was westward bound. These metal monsters must surely be bound to defend the continent against possible invasion. That meant the coast. Probably the coast of Belgium or France.

I lifted the netting and slithered beneath the silent behemoth. Lying prone between the tank's treads I was out of sight from unfriendly eyes. But it was still night time. The tank's body had a high enough ground clearance that, by daylight, someone might notice the inert body. I decided to search for a better place.

Inside the tank?

The plan seemed totally audacious—which was why I loved it. The top hatch would be covered by the netting tied down tightly over it. But I was pretty sure that some American tanks feature escape hatches in their bellies. Did German designers do the same?

That would be appropriate. I'm escaping. Why not use an escape hatch?

My fingers glided over the cold armor plating. In the gloom they did locate something that I believed might be a handle. However, when I tried to twist it, whatever it was wouldn't budge. Either it wasn't a handle at all, or else it was secured from inside. I gave up and slid out from under the netting to search for a better spot.

Then I found it. The perfect setup. Ahead of the flatcars was an area with neither voices nor lights. Just sealed freight cars waiting to roll westward.

There's the ticket I need!

When I was positive that nobody was near, I reached up and unfastened the metal latch. The door slid open on well-oiled rollers that made little sound.

My original thought had been to quickly hop inside and roll the door shut again. That quickly proved impossible. Long, wooden crates were stacked almost to the doorway. However, I thought I spied an empty space above these, so, peering left and right a last time, I scaled the stack and wriggled myself onto the top. That done, I turned and deftly pulled the door shut again. Success!

The opening strains of Handel's "Hallelujah Chorus" welled up inside me.

Thank You, God! I may not be traveling first class, but I'm aboard a train, it's pointed the way I want to go, and no one saw me crawl in here. No more walking!

However, I wasn't throwing away all the caution that had become an intricate part of my existence. Snaking my way on hands and knees over the top of the cargo, I sought a resting place farther away from the door, just in case someone should open it before departure. In the back of the car I discovered a stack of smaller crates. These weren't piled quite so high as the others, so when I eased myself down onto them, I had a little more headroom.

As delighted as a boy in his first tree house, I made myself comfortable and pulled off my boots. During the night my feet had felt the "hot spots" that warn of the onset of blisters. Now as I lay on my back, I blissfully wiggled my toes and aired my feet as I waited for the journey to begin.

I wondered about the contents of the crates beneath me, but it made no difference. My bare hands couldn't pry up the lids. They might hold gold bullion for all I knew, but without a crowbar or a hammer, I had no way to get inside them. Most likely they contained artillery shells.

Then a new worry surfaced:

What if they weigh these cars? By coming in here, I just added to the weight.

I fretted over this new angle. Ultimately, though, I shrugged and decided to sit tight. The sun would soon be rising. I was committed. It was too late to change plans now.

Besides, once we get moving, I can slide the door open a little and shove out a crate or two. That will lessen the weight, which they might not check anyway.

This scheme put my heart at ease. Relaxing, I even dozed off.

After I don't know how long, a sharp metallic clank jerked me awake. Tensing, I half expected to see sunlight flooding the car as someone rolled the door open. But no such thing happened. What the clank was I didn't know, and the sound wasn't repeated. I settled down again, but not quite as peacefully as before. Through a crack in the wooden wall, a slender shaft of sunshine delivered some morning cheer.

Come on. Let's get moving. Doesn't this thing have a schedule to keep?

As if in response to my wish, within minutes I heard and felt the first jolt of movement as the unseen locomotive surged forward, jerking each car in turn behind it. Among all those tons of German cargo sat one foot-weary American, grinning like an idiot in the darkness.

"This is more like it," I said aloud after our speed had picked up. With the incessant *click-clack, click-clack* of wheels on rails beneath me, I sang again, "When you hear the whistle blowin' . . ." ending with "Woo-woo, Chattanooga, there you are!"

"Whoa there, Yoder," I said aloud. "You're getting way ahead of yourself. You haven't even figured out how to get yourself back to England. Tennessee might as well be on the moon."

As sobering as this reminder was, it still couldn't dampen my enthusiasm. Sneaking aboard this train was the absolute best turn of events that I could have hoped for. My spirits were soaring at about twenty thousand feet, right up there with *American Pride,* wherever she might be flying.

"If only the guys could see me now! At night around the stove they probably tell the newcomers about 'poor old Yoder' who must be rotting away in a POW camp."

After so many nights of prowling the darkness in apprehensive silence, it felt terrific to talk out loud again, even if only to myself. So I talked, laughed, and sang songs at the top of my lungs to pass the time. I wasn't worried one bit about discovery. A speeding train makes plenty of racket. I knew that no ears could overhear me unless they came right into my boxcar.

For the first time in years, I sang the old hymns "Amazing Grace," "The Old Rugged Cross," and anything else I could halfway recall. I must have mangled the words, but I sang them as best I could. The lines I came up with fit the melodies, and I figured God wouldn't mind even if the hymn writers were turning over in their graves.

Later I remembered my plan to pitch a crate or two out the door to reduce the car's weight. Moving on elbows and knees, I slithered my way over to the door. Once there, I found just enough space between the crates and the door to ease myself to the floor of the car.

Not wanting to fall off a moving train, I firmly gripped a heavy crate, and then pushed the door to slide it open. It didn't budge. Was I pushing it the wrong direction? Now I shoved it with both hands. Nothing.

Finally the truth dawned on me. The clank that woke me up before the train pulled out—some worker must have noticed the unhooked latch and flipped it shut. I was locked in!

Once again I found myself a prisoner of the Nazis—but this time they didn't even know they had me.

I ran my fingers along the inside of the freight car's door as I searched for an interior handle or latch. Of course, there wasn't one. These cars were designed to shuttle nonliving cargo, not human beings.

Like a Liberator with two shot-out engines, my spirits sank from their earlier heights but didn't quite crash and burn. I snaked my way back to my previous spot to reflect on this new development. Had God let me down? After all, what was the point of letting me succeed at climbing into this boxcar if there was no way of escape? Why hadn't He blinded the eyes of the brakeman or whoever had flipped that latch? Or was this all some huge cosmic joke at the expense of me, an insignificant Hoosier?

I had no reply to these questions, but I refused to get mad at God again. Even if I couldn't comprehend why He allowed this to happen, I wasn't going to bail out on Him just because my personal plans fell through.

No, just sit tight and take this step by step.

At that point I did recall a tidbit of Bible knowledge that had once struck me during a Sunday school lesson. I recollected how, in the Bible's book of Job, this man of God endured trial after trial, affliction after affliction. But despite sheer misery, Job still declared something like, "Even if God kills me, I'm still going to trust in Him." I couldn't recall most of that lesson, but I was sure Job had a happy ending.

Maybe I should try that. Trusting God, even when life seems rotten?

I settled down for the ride.

Okay, so the door's locked. Big deal. They locked me up once before, and I got out, right?

Still my mood was more subdued now.

Periodically the train would slow to a halt, although I was never sure why. Possibly passengers were boarding, if this train included passenger cars. Or perhaps the engineer needed to refill his water supply for the thirsty locomotive.

Since fretting won't help, why fret? You have no choice but to sit tight.

In a way, I hoped that the train stops were due to damaged rails, either from bomb strikes, or anti-Hitler partisans. That would make friendly forces seem not so far away. The first possibility I considered quite real, but I had to admit to myself that the odds of citizens of the Reich opposing the Führer by sabotaging railroad tracks seemed pretty slim.

Inevitably, my thoughts drifted across the Atlantic toward home. What would Dad be doing today? Delivering mail, I supposed, unless it was Sunday. It might actually be Sunday. I had lost all track of the date.

I chuckled as I remembered a joke Dan Carlson had once made in the mess hut. He had pointed out that, in a sense, I had followed in Dad's footsteps and become a mailman too.

"What do you mean by that?" I had asked.

"We're all mailmen here. The difference is that our crew delivers only special-delivery packages—all of them addressed to the Third Reich!"

That had sparked a good laugh around our table. I had forgotten to write that in my last letter to Dad.

Next, visions of Margo floated into my mind. What would she be doing these days?

By now, it must be well into June. The class of 1943 has graduated, so Margo should be done with high school.

Those last two words stuck in my mind.

High school. Was it really just one year ago that I graduated? So much has happened in the past year.

My senior year seemed like a decade ago. The military, the missions, and my escape combined to make me feel much older than I really was.

In my imagination, I relived the time Margo and I had spent together in those last days before Uncle Sam sent me to basic training. We really hadn't done much without other people around. Mostly I had visited the Laces' home or helped Margo at the fruit stand. Strangely, though, I hadn't minded the informal chaperones. When Margo was close, everything and everyone else faded into the background. I didn't even mind when Pastor Lace asked me to help him tune up his Studebaker. As long as Margo and her beautiful green eyes lingered nearby or served ice-cold lemonade, I would have helped him to rebuild the whole engine.

Clint, though, was the typical kid brother. When Margo and I sat on the swing after supper, he would spy on us from around the corner and sometimes pipe up with comments, such as, "Hey, Jim, are you gonna kiss her tonight?" Of course, Margo would shoo him away, but eventually Clint would drift back. Somehow even his mischief didn't annoy me. As an only child, I thought having Clint around was kind of fun. The day I took him for his first motorcycle ride, he got more excited than if I had handed him the keys to Fort Knox.

Reliving these memories relaxed me. Eventually I found myself growing drowsy. The rhythmical swaying of the car plus the incessant *click-clack* of metal wheels on rails worked their magic on me. Now and then the engineer would blow his whistle. Some part of my brain was aware of the high-pitched toots, but as long as the train kept *click-clacking* along, I had no trouble dozing.

At some point in the day I awoke when the train slowed and halted. Putting my eye to the crack in the wall, I got a glimpse of a ruddy-brown freight car standing motionless alongside. Voices were audible as men walked to and fro outside. My impression was that we had entered another marshalling yard.

No sweat, I thought to myself. *They'll hook on a few cars or take off a few, and we'll pull out again.*

However, my expectations for a brief stop proved wrong. We sat there for several hours. Or at least it seemed so to me. The voices outside were unintelligible, as the words were still in the language of the Reich. But their tone struck me as the ordinary, everyday sound of workers going about their jobs and not of soldiers barking orders. I remained optimistic—or as optimistic as could be while locked inside my cage.

I unscrewed the cap to my flask and wetted my tongue with the last few drops of water. This action conjured up a new worry. I knew from biology class that a human body could survive for weeks without food, if need be. Not so with water. Deprive a man of liquid, and he'll become a withering corpse in a matter of days.

How long would my train car stay locked? It was impossible to predict.

Wouldn't it be ironic if I succeeded in traveling so far undetected, only to end up feebly knocking on the door and exchanging my freedom for a tin cup of water?

"God," I whispered, "I need some water."

The supply sergeants back in England didn't much care what we needed, but I hoped God would take a more personal interest.

I lay back and stared toward the ceiling of the car. With nothing to do, I let my mind wander and nearly dozed off again when a distant sound crept into my consciousness. It was a far-off sound, at first barely audible through the crack in the wall, but it steadily droned closer, louder.

A man's voice outside uttered a guttural curse, and then footsteps broke into a run. Immediately, I was on full alert.

I realized the nature of the sound at the same time an air-raid siren broke into a wail. *Bombers! And it's daytime, so that's our Eighth Army Air Force, not the RAF! Go get 'em, you guys!*

I was giddy with excitement. Airmen—fellow Americans—were going to pass overhead. In my imagination I could picture myself up there with them, manning a waist gun as usual. If there had been enough room to dance a jig inside my hiding place, I would have done it.

Today's weather forecast for the Third Reich—solid aluminum overcast, with 100% chance of bombs. Better take your umbrella!

By now the crescendo of hundreds of propellers sounded like they were directly overhead. I wished with all my might that I could poke my head out and watch them pass. I pressed my eye to the crack, but saw little more than a tiny patch of pale blue above the neighboring freight car. Now the staccato bursts of antiaircraft guns erupted in the distance, and I truly felt sorry for the fliers on the receiving end of it.

Not until my ears detected the high-pitched whine from overhead did the truth dawn on me. These bombers weren't on the way to their target for the day. They were already above it—this railroad yard!

Explosions erupted all around me. Massive concussions bounced me right off the wooden crates and slammed my skull against the ceiling. In rapid succession, detonating bombs both near and far rocked and jolted the entire freight car, including the cargo beneath me. It was the first time I'd been on the receiving end of a bombing, and it was my own countrymen dishing out the punishment.

"God, don't let one land on me! I've come too far to die like this!"

Even as I blurted the prayer, I hoped that none of the aircraft up there was hauling incendiaries. If so, they wouldn't need to score a direct hit to snuff me out. The magnesium sticks would ignite fires that would fry me to a blackened cinder, while the local German population huddled safely in their bomb shelters.

Gasping for breath amidst swirling dust, I crawled and bounced my way toward the door. I wasn't thinking anymore, just reacting to the pummeling I was receiving. More than anything, I wanted out of that overgrown coffin. I was willing to kick and punch the door until either it gave way or I wore my arms and legs to bloody stumps trying.

To my astonishment, no sooner had I dropped into the narrow gap near the door than another figure from the opposite end of the train car did the same. He was a shorter, gaunt fellow with dark hair.

"*Vite, vite!*" he shouted in French, shoving me back to give himself room.

I understood his meaning, "Quickly, quickly!" but it was my bewilderment that let this skinny fellow elbow me away from the doorway. Where had he come from?

In the meager light that glimmered through the crack around the door, I watched as my unexpected companion wielded a bent piece of wire about the thickness of a coat hanger. Deftly, and with a skill that spoke of experience, he poked one end out the crack and repeated a series of quick jerking motions until he had achieved his purpose: the latch outside flipped open. My cohort rolled the door open.

"*Vite! Avec moi!*"

He leaped to the ground, and the next concussion bucked the freight car with such force that I toppled after him faster than I'd intended. Scrambling on all fours, the stranger scuttled underneath the car's protective mass. I was right behind him.

Where had my rescuer come from?

"*D'où venez vous?*" I shouted, straining to be heard above the cacophony of plane engines, antiaircraft guns, exploding bombs, and flying debris.

The newcomer, however, ignored me. Far from replying, he hunkered face-down on the oil-grimed railroad ties with both hands clapped over his ears. Seeing the foolishness of trying to communicate over the tumult, I followed his example.

Instinct urged me to run for my life, but that would be foolish. Being caught in the open amidst the flying shrapnel would be much more dangerous than sheltering under the freight car.

I was petrified. Any moment my body could be atomized into unrecognizable bits, and even the clean-up crew would never guess that an escaped Allied airman had died in their midst.

Peeking at my cohort, I saw that he hadn't moved a muscle. If I believed in witchcraft, I could've conceived that some spell had transformed him to stone, with his face earthward and his ears covered.

I judged the man to be about thirty years old. His oily hair might never have enjoyed the touch of a comb from what I could see. He had a thin mustache surrounded by a wealth of black whiskers that hadn't been shaved in a week or two. His clothing bore food stains and was threadbare around the cuffs and elbows.

Something about this man struck me as disagreeable. There was nothing wholesome about his appearance. On the other hand, I asked myself, how must I look in *his* eyes? My chin and cheeks sported the beginnings of a scraggly beard, and even though I washed in rivers, no soap had graced my body for weeks. Also, I probably had dark circles under my eyes from lack of proper sleep.

As quickly as the bombing began, it halted. An eerie silence settled over the train yard. Peering from behind the huge metal wheel that had been my shield, I saw thick dust swirling everywhere.

The spell broken, the figure beside me raised his head. With a furtive glance left and right, he burst into hysterical laughter and clapped a hand on my shoulder. *"Quelle bonne chance, non?"*

I replied. "Not luck—prayer! I was praying hard!"

"Ah, yes, yes," he agreed amiably in his tongue. With his right hand he crossed himself in the Catholic manner.

I wasn't sure whether he was serious or mocking.

"Wait inside," he said, pointing overhead to the train car we had so recently vacated. "There's no time. I will return quickly."

With the agility of a spider, he scuttled out, leaped to his feet, and scurried into the devastated rail yard.

"Wait!" I called. "Where are you going?"

Too late. The gaunt figure vanished.

What a predicament! I barely escape an air raid with my life intact, and now some sleazy-looking fellow who knows about me runs away with no explanation.

Not willing to trust anyone, I considered heading for the hills before the locals crept from their bomb shelters. But how far could I run in daylight? Not very far. Although I harbored serious misgivings about the stranger, I reminded myself that he spoke French, and without the slightest trace of a German accent. In the end, I climbed back into the boxcar and slid the door shut, except for the last three inches. Through this gap I kept watch from atop the wooden crates.

My fears soon seemed groundless. The short fellow jogged back with a self-satisfied grin on his face. In his hands he held no fewer than four lunch boxes such as workmen carry to their jobs.

"Food for the road!" he explained as handed up the spoils of his treasure hunting. After he had climbed aboard, he slid the door shut.

"Bon appétit!" he said gaily.

I accepted the two boxes he offered me.

Whoever my newfound comrade was, he was slick. He also possessed a generous supply of guts. Best of all, like me, he seemed bent on avoiding German eyes.

So what was it about this man that I still didn't trust?

Over our meal, my companion and I quietly chatted. He gave his name as Henri. He had already concluded that I was American, so I went ahead and told him the rest of my story—about the bomb run on Kiel, about escaping from my Nazi captors, and how I had been wearing out my boots walking the rails until I managed to sneak aboard this boxcar.

"Those are not American boots," he noted. His tone was flat, but I imagined the ghost of an accusation in them.

I agreed. "I needed shoes when I escaped. I took these from the Germans."

Henri gave me a wink. Evidently he took this as a superb way to tweak the nose of the so-called "superior Aryan race." Henri never referred to them as Germans. To him—and, I learned, to many speakers of French on the continent—the Germans were *les Boches,* a derogatory term I had never heard before. But I figured it rated about as low as the green scum that grows in stagnant ponds.

Henri told me that we were now in the city of Cologne, near Germany's western border. With the air of a seasoned traveler, he stated that this shipment was headed westward, toward Belgium, which was his native land. When I asked if he was an escaped prisoner like me, he flashed a mischievous grin and mumbled, "Not this time," while munching a mouthful of buttered bread and cheese. After he had washed this down with a swallow of German beer, he explained that he had once been sent to Germany for compulsory labor. Like a slippery eel, he somehow escaped, and made his way home via train.

"Then, you're in the Resistance?" I asked, eager to make contact with any underground organization.

"In a way," Henri replied, wiping his shirtsleeve across his mouth. "The Resistance needs weapons. These crates on which we lay contain rifles. When we reach a certain location east of Brussels, I will open the door and push out a few crates. So the Resistance will get rifles, and Henri will line his pockets with Belgian francs."

Now the picture came into sharper focus. Apparently Henri was a profiteer. He had no sympathy for the German occupation of his homeland. On the other hand, he wasn't so devoted to Belgium that he would resist the Nazis personally. Instead, he was content to steal arms and sell them to the true patriots. He claimed this was his third such undercover trip.

It didn't take long before the deathly silent rail yard transformed into a bustling work site. An army of workmen scurried about, clanging, banging, hammering, sawing, and shouting to each other. Henri took all this in stride, explaining in hushed tones that the railway system was crucial to the Nazi war effort and that the damaged rails and bomb craters would be speedily repaired.

"We will not be here for long," he promised. "You will see. Soon we will continue on our way to *Belgique.*"

When I asked how long Henri had been in the boxcar, he grinned again.

"I was hiding here before you entered. But since you crawled to the other end and did not bother me, I decided not to bother you either. But if you had been a Boche trying to arrest me . . ."

He pulled a narrow dagger from an unseen sheath and made a slicing motion across his throat.

"Later, when you talked and sang songs in English, I understood that you were either English or American. You have a good voice," he added.

Despite the compliment, I was embarrassed to learn that I'd had an audience throughout the time that I thought I was alone.

And my skin crawled when I realized that I could have been knifed in the dark.

"So, *mon ami*," Henri said, "did you jump from a *forteresse volante?*"

I had never heard or thought about the literal translation of Flying Fortress in French, and it sounded odd, but I immediately grasped his meaning.

"*Non,*" I responded. "I come from a *Liberateur.*" I liked the way the word for my B-24 sounded in Henri's tongue, and he nodded approvingly. No doubt, to the citizens of the enormous prison that Hitler had carved out of Europe, the meaning of the word "Liberator" bore even more significance than it did to us airmen.

On the subject of my French, Henri was curious. Did my ancestors hail from France or from Belgium, or perhaps Canada?

"I have absolutely no French blood in my veins," I explained.

I explained how my neighbor in Elkhart, Dr. Scoville, had married a French woman sometime after the Great War of 1914–1918. From the time I was an infant, Madame Scoville often babysat me, crooning French folk songs and talking to me in her native tongue. Later, when I was a boy, I was in the Scoville home playing with their son Jack—she pronounced it Jacques—as often as I was in my own. Madame Scoville always spoke to both of us in French, as if that were the most natural thing in the world. So I grew up hearing and speaking that language. Not until high school, though, did I learn how to read and write in French, complete with all its acute accents and circumflex marks.

Henri seemed disappointed to hear that few Americans know more than a handful of words in his language. Until then, he seemed to admire *les américains* as capable of nearly anything.

True to my companion's prediction, shortly after nightfall our boxcar was coupled to a new string of cars, and we slowly chugged out of Cologne.

Once we were underway again, Henri lost interest in conversation. He wished me a "*Bonsoir*" and turned away to catch some sleep. For a while I lay there reviewing every scrap of information I had gleaned from him.

Well, he might not have the noblest character in the world, but at least now I know where I am and that I'm headed in the direction

I want to go. And, praise God, I have some food. Best of all, even if Henri isn't part of the Resistance, he has contacts. He can lead me to them!

Eventually I closed my eyes and breathed a brief prayer. The rhythmical *click-clack* of wheels on rails, plus the gentle swaying of the train, lulled me to sleep once more. At last my escape seemed to be picking up the pace and making genuine progress. I breathed easier, assured that I was heading westward toward friends and freedom.

Sometime during the journey I awoke to the sensation of the train braking to a stop. Even without being able to see Henri in the darkness, I sensed that he was sitting up and tense.

"Where are we?" I asked.

Henri answered with a shushing sound. He was listening.

Outside were muffled voices, some of them harsh and guttural, but others softer, with the familiar French smoothness. Outside the train, people were walking up and down.

Soon my companion gave me a poke in the shoulder. "Welcome to my country. Ici Belgique."

So I had already made my first border crossing—and done it in my sleep.

Thank God, I thought. *This escaping business is a snap!*

However, Henri was taking no chances. Evidently he knew something I didn't, because he took a wine bottle that he had filled with fuel oil and some other smelly substance. Pulling the cork, he crept to the door and dribbled some of the concoction all around the entrance. Then he proceeded to flick droplets from the bottle around the cargo, too, including himself and me.

"Pour les chiens," he explained in a whisper.

Dogs? This had been my chief fear all during my escape, and now some hound might pick up our scent?

We lay low, and sure enough—the door banged open. Loud barking erupted, which struck terror into my heart. I heard snuffling, some German voices, and then the door slammed shut again.

"The dogs do not like the smell," Henri confided. "If you do not give them a reason to go away, they will smell you and catch you."

After a short delay, the engineer gave a blast on his steam whistle, and the train jerked forward again.

"How far to Brussels?" I asked.

"Maybe one hundred kilometers. I think a little less."

Roughly sixty miles. Yoder, I think you're going to make it!

I wanted to ask Henri if they really grow Brussels sprouts in Brussels, but I didn't know the French name of that particular vegetable. Back home, Madame Scoville had never served it. Hot Brussels sprouts were evidently extremely popular in England, as they kept appearing in our mess hall. Most of us American airmen, though, grew to despise the things. I even heard that one commander had given the order, "If pilots of damaged aircraft must crash land on return to England, please do so in a field of Brussels sprouts!"

Unfortunately, there was still a danger. If patriots of the Belgian Resistance were to remove just one steel rail from the track, it could derail an entire train. For the first time, I hoped with all my heart that the Belgian underground wouldn't tamper with the rail line. At least not today. The farther I traveled, the more excited I became. I didn't want any unnecessary delays or accidents.

About an hour later, Henri crawled to the door and worked his magic with the wire trick. He shoved the door open. Tree-clad hills, meadows, and homes glided past as we click-clacked westward.

As we rolled along, I asked Henri questions about his country, and he was happy to quench my curiosity. In the northern Ardennes region, he informed me, a stranger like myself could easily become lost and swallowed up in the ancient peat moors and bogs that lie there. I was glad to have entered the country this way, by rail, and avoided inhospitable terrain.

"Belgium is at the crossroads of Europe," my guide boasted. "We have beautiful nature, ornate tapestries, statues, castles . . . No other land is like it!"

"Does everyone in Belgium speak French?"

"Not everyone. Some speak Flemish. You would not understand them." He paused. "You know, even though your French is not bad, you do not sound like a true Belgian. Except for a little accent, you could almost pass for a Parisian. Your Madame Scoville taught you well."

Obviously no novice to the area we were now passing through, Henri studied the landscape, picking out landmarks to gauge our progress. From time to time he would nod or say, "Bon, bon." I lay beside him and watched too, but I could have been back inside of Germany for all I knew. To me the scenery looked very similar.

Finally Henri poked my shoulder excitedly. "We are almost home!"

I grinned back, but I didn't voice my thought that "home" for Henri was still a long way from home for Jim Yoder.

The shoulder-poking routine seemed to be typical for this skinny guy, as he often did it. For my part, I found it irksome. Still, he was my guide and my sole link to the Resistance. I wasn't about to alienate him now by complaining. Besides, I had never been in continental Europe before. Was shoulder poking a common gesture? I had no clue.

As we approached a certain curve in the tracks, Henri slid down from the crates and shoved the door all the way open.

"Vite! Help me."

The moment our boxcar began the bend, Henri and I began heaving crates of rifles overboard. We managed to shove a dozen or so out the opening before we rounded the curve and began picking up speed again.

"Now, follow me!"

To my surprise, Henri leaped out the door. I saw him tumble to the ground and roll to a stop. Imitating his example, I sucked in a breath and launched myself out the door. I actually managed to land on my feet, but my momentum carried me forward. I landed in a crumpled heap. Rising to my feet, I was spitting dirt and grass. My right knee ached too.

A too-familiar finger was soon poking me on the shoulder. "*Très bien,* Jim! And that was your first time, *oui?* Ah, but you jump from Liberateurs, so maybe this little hop from a train is not difficult for you."

From under a huddle of oak trees several men appeared, striding straight toward us. Alarmed, I prepared to bolt. Henri must have sensed my apprehension, for he tugged me by the sleeve.

"Do not worry. These are friends."

"Resistance?" I asked.

"Oui."

Henri's one-word reply filled my heart with joy.

At last!

"Come," Henri said, tugging at my sleeve again. "We must help."

The four newcomers were silently retrieving the crates we had jettisoned from the freight car. Clearly, our arrival—or Henri's arrival, at least—had been expected. I interpreted all this as the signs of an efficient and smoothly organized Resistance operation.

While lending a hand lifting a crate onto a horse-drawn wagon, I heard one of the men whisper an inquiry about me to Henri. I didn't hear all the reply, but did make out the words "*un aviateur de l'Amerique.*" I realized that my presence and their helping me to escape would pose new dangers for any citizens involved in the underground. As a result, I really put my back into lifting and stacking those valuable rifles. I wanted to demonstrate that I was just as patriotic as they and that I was worth any trouble my arrival might cause.

When twelve wooden crates were safely loaded onto the wagon, we hopped up too.

"Welcome to Belgique," one of men said. He offered his hand.

The stale odor of alcohol on his breath surprised me. I would have expected Resistance agents to abstain from drinking, at least while engaged on a mission such as this one. But once again, I was new to the people and customs of the land. I kept my impressions to myself.

"Do you have any American cigarettes?" my other neighbor asked.

"Sorry, no. I don't smoke."

"What a shame." He sighed with disappointment. "I would like to try one."

I was disappointed too, but for a different reason. His question made me realize that I no longer had anything—not just no cigarettes, but even the sack that I used to carry my water flask and dwindling food supply was gone, still barreling down the railway.

Oh, well. You're in good hands now. You won't need those things anymore.

We hadn't gone more than a mile before the driver halted at a large building that appeared to be a warehouse. Two of the men sitting with me hopped to the ground and swung open large, double doors. The driver dismounted too, and led the horse—wagon and all—into the building.

I saw that we were in a medium-sized warehouse. Along both sides were sturdy wooden shelves, mostly bare, except for dust.

"Come, mon ami!" called one of the newcomers, whose name turned out to be Marc. "You must be hungry. We have food on the stove and a bottle of wine to share."

I followed the group to a door in the rear of the building. As we walked across the cement floor, the other three men introduced themselves. Their names were Gérard, Albert, and Claude. Claude lingered behind to unhitch the horse.

I couldn't help feeling less than impressed with my new companions. I had imagined that Resistance operatives would be doctors, schoolteachers, sympathetic policemen, and former soldiers. Instead, each of the four fellows who now chatted with Henri and asked about his latest adventure exhibited the same oily hair and unkempt appearance that I had noted about Henri himself. Back home, I would have been nervous to have any one of them following me down a street after sunset.

This is an occupied country during wartime, I reminded myself. *You can't expect everyone to look like prosperous Americans.*

Stepping through a door, we entered what must have once been an office area. In place of desks and files, however, the room now featured some rough wooden chairs and a table that looked homemade.

A woman was there too, stirring a dented pot over a makeshift stove. Her dress wasn't new, but her long, sand-colored hair was clean and neatly braided. She offered a much more pleasant image than any of my male cohorts. Judging by her appearance, I guessed that she was a year or two older than I—perhaps twenty-one or twenty-two. Glancing up, she did a double take and appeared startled to see an unknown face among the others.

"Brigitte," called Albert. "Meet an American aviateur. Henri rescued him from the Boches' land and brought him here, to civilization!"

"*Enchanté,*" I said, offering Brigitte a friendly smile. "Glad to make your acquaintance."

"Ah, be careful of this one!" joked Gérard, a stocky fellow with red hair. "He speaks French like a poet and sounds like a ladies' man to me. I will bet monsieur aviateur has plenty of experience chasing skirts!"

Brigitte blushed, and all the males—except me—guffawed at her expense.

"Brigitte is my younger sister," explained Marc, a thin man who sported the same sand-colored hair that she did. "The meals that Brigitte prepares are *magnifiques!*"

The aroma rising from my steaming bowl of onion soup was enticing. I hadn't even realized I was hungry until I sipped the first tantalizing spoonful. Then I dug into the meal with such gusto that the others laughed and pointed. I didn't care. And I didn't mind that the meal was simple. This was my first hot dish since England. That soup, plus the hearty bread that accompanied it, truly did make me feel like I was back in civilization.

No more raw potatoes for me!

I was so enraptured by the delectable smell and taste of my soup that I scarcely noticed when Claude rose and ambled away. Of all the men, Claude looked to be the strongest physically, but he was also the least social. Somewhat sullen in attitude, he ate sparingly and exchanged quiet comments with Henri. The most remarkable thing about Claude was his eyes. The glint in them was cold and hard as granite. They say a person's eyes are the window to his soul, but Claude's eyes revealed no soul. If I thought anything at all when he stood and lumbered away, I assumed he was on his way to a bathroom, or perhaps to tend to the horse.

As I spooned yet another swallow of the delicious soup past my lips, I closed my eyes and savored the taste.

Suddenly, something jerked tightly across my stomach. In a flash, my eyes flew open. Someone—Claude—was behind me and tightening a rope around both the chair and me. Gérard, Marc, and Albert simultaneously leaped from their places. They pinned down my hands and feet until Claude could secure them with other lengths of rope.

In the background, Brigitte was as caught off guard as I was. She kept shouting, "What are you doing? Why are you doing that to him?"

Meanwhile I was thrashing and trying to fight back, all the while shouting in English, "Knock it off! Get away from me!"

At one point I succeeded in butting the crown of my head into Gérard's face, which gave him a bloody nose. He retaliated by punching me in the stomach. The blow sent me reeling backward, chair and all, onto the cement floor. By then the fight—if you could call it that—was over. I was trussed up tighter than a calf in a rodeo roping event.

Henri bent over my face. "Pardon us, Jim Yoder. We did not mean to hurt you. But you should not have struggled so valiantly."

Claude and Albert picked me up and set the chair back on its four legs. Gérard dabbed at his nose with a soiled handkerchief. The crimson trickle from one nostril clashed with his ruddy red hair.

Brigitte was nearly frantic, her eyes large and frightened-looking. "But he is américain," she kept repeating.

Her brother Marc was shushing her. Albert had already settled back into his own seat and continued eating as calmly as if he had simply stood to fetch a napkin.

"Why are you doing this?" I barked, remembering to speak in French this time. "Henri, you said these men were in the Resistance. We're Allies! I'm not Boche!"

"The answer is simple, mon ami," Henri replied. "We do not love the Boches, but my companions and I are not Resistance. You see—I lied. Our little group steals what we can, and then we sell to anyone who will buy. That is how we survive."

"What's that got to do with me?"

"Ah, well, you know how you and I stole rifles from the Boches? The Resistance will pay well for them. However, the Boches have money too. We cannot sell them their own rifles, but I believe they will reward us if we deliver to them a different sort of prize. Let us say, an escaping aviateur who has dropped bombs on their nation?"

His lopsided smirk was devilish.

I glared. "You're a traitor! You're an enemy to the people of Belgium!"

Everyone but Brigitte chuckled at my remark.

"*Non, cher* Jim Yoder," Henri said with a sinister smile. "I am quite faithful—to myself and to my friends. Who are my people? Only the ones you see in this room. Before the war, the gendarmes put us in jail. Now we are free, and we are going to stay that way. I would sell my own mother to the Devil for the right price."

"It won't work!" I blurted. "I know too much for you to sell me to the Nazis. Don't you think they would like to find out who is stealing from their trains? They'll miss those rifles. I'm the one person who will be able to say who took them. Why, you even helped me to escape! They might find that little fact interesting too."

For the first time, Henri leaned back in his chair with a slightly perplexed expression. He played with the corners of his mustache while the other men whispered to each other. Obviously, they hadn't considered this flaw in Henri's scheme.

"You are right," Henri admitted at last. "If we simply sell you to the Boches, you will talk. The Gestapo is very talented at persuading reluctant people into conversation. You know too much for us to let that happen. . . ." He let that last sentence trail off.

"And . . . ?" I questioned.

He grinned, but with no humor in his eyes. "That is why I am glad you enjoyed your meal so much. I am afraid it must be your last. The Boches will not mind if you are not breathing when we hand you over."

I stared, not believing he could be serious.

Gérard leaned close to me, his red-soaked handkerchief still clutched to one nostril. His face so close to mine that I could smell the garlic on his breath, he breathed, *"Les morts ne racontent pas de secrets."*

The translation chilled me to the marrow: "The dead do not reveal secrets."

Henri and his gang showed no signs of being in a hurry to slit my throat. I wanted to believe they had changed their minds. More likely, though, they didn't want a corpse smelling up their hideout. Time was on their side, not mine. As long as I was safely bound hand and foot, they had no need to rush. Lying on the cement floor that night, I couldn't do more than doze fitfully. The knowledge that Henri planned to murder me, coupled with the rock-hard cement beneath me, made genuine slumber impossible.

The next morning, Albert and Marc complied with my request to use the restroom. They untied the rope binding my feet. My hands, however, remained bound in front of me at the wrists.

"That stays," Marc said, pointing to my hemp manacles. "You will have to manage as best you can."

Both of them, knives held at the ready, accompanied me through the rear door. The warehouse apparently featured no plumbing, but behind the building was a crude latrine of rough, brown bricks and sloppy mortar. Three times that day I requested a trip to the outhouse, and each time I hoped that my escorts would relax their vigilance enough for me to bolt. Unfortunately, they remained on guard for each excursion. I had no choice but to plod back to the main building, where they would truss me up again.

Meanwhile Henri, Gérard, and the ever-sullen Claude had disappeared early, taking the wagon and rifles with them. Brigitte rarely spoke directly to me, but I sometimes caught her looking my way. She would take a cracked mug and fetch cool water from a hand pump when I was thirsty. She also broke off part of a loaf of bread and set it before me to eat off the floor. Despite Henri's words that I had eaten my last meal, she provided this bit of sustenance, and neither Marc nor Albert ordered her to stop.

The light in Brigitte's brown eyes was not unkind. I believed I detected sympathy.

Could she, like me, be a prisoner of these criminals despite the fact that she's Marc's sister?

My best efforts to loosen my bonds proved fruitless. I recalled from my boyhood reading that Harry Houdini used to have a knack for escaping from ropes, but I couldn't figure out the trick. No matter how I twisted my wrists, the knots held fast, and the hemp dug into my skin. Worse, Albert glanced up from the card game he and Marc were playing and spotted me trying to wriggle free.

"Non, non, monsieur aviateur," he warned, wagging a finger my way. "Marc and me, we play the only game in this room. You just sit quietly and enjoy your final hours."

Marc chuckled.

Busy threatening me, Albert didn't notice his pal filch an extra card from the deck.

I dropped my head and closed my eyes.

Dear Lord, I prayed. *Here I've been sweating and scheming, trying to get out of here on my own, and it's not working. It seems like I'm always asking You for something, and I haven't had a single chance to do anything for You in return. But did You really bring me so far just to let these cutthroats betray me for a handful of francs?*

That thought made me pause. Jesus had been betrayed for money too. For thirty pieces of silver. Right from the beginning I had felt slightly uncomfortable with Henri. I never considered him a friend even though I had trusted him for contacts. Judas, on the other hand, had been a close companion and friend to Jesus Christ.

That has to hurt, having an actual friend betray you with a kiss!

"Eh, you, what are you doing?" Marc asked me. "Sleeping?"

I opened one eye. "I'm thinking. And praying."

Albert cackled. "You're praying? That is good. Go ahead; pray. Straighten out your life with God. The man who once owned this warehouse did not have time to prepare his soul before Claude twisted his neck. What a shame."

Marc threw back his head and chortled at his buddy's remark. Across the room, Brigitte turned her face away.

That day crept by with agonizing slowness. Between prayers I stared listlessly at the flies that wove endless circles around the room. Later I studied a roach that spent hours exploring the floor and walls. I had no idea where Henri, Claude, and Gérard had gone with those rifles. But my captors took it in stride when their partners did not return by sundown.

"You sleep on the floor again," Marc informed me. "I am sorry we have no mattress for you. But what can I do?" He waved his hands uselessly. "After all, this is not the Hotel Metropole. For that, you must go to the city center, into Brussels."

I made no reply. Their brand of humor wasn't entertaining. Instead, I simply slumped sideways onto the floor. Brigitte had already retired somewhere for the night. After Albert left, Marc turned down the wick on a kerosene lantern and leaned his chair against the wall. As on the previous night, I was not to be left unguarded.

By now the lack of sleep was sapping my energy. I closed my eyes and let my mind wander to Mom, Dad, my crew mates aboard *American Pride,* the friends I had known in high school, and of course to Margo. The vision of her smiling face and dancing eyes comforted me.

It's odd, but in a way I reconciled myself to the grisly fate that awaited me. My main regret was that Margo would never know I had put my trust in Jesus and made my peace with God. I couldn't even write her a farewell letter. As far as she was concerned, Jim Yoder would just suddenly disappear from the earth, never to be heard from again. On the other hand, I would soon see Mom again in Heaven.

Lying there, I wondered what exactly Heaven would be like. Somewhere, I recalled, there was a Bible verse that claimed no eye had ever seen and no ear had ever heard what marvelous things await God's people in Heaven. Now, unexpectedly, I stood on the threshold of that celestial kingdom . . . At last sleep overtook me.

How long I slept I have no idea. But I jerked back to consciousness when a hand clamped over my mouth. Parting my sleep-fogged eyes, I spotted the glitter of a knife blade hovering near my face. Instinctively I arched backward in horror.

"Shh!"

To my amazement, the person wielding the knife was not Marc, Albert, Gérard, Claude, or even Henri. It was Brigitte.

"Nous partons," she whispered, glancing at Marc's sleeping form in the chair. "We are leaving."

Removing the hand from my mouth, she sliced into the knots binding my wrists. She must have sharpened the kitchen knife especially for this task, for my hands were free within seconds. I rubbed them together, restoring full circulation while Brigitte went to work on the rope binding my ankles.

Once I was free, she pressed the knife into my palm and held a finger to her lips. She looked terrified. I can only guess where she found the courage to aid me against the men's wishes.

Out the door we tiptoed, first into the cavernous blackness of the warehouse, then out the rear door I had passed through during my trips to the outhouse. Leading me by the hand, Brigitte guided me around the building and into the rutted lane out front.

"I will help you," she finally dared to whisper. "First, we must get away from here quickly."

She wasn't going to get any argument from me on that score. "Lead the way."

The warehouse was on the outskirts of Brussels, and Brigitte led me, not away from the city, but down a hedge-lined lane toward it. As we made our way along a hedgerow, I smelled a delicate fragrance suspended in the still night air. Lilacs were in bloom. Back in Indiana, Margo's favorite perfume smelled just like lilacs, and in the darkness I could almost imagine it was she, and not Brigitte, who walked by my side. How ironic that I had never gone on a private stroll with Margo even in the daylight. Here I was out walking with a woman I didn't even know, well past midnight.

As we slunk through alleys and crossed lanes, I was growing more nervous by the minute.

"Where are we going?" I asked. "Do you know someone in the Resistance?"

"Non. But I know someone else who might. Please don't think that all Belgians are like Henri and his companions. Most Belgians are loyal to the Allies. A few are criminals, oui, and some welcome the Nazi invaders with open arms. But most Belgians would consider it an honor to help the British and Americans. I believe there will be no problem finding someone to hide us."

"Us? But the Germans aren't searching for you, Brigitte. You don't have to hide."

She laughed softly, with a touch of bitterness. "Oui, now I do. My parents are dead. Marc is only my half brother, not my real brother. He met Henri in prison. He and the others have no fondness for me. As long as I cooked, washed their clothes, and held my tongue about their thievery, they gave me food and a few francs to spend. I'm not sure what they would do to me for taking you away, but it would not be pleasant."

I felt mingled admiration and pity for this girl. From her description, I gathered that her life had been miserable for a long time. I wished I could protect her, and yet, here she was, protecting and aiding me instead.

A motorcycle roared down the street, and Brigitte pulled me into an alley until it passed. "Curfew," she explained. "That was a Boche courier. If the Germans see a civilian out so late, they might shoot without asking questions."

Brigitte led me from the cobblestone street, past a barbershop and down an alley to the rear of the shop. The building was larger than it appeared from the front. It seemed to be a combination home and business.

"The barber who lives here is a good man. His name is Charles Rousseau—a true Belgian. He was a friend of my father's. Monsieur Rousseau knows many people and listens to all who sit in his chair. He might be able to help us."

She tapped lightly on the rear door. Nothing happened. Brigitte continued tapping, slightly louder now. At last a dim light appeared through the window and a muffled voice asked, "Who is there?"

"I am Brigitte, the daughter of Marcel de Coster."

The door cracked, and a middle-aged man wearing pajamas peered out with bleary eyes. In his hand he held a kerosene lamp. "Little Brigitte! I haven't seen you in ages. But who is that behind you?"

"A friend. He has come a long, long way. He needs help."

The barber hesitated. "A friend, you say? From a long, long way?" He regarded me suspiciously in the lantern's orange glow.

I was painfully aware of the thick stubble on my face and my unwashed condition. By now I must look just as much a scoundrel as Henri himself.

"*Des États-Unis,*" I whispered. "From the United States. I'm an aviateur."

Like magic, the barber's demeanor instantly changed. The door swung wide, and he ushered us in with much waving of his hand. The man led us to a small parlor, where he set the lamp on the table. While he pulled chairs together, I noted that the room did feature electric lights even though he wasn't using them. I assumed that he didn't want to arouse attention by having bright lights glimmering through his window at such an unusual hour.

A woman wrapped in a drab maroon robe entered from a darkened doorway. "Charles? What is happening?" she asked.

"Visitors, Justine," he explained to his wife. "Very important visitors. Come, join us."

I stood there awkwardly, not knowing what to do.

"Sit, sit," the man urged Brigitte and me, indicating a short divan. "How can I help?"

Briefly I recounted the mission to Kiel, how an accident sent me tumbling from my heavy bomber, and about finally escaping from Germany by train along with Henri. Next Brigitte picked up where I left off. In rapid-fire French that I couldn't always follow, she brought Monsieur and Madame Rousseau up to date on the sad turn of events in her life, about Henri and his gang, and how she had helped me to escape from them.

The barber and his wife had listened to my saga in rapt fascination. During Brigitte's portion of the story, tears welled in their eyes.

"Ah, Brigitte, Brigitte," sighed the barber. "You should have come to us sooner. We had no idea."

"You will both stay with us until we can decide what to do," Madame Rousseau stated. "Brigitte can stay in the spare bedroom. Monsieur Yoder can sleep on the *lit-canapé.*" The word was unfamiliar, but I hid my ignorance.

"Yes, of course," the barber agreed. "Tomorrow I will make some quiet inquiries about helping our aviateur friend."

The divan, which I at first assumed was merely for sitting, actually opened into a lit-canapé—a sofa bed. Madame Rousseau adorned it with sheets and a comforter, while I luxuriated in a hot bath, my first in ages. I scrubbed and rescrubbed, removing every speck of grime I had picked up during my wanderings. Then I just lay and soaked until the water began to cool. Back home, I had never truly appreciated a tub of clean, steaming water the way I did in that humble barber's home.

Later, when my head at last settled into the heavy goose-feather pillow, I felt like I had died and floated into eternal bliss.

My first real bed in weeks!

In fact, because the biscuit-cushions we slept on in England were so hideously uncomfortable, I considered this my first decent bed since I'd left McDill Air Base in Florida.

Moved in my soul, I slipped out of the bed and slid to my knees. "Thank You, God. Thank You for Your guidance and protection. Thank You for bringing me to this home and to these kind people." I couldn't think of any other words to say, but just overflowed with thankfulness for this latest turn of events in my undesired adventure.

The next morning, Monsieur Rousseau treated me to another luxury: a much-overdue haircut. He even insisted on shaving me.

"Non," he said in response to my protests, "you are my guest. It will be my privilege to serve an Allied aviateur. Vive l'Amérique!"

It felt both wonderful and odd to have a smooth chin and upper lip again. Frequently that day I caught myself gliding my fingertips over my baby-smooth skin. Until I'd landed in Germany, I'd never had a beard before. Now the sensation of not having whiskers felt almost odd.

My reflection in the hallway mirror shocked me. Having trekked so many miles on meager rations, I had lost much weight. My cheeks were hollow, and my eyes looked dark and sunken.

"You are so thin," Madame Rousseau lamented, watching me study my image.

Even though I was positive this good couple had little to spare, she promptly launched into a program to fatten me up. At each meal, my portion would be larger than the others. In between meals too, she would bring me a thick slab of bread with cheese on it, or perhaps a rare bit of hard candy.

On my first night there, this fine lady of the house had also scrubbed my soiled flight coveralls until they looked nearly new again. However, Monsieur Rousseau locked his barbershop at noon and returned with new socks, a shirt, and a pair of pants that fit remarkably well. He had also traced my feet on a sheet of paper, and with this pattern had purchased the most priceless gift of all—brown leather shoes that actually fit! The shoes were used, but I didn't care. I cheerfully discarded the oversized Wehrmacht boots forever.

Because I carried no money, I had no way to reimburse the pair for all their kindness to me. Even though they insisted no payment was needed, I began sweeping floors and polishing doorknobs, silverware, and metal fixtures around the home until they glistened. In addition to showing my gratitude, this activity helped me to while away the hours. I had always thrived on busyness, both in school and in the Air Force. I enjoy working with my hands. I was determined not to sit around twiddling my thumbs while everyone else accomplished something useful.

Brigitte had the advantage over me. As a native Belgian, she could leave the house and run errands for Madame Rousseau. Taking the required ration stamps, she would stand in long lines at the butcher shop and the bakery to receive the legal allotment of meat and bread. Of course, the goods that she brought home were sufficient for only two people, the barber and his wife, so the arrival of two guests put a serious crimp in the food situation. In time Brigitte could receive her own ration stamps, but none would be available for a foreign flyer.

Then Brigitte heard of Rue des Radis, a street in the poorest section of Brussels. A thriving black market operated there.

According to rumors, illegal vendors spread blankets on the sidewalks and laded them with butter, sugar, meats, and even that rarest of treasures—chocolate. But the prices were outrageous. Unroasted coffee cost the equivalent of a worker's monthly salary.

"I was looking at all these treasures in amazement," Brigitte recounted, "when lookouts shouted that a German patrol was coming. The vendors grabbed their blankets by the four corners, threw them over their shoulders like sacks, and scattered in all directions! I ran too, because I had bought this." She held out a small package of sugar, which Madame Rousseau accepted with tears in her eyes.

I appreciated Brigitte's successes on our behalf, but I was worried.

"Isn't there a danger that Marc, Henri, or the others might spot you in public?"

She laughed off my fears. "Those cowards? They will be afraid to show themselves openly. By now they will be hiding in a new hole, afraid that I will send an anonymous note about their activities to the Nazi authorities."

Of course, I wanted information on how the war was going. I especially wanted details on all daylight bombing missions, since that would be my own Eighth Army Air Force. The main newspaper in Brussels, *Le Soir*, provided some information, but I read it with skepticism. The Nazi occupiers had seized control of the paper and edited every story with a pro-German slant. Still, by reading between the lines of propaganda, I was able to piece together some information.

I was pleasantly surprised to learn that Axis forces in Africa had surrendered over a month earlier, on May 13—the day before I had accidentally tumbled into the Fatherland. Also, my spirits really soared as I read how American and British bomber forces were increasing their attacks. On the other hand, the reports left no doubt that the Germans had successfully squashed some sort of uprising in Warsaw, Poland.

In his off hours, Monsieur Rousseau delighted in bringing me up to date on other campaigns that I had missed during my trek across Germany. Because I served aboard a bomber, he took special glee in relating a tale about a squadron of RAF planes that had dropped "bouncing bombs" on the waters of the Mohne and Eder Rivers and destroyed dams that provided electricity and water to the Ruhr area.

"Bouncing bombs?" I repeated. "Monsieur, it makes a nice story, but I've never heard of bombs that bounce on water. And I should know; I serve aboard a bomber."

"It is true! Not all the details were in the paper, but we hear things. The BBC told about it too."

I didn't want to argue, so I changed the subject. "Let me ask you something. Out of all the Allied actions thus far in the war, which one has been the most inspirational to you? Which one has given you the most hope?"

The barber's lips parted into that grin I had come to appreciate so well. I knew he was about to regale me with yet another marvelous story.

"The most inspirational, most heroic moment for us Belgians was the work of one man: Jean de Selys-Longchamp. He is Belgian, but he went to England when our country capitulated to the Nazis. There he volunteered to join the RAF and became a fighter pilot, but do not ask me what kind of airplane he flies. On January 20 of this year, while on a mission over Belgium, he added a second mission of his own—to attack the Gestapo single-handedly!"

"I've never heard of him. What did this de Selys-Longchamp do?"

Monsieur Rousseau's eyes were moist with emotion. He also began illustrating his account with broad, sweeping motions of his hands. "After completing his main mission, he flew very low to avoid radar, straight toward 453 Avenue Louise in Brussels. It is a twelve-story building used by the Gestapo. He flew toward it, barely above the rooftops. As de Selys pulled his fighter up, he raked the entire building with machine guns and cannons. Shattered glass and concrete flew everywhere! A dozen Gestapo agents were wounded, and several Boches were killed in the attack, including one of their highest-ranking officers. As a final gesture, de Selys threw two flags from his cockpit—the flag of England and the flag of Belgium. Then he flew away."

I let out a low whistle of admiration.

"In those few seconds, one man—a Belgian—proved to our whole nation that the invincible invaders are not so invincible after all! Faster than electricity, news of his exploit raced through the countryside. That night the BBC told the pilot's name and more details. The next day Avenue Louise was crowded with people wanting to see the bullet holes or to pick up a scrap of glass as a souvenir. Irate German guards would not let anyone go near. I hope Jean de Selys-Longchamp received a medal for his actions. He deserves one!"

As gripping as all these accounts were, they sparked mixed emotions in me that lasted far longer than that one conversation. On one hand, the barber's stories made me feel like the war was passing by while I sat on the sidelines and accomplished nothing. Jean de Selys-Longchamp was only one man; yet he had inspired an entire nation. I was one man too. Unlike him, however, I was not inspiring anyone. I was no longer even actively engaged in the struggle. Was I a coward? Was I just trying to keep my skin intact while others fought and died for a noble cause?

But it's different with me, I argued with myself. That Belgian pilot was in an RAF fighter plane. All I have are my two hands. What am I supposed to do?

I still believed that escaping was more than just personal desire. It was my duty. Would I be endangering that duty if I risked clashes with the enemy? I could stay in Belgium and fight the Nazis alongside local underground fighters. But would that decision make me a hero, or a fool? I had no answer to these questions. I even prayed about it, but received no instructions from Heaven. How I would have loved to get my hands on a copy of *Stars and Stripes,* our U.S. military newspaper.

If only I could read some real, solid news, it might help me in knowing which way to turn. Or at least how to think.

Brigitte helped in the kitchen, but the two of us still found time to chat. One evening she told me about her childhood and about the schools she had attended. When Brigitte was still an adolescent, her mother had died in childbirth. Her father bottled his anguish inside himself, but he had already suffered from a weak heart for many years. One morning she found him waxy cold and lifeless in his bed.

I could certainly sympathize. I had lived in anger over my mother's untimely death, but at least I still had a father at home. Brigitte was left with no one.

"How did you live?" I asked her.

"I had a job for a time," she explained. "I was housekeeper for a wine merchant. I cooked and cleaned for him. In return, he let me live in a small room and paid me a modest salary. But . . ." Her voice trailed off, and suddenly she found the rug worth studying.

"But . . . ?" I echoed.

"One evening he came home late. He was drunk. I had to flee from him." She winced and shook her head. "With nowhere else to go, I ended up at Marc's house."

Twin trails of tears were starting down Brigitte's cheeks, and she hung her head.

I hate it when women cry, and seeing Brigitte's tears falling made me feel incompetent. What was I supposed to say? What could I do? I was afraid to ask for more details of why she had to flee. Clearly the memory was painful to her.

"I'm glad you escaped from Marc and those criminals, Brigitte. You deserve a better life than that." The statement sounded feeble, but it was better than nothing.

She sniffed and wiped her nose with a handkerchief. "And I am glad you escaped from the Boches, Jim Yoder. You deserve a better life than a prisoner of war camp." Then she was gone.

I sat there by myself still feeling awkward. With tools and motors I felt at home. But in social situations where people shared their personal feelings and problems I often didn't know how to respond. But one thing Brigitte's conversation accomplished was to remind me that I wasn't the only one in the world with problems. I had been consumed with my own situation, but the world was full of people enduring tragedies, and not all of them from the war. My desire to be free and back home with Margo was unimportant compared to bigger issues all around the globe.

Margo! I have so many things to tell you. I wish I could be with you now. Will I ever get to see you again?

Like an ominous cloud, a dark fear settled over my heart. Margo was undeniably a beauty, and other men had eyesight as good as mine. In my opinion, it was a miracle that she didn't already have a boyfriend when I met her. However, as far as Margo knew, Jim Yoder was still far from being the Christian she would ever want for a boyfriend—let alone a husband. So why shouldn't she date church-going men who hadn't marched off to war?

The very thought made my chest feel tight, like it was being squeezed in a vice. I buried my face in my pillow.

Not until my seventh day in the barber's home did Charles Rousseau lock his shop door and come into the house with an uncontrollable grin. He plopped onto a chair looking very pleased with himself.

"Jim Yoder," he said, "I believe your prayers are answered. These are dangerous times, and a person seeking help from the underground does not dare to say too much too loudly. So I have moved cautiously. But now I believe we have a contact."

He had my full attention. "Really? Tell me more."

"I do not know much myself. But one of my customers was once an army officer. Now he works in construction, building houses. But once a patriot, always a patriot. He promises he can help you. He knows the right people."

Hope rose up inside me. "At last! What's the next step?"

"We wait. When someone enters the barbershop asking directions to Rue Lafayette, that will be our man. I will bring him to you."

Justine Rousseau beamed. "Oh, Charles. I knew you could find someone."

I couldn't help being excited, but I didn't want to set myself up for a huge disappointment. I was about to say, "Let's not count our chickens before they're hatched," but stopped when I realized I had no inkling what the verb for "hatch" might be.

"Congratulations, Jim," Brigitte said. "You will soon be with your friends again."

"I'm already among friends, Brigitte. But my duty calls me home."

Monsieur and Madame Rousseau laughed at my reply, and we shared hugs all around.

The next afternoon, a Wednesday, I was sitting in the kitchen reading *Le Soir* when Charles Rousseau opened the door that divided the kitchen from the barbershop.

"Mon ami, I have a gentleman here who needs directions to Rue Lafayette. Perhaps you can help him?"

My heart lurched, and Monsieur Rousseau evidently enjoyed the expression on my face. He chuckled and flashed two fingers in a V for victory.

From behind him a stranger stepped into the kitchen. The newcomer looked to be in his thirties. With a wink, the barber returned to his customers.

"*Bonjour,*" I greeted, offering my hand. "*Je m'appelle* Jim."

"Call me Jacques," the man replied in English with an accent that sounded like he had been schooled in Oxford. "That is not my real name, but it is the name for my 'side business.' "

I instinctively liked Jacques. His handshake was strong, and the skin of his palm was tough, as if from much working with tools. His face was well tanned, and I concluded that this man must also be in the construction trade, like Monsieur Rousseau's former officer friend. Jacques had steel-gray eyes and a square chin. His whole bearing suggested strength and determination. I wouldn't have wanted to climb into a boxing ring with him.

We sat down, and Jacques asked me my whole name and wanted to hear the entire story of where I was from and how I ended up in Brussels. Just talking in my own language was refreshing, so I spilled out my story. When I mentioned the raid on Kiel, he nodded. "I heard about that. The Americans lost many planes. But it was successful. You did much damage to the shipyards."

He immediately got down to business. "You need a new name for your journey. No one born in Belgium or France is called Jim Yoder. From now on you are Gaston Bosman. Understand?"

Chapter 17

"Perfectly. I am Gaston Bosman."

Inside, I cringed a little at the name Gaston. To me it sounded like the name of a butler in a cheap dime-store detective novel. But who was I to argue with the underground?

"Good. On Friday afternoon a small truck will stop in front of the barbershop. If I am not in it, the driver will ask Monsieur Rousseau if his cousin still needs a ride. Get in the vehicle, and bring your belongings with you. You will not be returning."

I was impressed with how fast plans were moving ahead. Surely I would be home in no time. "No problem. I have no belongings."

"Good. It is easier to travel light. Do you carry a weapon?"

The question surprised me. "No. I had a pistol when I parachuted into Germany, but the Boches took it away."

The man reached under his shirt and pulled a battered-looking pistol out of his belt. It was a vintage model I didn't recognize. Probably of Belgian origin. But it was clean and well polished.

He slapped it into my hand. "This is from the Great War. Now you have a weapon. Do not lose it. You may need this if you want to see your home again."

That evening at the supper table, Monsieur Rousseau asked me to repeat every portion of my conversation with the visitor called Jacques. The barber was vicariously living my adventure through the story. When I finished sharing the brief conversation, he rubbed his hands together with excitement.

"Marvelous. May we see your pistol?"

I lifted the previous day's copy of *Le Soir* from a stool and revealed the weapon it had concealed.

The barber nodded, an appreciative glint in his eyes. "I wish I were young enough to fight against the Boches. You have been out of the war for a little while, Jim, but now you are back in the fight. Congratulations! May many of the enemy die from this weapon!"

I didn't have the heart to tell my host that I had no desire to stick around Europe long enough to use the pistol, as least not extensively. Maybe he could picture me leading a host of underground volunteers against Nazi strongholds with my one handgun, but I couldn't. My main goal was unchanged—to get back to England and survive this insane war.

Just carrying the weapon was a concern. As an escaped soldier in uniform, I would have been entitled to certain rights under international agreements. Now, though, dressed in civilian clothes and carrying a gun, I had zero rights under international laws. The Germans could execute me as a spy and still be within the Geneva Convention.

By the time dusk was deepening Friday evening, anticipation hung heavy in the sitting room of the Rousseau home. All day I had been unable to concentrate. I would pick up *Le Soir* and run my eyes over the lines, but midway through an article I would realize I had no idea what I had just read and then start at the top again.

At last we heard a light knock on the rear door. Monsieur Rousseau went to answer it.

Instead of an adult figure, a slim boy of about twelve stood on the rear porch. He fished a scrap of paper from a pocket and presented it to the barber. *"Au revoir,"* the lad said. He climbed onto a bicycle and pedaled away without any explanation.

The rest of us gathered around while Monsieur Rousseau unfolded the paper. It said simply, "Necessary to change plans to Saturday. Good luck. Jacques."

"Another delay," I moaned.

"But just one more day," Madame Rousseau consoled. "Perhaps the vehicle was not available?"

The barber grunted. He was definitely a patriot, and I'm sure he felt this holdup somehow stained the honor of Belgium in the eyes of an Allied airman.

"Oh, well, we wait for tomorrow," I commented. *"C'est la vie."*

"C'est la guerre," Brigitte replied. "That is war."

Our threesome spent the rest of the evening talking and speculating on the war while Justine Rousseau darned the holes in her husband's socks. The Rousseau home had no radio for listening in to BBC broadcasts. However, the barber knew a good bit more than was printed in *Le Soir.* I assumed that some of his customers listened to British broadcasts, even though the Nazi occupiers strictly forbade it. When we finally ran out of topics for chit chat, we each wished each other a good night and went to bed.

Later, in my dreams I was back aboard *American Pride.* In the crazy way dreams go, I would shoot off a few bursts at attacking Messerschmitts and then shout at George Baker to throw away his Captain America comic book and get into the ball turret to help us shoot. But George would calmly turn the page and say, "In a minute, Jim. I'm right at a good part." Seething with anger, I dropped my gun and prepared to stuff George bodily into his turret. Suddenly I heard and felt a deafening explosion that rocked *American Pride* . . .

In the next instant I jerked upright and my eyes shot open. Instantly my imaginary mission evaporated. I found myself whisked back to the lit-canapé of the Rousseau home, where near darkness reigned in the sitting room. The only sound was the monotonous ticking of the wall clock. My skin was cold and wet with sweat.

I had had wild dreams about missions before, back in my hut at Shipdham. Maybe all of us airmen had them. I didn't know. We never talked about them, but judging from an occasional shout in the middle of the night or thrashing of blankets, I had suspected I wasn't the only one who endured such nightmares.

But I had been on the ground for weeks now. I would have thought that such dreams would have passed by this time.

"Will I ever be the same person I was before the war?" I asked myself as I flipped over my pillow.

In the back of my mind I already knew the answer. No, I would never again be the same innocent Hoosier I once was. I had seen too much, experienced too much. The visions of exploding aircraft and dying men would always be a part of me, no matter how hard I tried to repress the memories.

"You don't have a right to forget them," a voice seemed to say in my head. "They sacrificed their all. They deserve to be remembered."

But would the nightmares stop after I got back home?

"Whoa, Yoder," I muttered aloud. "You've got a long way to go before you can even think about home. For right now, you better worry about getting out of Europe in one piece."

The next day, I tried to forget that I was supposed to leave the Rousseau home that day. Anticipation and boredom make a killer combination. I pretended this was just another day of hiding out. So I passed the time by dusting every nook and cranny and washing the windows—but only on the inside. I hadn't shown my face outdoors since my arrival, and I wasn't going to take any risks now.

I did have a chance to share a little about my newfound faith with Brigitte. She listened politely, but didn't truly seem to comprehend a personal relationship with God. For her, "religion" equaled the outward formalities of attending church and going through various rituals. But she did let me close our chat with a word of prayer for both our futures.

Madame Rousseau had long since given up her attempts to curb my housework. She must have realized that I needed to channel some nervous energy. For the afternoon, I had set aside a copy of *Le Soir*. That was a good way to improve my vocabulary and to distract myself at the same time. The downside was that the paper often used abbreviations for Belgian businesses or associations. I sometimes had to struggle to figure out exactly what an article was describing.

However, during lunch there came a knock on the rear door, and the three of us—Madame Rousseau, Brigitte, and I—froze in midbite. The barber was still in his shop, finishing a haircut, so Madame Rousseau went to answer.

From around the corner I heard a male voice ask, "Is your cousin ready to leave for Rue Lafayette?"

It was Jacques.

"You're earlier than I expected!" I exclaimed.

Jacques wasn't smiling. "I had no choice. The enemy has arrested a member of our circle. It was the driver who was to pick you up tonight. I was on my way to his house when I saw soldiers lead him out his door and push him into a black Citroen."

A deathly chill gripped my heart. If the Germans had waited a few hours and tailed their quarry instead of arresting him at home, this entire household would have ended up in Gestapo hands.

"How much does that man know?" I asked.

"About you, nothing," Jacques replied. "I was going to pass him the barber's address when I reached his home. But about me—he knows everything they would want to know. He is a good man and won't betray me intentionally, but the Germans have ways of squeezing information out of a person. I cannot return home, so I will escort you to the border personally."

As devastating as this news was, I found comfort in the fact that it was Jacques who would accompany me rather than some stranger.

"But what about your family?" Brigitte wanted to know. "Are they not in danger too?"

"I live alone. If the Nazis go to my apartment, they will find nothing and nobody." He grinned in a defiant way that I couldn't help admiring.

"All right. I'll get my pistol; then we can go."

Madame Rousseau sprang into action. "No, wait. You haven't even finished lunch. I will put some things in a sack for both of you."

Of course, I couldn't leave without bidding farewell to my generous host. Justine Rousseau hadn't finished her task before her husband stepped in for his noon break and learned I was leaving.

"*Bonne chance,* Jim!" he said, wishing me luck and clasping my hand. The glint in his eye and the set of his jaw told me he was proud of me. Probably he was also proud of himself for his role in defying the occupiers of his nation.

"We will miss you," Madame Rousseau said in turn. "The house has never been scrubbed so clean!"

I laughed and turned to Brigitte. She took my hand in both of hers.

"May God go with you, Jim. Greet your Margo for us."

"And God be with you too, Brigitte."

I turned to my new traveling companion. "I'm ready."

Jacques led the way out the rear door and down the alley. Then, surprising me, he led me around a corner right onto a busy sidewalk. Half a dozen bicycles were chained there. Jacques calmly unlocked two light-blue ones.

I raised my eyebrows in a silent question.

He shrugged. "This was not the original plan," he said in an undertone. "But with Paul under arrest, the truck is lost to us. So we ride these." He tilted the handlebars of one bicycle toward me. "Do not worry. You do not look American. In those clothes you look as Belgian as I do. Just relax and act like you have done this a thousand times. Do not stare at anything."

Unsure how to pedal and also hold the paper sack that Madame Rousseau had prepared for us, I unfastened a couple buttons and stuffed the bag inside my shirt.

Seconds later, we were wheeling down the boulevard in brilliant sunshine. After more than five weeks of living in darkness or being cooped up indoors, I found the experience exhilarating. At first I felt as conspicuous as a giraffe in a dog show, but no one showed the slightest interest in me. We wove in and out of traffic and passed throngs of Belgians on the sidewalks and in the cafés.

Here was life! Men, women, and children walked or drove all around. Like us, other bicyclists maneuvered in and out of traffic. Going from practical house arrest to the sights, sounds, and smells of a bustling society was intoxicating.

If only I could ride my motorcycle instead of pumping pedals!

I held my breath when I realized we were approaching four uniformed soldiers of the Wehrmacht who were crossing the street. But they didn't shout or pull their weapons. In fact, they barely glanced at Jacques and me. We shot past, and my confidence level soared.

Pedaling along, I started grinning like a child with his first tricycle. But then I decided that even grinning might make me stand out in a crowd. After all, do the citizens of an occupied country have anything to grin about in public? From then on, I tried to enjoy the scenery without displaying my enthusiasm.

The store windows I saw pleasantly surprised me. I had expected to see empty shelves and long lines, but the city center looked fairly busy. Seeing the architecture and obvious history of my first European city—that is, my first city from less than twenty thousand feet—enthralled me.

When traffic allowed it, Jacques would pedal alongside me. He nodded his approval at how naturally I conducted myself. Occasionally he would name a historic cathedral or park as we wheeled past, but mostly we rode in silence. That suited me, since Brussels was a huge city, and I wanted to soak up as many sights as I could without gawking. However, red flags adorned with black swastikas hanging from buildings were solemn reminders that this was no holiday.

Later, when we reached what I assumed must be the western side of Brussels, Jacques pointed to a café up ahead. "Let's stop for a drink."

I followed his example as he braked and then leaned his bicycle against a wrought-iron post. We settled onto chairs at an outside table. I was glad for the rest. Pedaling was using muscles that I hadn't exercised for quite a while.

"For me, a beer," Jacques told the waiter who came for our order.

The waiter looked at me expectantly. My mind went blank. What would a Belgian café have on hand in wartime? Lemonade? Fruit juice?

"For me, tea," I pronounced in my best accent.

Jacques halfway raised one eyebrow at me, but the waiter nodded and said, "If you can afford genuine tea, monsieur, we still have some." He left to fetch our drinks.

Jacques leaned closer. "I knew the British loved their tea, but I didn't know that Americans do too."

I realized I'd goofed. The truth be told, I'd been picturing a chilled glass of iced tea to cool me down from pedaling under the summer sun. Jacques's comment reminded me that iced tea was an American beverage that hadn't caught on in Europe. So instead of a drink to cool me down, I would be sitting here in late June with perspiration beading my forehead and sipping a piping-hot beverage.

Along with the drinks we ate the buttered bread and cheese sandwiches from my paper sack. I was feeling totally relaxed now as I leaned back and relished the opportunity to feel truly like a part of Belgium. It was great to forget the war for a few minutes and pretend I wasn't a hunted animal.

A military vehicle with screechy brakes pulled to the curb, and three men in German uniforms stepped out of it. I stiffened, but Jacques casually shrugged and sipped his brew. Why not? This must happen every day all over occupied Belgium. I followed my companion's lead and ignored the newcomers, who sat at a table off to the side.

The Germans were soon in loud, animated conversation. I wished again that I understood their tongue. Were they discussing anything that Bomber Command in England would like to know?

Suddenly Jacques cleared his throat, just loud enough for me to hear but not enough to attract attention. He looked alarmed and kept glancing at my pant legs. I looked down, but I couldn't understand what the problem was. There were no stains, no American insignia. These were pants Monsieur Rousseau had bought for me locally. Then it struck me—I was so relaxed that I had leaned back and crossed my legs, just the way I would do back home. I was the only man in sight sitting with one ankle crossed over the opposite knee in typical American style!

I quickly adjusted my posture, crossing my legs knee over knee, the European way.

What a blunder, I berated myself. *If you don't be careful, Yoder, you're going to get yourself arrested yet.*

Fortunately, the German patrons were so engrossed in their own mugs and conversation that they hadn't noticed. For my part, though, I was wishing a breeze would spring up. I was suddenly feeling very hot and couldn't wait to get away.

"Garçon," Jacques called to the waiter. He paid our bill, and we stood to leave.

I was just climbing aboard my bicycle again when the waiter reappeared and, bypassing Jacques, slipped a folded scrap of paper into my hand. *"Merci,"* he said politely, then began wiping our table.

Jacques and I were both curious, but I didn't dare to linger after my recent faux pas. We pedaled away as casually as we had arrived. Once around the corner, however, I unfolded the paper. One startling sentence was hastily scrawled in pencil: "Vive l'Amérique!"

I passed the message to Jacques, who burst into laughter. But the waiter's "Long live America!" made me feel foolish. Right at the moment when I had considered myself most at ease, I had committed a near-fatal gaffe.

Yoder, if some intelligence officer ever recommends that you become an international spy, just say no. You would never survive.

All during that long afternoon, Jacques kept the information about our destination to himself. When I asked outright where he was taking me, he grinned mischievously and said simply, "Toward France."

I hated not knowing things that involved me. I realized that the underground has to operate in secret, but this was one secret that affected me personally. What if something went wrong? What if a car sideswiped Jacques? Or what if he got caught in a German ambush and I escaped? I wanted to know at least some of the plan in case I needed to act alone, but Jacques shook his head.

"No, my friend. Information is a dangerous burden. Let me carry that weight for you. The less you know, the better for all concerned."

I saw the wisdom in this, of course. Still, I felt like a toddler being shuttled from place to place with no clue about my route or exact destination.

As we pedaled side by side, I gave the matter one more try. "Jacques, what if both of us get captured? The Gestapo will never believe I'm totally ignorant. If I don't give them some useless little piece of information, they'll think I'm holding back and try to torture it out of me."

Jacques grinned. "That's a risk I'm willing to take."

These Resistance people sure are a closed-mouth bunch. If Jacques's friend Paul is anything like him, the Gestapo will be wasting their time on him.

At least with Jacques I could speak English once we got away from the capital. My language skills had made great strides in recent days, especially since no one around me knew more than a smattering of English words. I had to speak French and listen to it whether I wanted to or not. But my American brain yearned for my native tongue, especially in the evenings, when I was tired.

Once we were away from the city and out in the countryside I let my mind wander. I was glad that Monsieur Rousseau had found a job for Brigitte. On Monday morning she was to begin work in a tailor shop owned by one of the barber's customers. Soon she should be able to move into a small apartment on her own and not feel like a perpetual houseguest. I was already happy for her new life.

Jacques and I pedaled all that Saturday afternoon. What had initially been a welcome escape from "house arrest" turned into a strenuous challenge for me. I wasn't accustomed to bicycling. Endlessly pumping my legs up and down made my thigh muscles ache. On uphill slopes the struggle to keep up with Jacques made them burn like fire, especially above the knees. For hill climbing, I rose off the seat and used my whole body weight to push down the pedals. Meanwhile, Jacques pumped away with sinews of steel. Clearly, this man was no stranger to bicycles.

"Jim, I thought Americans were big and strong athletes. What is wrong?" He was smiling mischievously.

"I haven't had time to recuperate from my escape out of the Fatherland. Besides, I'm one American who's used to flying, not bicycling."

"Ah, that is right. You are a flier. Very well. Flap your arms and fly ahead if you want. Wait for me when you reach the border." Again that infectious smile of his.

I laughed despite my throbbing muscles.

Finally, around dusk we cycled through a small village and down a dirt track that bore few signs of automobile traffic. At the end of this lane was a weather-beaten cottage in desperate need of repainting.

"Our luck is good," Jacques said. "We have come all the way."
I dismounted on wobbly legs. "You mean, we're in France?"

"No, of course not. We are still in Belgium. But we are close to the border here. Very close. This is where we spend the night."

He stepped to the old-fashioned well and cranked up a bucketful of water. The cool liquid tasted sweet as I drank my fill. We both wetted handkerchiefs to wipe our faces and necks.

Refreshed, Jacques strolled to the door and gave four rapid knocks, followed by a pause, then one last knock. The door opened, revealing a gray-haired matron with a wealth of wrinkles.

"Ah, you decided to come after all? We were expecting you yesterday." Just as I figured, we were plunged back into French conversation.

"There was a delay," my escort explained without going into details.

She looked past Jacques at me. "Is this the 'package' that needs delivering?"

"Oui. This is the package. Meet Gaston. He is américain. Gaston, this is Grand-mère. Is Grand-père home?"

"Yes, yes, he is home. Come inside. No need to stand out here like strangers."

Stepping indoors, I said, "Very nice to meet you. I didn't realize until now that I would be visiting my friend's grandparents."

She cackled. "We are not family. Around here, everyone calls me Grand-mère and my husband Grand-père. We have lived here so long that we are part of the landscape."

Into the main room shuffled Grand-père, as aged as his wife in years, but moving more slowly on crutches—his right leg was missing from the knee down. At the sight of me, his face lit up. "Ah, the next package has arrived. Good! Welcome to our home."

"Have you handled many packages?" I asked.

The man's grin deepened some of his wrinkles. "Not enough."

He pointed at his stump of a leg. "I lost that to a German cannon over twenty-five years ago in the Battle of the Somme. When they began this new war, I vowed to help the Allies if ever I could. Let them arrest me! We're too old to live much longer anyway."

His feisty attitude inspired my heart.

That evening for supper Grand-mère cooked up the fish her husband had caught earlier that afternoon. I had never been a big fan of fish, but this elderly woman had a knack for baking them in a way that even I enjoyed. Or perhaps I had grown less picky during my recent misadventures.

Over the meal, Jacques finally shared with me that, from this cottage, three airmen had already been smuggled over the border into free France.

"They were all British," Grand-mère said. "You are the first package from America we have seen.

"Is the border crossing difficult?" I asked.

Grand-père's face lit up. "It is supposed to be difficult. But for people who have lived here for a long while, this is not a big problem. The superior race is not as superior as they like to believe."

"Tomorrow I will visit the delivery boy," Grand-mère added. "We will make the arrangements then."

"Do you like to fish?" the old gentleman suddenly questioned.

"Yes, but I usually give all my fish away."

"Splendid. We'll go fishing tomorrow, while Grand-mère is away. These days I do not often have company at the stream."

"As for me," Jacques said, "I will bid you farewell after breakfast. I must be getting back to Brussels."

This was not welcome news. I had hoped Jacques would continue into France with me. "Won't it be dangerous for you in the capital? I mean, one of your colleagues was just arrested. Can't the same happen to you?"

"Of course. But Belgium needs men, not mice. I can still find ways to resist the Nazis."

The next morning we said good-bye to Jacques and watched as he pedaled down the lane. Because my own legs hadn't recovered from the previous day's grueling ordeal, I was glad I wouldn't be pedaling anywhere. Also, I felt comforted when Jacques agreed to check on Brigitte de Coster occasionally to make sure that she was all right.

True to his word, Grand-père took me fishing with him the next day. Or rather, I took him. Although his fishing hole wasn't far, at his age he struggled to travel very far on his crutches. So he showed me a contraption that looked like a cross between a wheelbarrow and a wheelchair that someone had cobbled together for him. He asked if I would mind pushing. I agreed, so off we went, with him carrying two poles.

At the stream, we both sat on a grassy bank and dropped our lines into the water. Grand-père was delighted to have some male companionship. In his rustic tongue, he told me stories of pranks he had played on villagers as a boy, about how he had courted and married Grand-mère when they were in their twenties, and about the Great War of 1914–1918.

Occasionally he would ask me questions about home and life in America. He was probably curious about my role in the American armed forces, but he tactfully steered clear of such subjects.

"This is a relaxing spot you have here," I commented between stories. I had peeled off my shirt and was soaking up morning sunshine. "Good thing the Germans don't come here."

"Ah, but they do."

"They do?" I swallowed hard and looked around, as if expecting to see a patrol marching by with rifles over their shoulders.

"Oui. Sometimes. There is one sergeant with the border guards. His French is abominable. Sometimes he fishes near here. Downstream, where the water is deeper, I have also seen Boches soldiers bathing."

Suddenly the two American dog tags dangling from the chain around my neck seemed as large and obvious as a theater marquee. I pulled my shirt back on.

"I leave them alone, and they leave me alone," Grand-père continued. "The Germans must think this one-legged old fellow is harmless. But you and I know better!" He punctuated his words with a wink.

We saw no sign of the enemy that day, which was fine with me. For a few hours I had been able to pretend there was no war and simply enjoyed nature. The nervous tension that built inside me from constantly being in hiding evaporated and blew away, leaving me refreshed and lighthearted.

It was Sunday. I would have relished a chance to slip into the back of a church, but that was out of the question. In the big city an unknown face in the crowd is common. In small towns and villages, a stranger arouses curiosity that I couldn't afford.

That afternoon, Grand-mère returned and announced, "Gaston, everything is arranged. The delivery boy will come this evening."

I laughed. "Is it really so simple?"

"This is not the first time, you know. We have some experience."

"I praise God for your experience—and for both of you."

We were just clearing the dishes after a late supper when several friendly raps sounded at the door. Without waiting for a reply, a young man with curly blond hair and ice-blue eyes stepped inside. He couldn't have been older than sixteen, which surprised me. I assumed an older man would guide me over the border.

Grand-père introduced the newcomer as Vincent.

"Are we ready to travel?" I asked.

"Not yet, monsieur. It is still too light outside. Once darkness is complete, we will leave."

More waiting. I was beginning to detest waiting as much as I hated flak. At least when the enemy was shooting flak at *American Pride,* I felt like our plane was accomplishing something. Here, I felt useless. Worse—like a dangerous burden. I was the hot potato everyone wanted to help, but nobody wanted to get caught with me. In late June, we would have to wait a long while for complete darkness.

I settled into a creaky rocking chair in the corner while Grand-père chatted with Vincent, asking about the health of his parents and about how the radishes, beets, and carrots were doing that summer. The old man scarcely heard Vincent's reply before launching into a barrage of gardening tips gleaned from his lifetime of experience. All the while, anxiety was churning in my gut. I wanted to cross the border and get it over with.

After a full day of conversing in a foreign tongue, my brain was shot. Impolite or not, I closed my eyes and clicked off my mind. I didn't even try to follow the conversation anymore. Foreign words swirled around and over me, but they were just sounds now. I became oblivious to their meaning.

When darkness finally arrived, it wasn't merely the obscurity of nightfall. Ominous, gray clouds rolled in from the west. Raindrops started to patter, just a few at first, but soon it sounded like thousands of miniature, soggy drumsticks *tat-tat-tatting* on the roof overhead.

Oh, great, I thought. *Just when we're ready to move, the weather turns against us.*

Vincent, on the other hand, was beaming with happiness. "Monsieur, luck is with us! Look at how hard it rains!"

I wasn't sure why he had to be so formal and was gracing me with the title monsieur. After all, I wasn't more than three years or so older than him. Instead of pointing this out, however, I groused about the weather instead.

"The rain is good? We're going to be wet as river rats the moment we step out the door!"

Vincent's smile was unquenchable. "*Oui, oui.* But rain covers the sound of footsteps under the trees. Also, it can make even dedicated guards huddle in their shelters to stay dry. Let us leave quickly!"

The truth of this young patriot's words humbled me. Instead of seeing God's hand of blessing in the rain, I had been grumbling out of my own discomfort.

Because I owned no hat, Grand-père fished one of his retired ones from a drawer and presented it to me.

I shook hands with the elderly couple. "Thank you so much. I'm sorry I have no way to repay you."

"Get back to England and help to end this war. That will be our payment," Grand-père said.

Then Vincent and I were out the door and scampering up a rain-soaked path through the woods. We forded the fishing stream by sloshing through a shallow spot and passed into what was, for me, unknown territory. Beyond the stream there was no more path—just tall trees tossing and swaying in the wind as they endured the onslaught of raindrops.

As I had predicted, Vincent and I were waterlogged in record time. Chill rain pasted my shirt to my back. My pant legs stuck uncomfortably to my legs. If my adrenaline hadn't been pumping, I would have felt absolutely miserable. I made a mental note to oil the pistol tucked into my belt the first chance I got.

As it turned out, Vincent was correct. Even if we had gone stomping through the woods as loudly as possible, this downpour would have drowned out the noise. Before long I lost all sense of direction, but Vincent flitted between the trees unerringly. He led me onward, pausing periodically to scan in all directions. I assumed he was keeping his eyes alert for German soldiers. I certainly was.

The storm may have been a timely blessing; however, the combination of rain and nightfall severely limited visibility under the canopy of dripping leaves. If any border guards were insane enough to be traipsing through the woods just then, we could have passed quite close without them seeing us, or vice versa.

When we reached a clearing, Vincent hunched low, peering left and right into the drizzle. I copied his example. The rain was slacking off now, and I believed my ears caught the distant sound of a car door slamming. Vincent tapped me on the shoulder, and then pointed ahead. Wordlessly, he half stood and hustled across the clearing, bent low as he jogged. I was hot on his heels.

A road passed through the clearing, and no sooner had we reached the far side than my left foot sank into some kind of animal hole, and I fell flat into the grass with a mushy *shwump* sound. Vincent turned and hugged the earth until he could figure out what happened to me. I heard no alarm, but I was petrified. All I wanted was to get out of this exposed area, dark though it was. In seconds I was back on my feet, and the two of us continued toward the far side. I was glad I hadn't sprained an ankle.

We gained the trees on the far side of the clearing and plunged between two massive trunks. My heart was thumping, not just from running, but also for fear of shouts or gunshots.

What's worse, facing flak in the air, or playing cat-and-mouse with the Germans on the ground week after week?

That's the silly thought that popped into my mind. The question remained unanswered as I trudged up a hillside behind my guide.

The trees were considerably thinner here, but we still had to strain our eyes for the fallen limbs and rotting logs that decorate the floors of forests everywhere.

After about thirty more minutes, we approached a small home from the rear. The dwelling looked squat in the dark.

Vincent and I circled to the front, where he knocked on the door. We waited, and when nothing happened, he knocked again.

"Who is there?" asked a muffled voice inside.

"It is me, Vincent. And a friend."

The door swung open, revealing deeper darkness inside. Vincent led the way. Not until the door shut again did someone light a match and touch it to the wick of a kerosene lantern. The man standing there wasn't young, but neither was he as elderly as my previous host and hostess.

"Grand-père sends you a package. This one is bound for America," Vincent declared proudly.

The man eyed me up and down. "It has been a while since my last package. But I will take good care of this one for you. Does he understand us?"

"Je parle français," I answered.

He nodded his approval. *"Très bien.* Welcome to Free France, monsieur." He shook my hand.

Vincent wanted to return immediately, but the owner of this home—whose name turned out to be Jean-Marc—wouldn't hear of letting him go until he sat him down for a few minutes and fed him some cheese and wine. I nibbled at the cheese too, but wasn't really hungry—just cold, sodden, and weary now that the dash over the border was completed. I let Vincent share the latest news from his village, plus give an update on the health of Grand-père and Grand-mère.

At last Vincent insisted that he must get back. I shook his hand at the door. "Merci, Vincent. You're a brave man. So I'm the fourth airman you have led over the border?"

"Oui." He nodded, both pleased and embarrassed at the praise.

"Tell me, how long did it take the others to reach England from here?"

"Oh, I have no idea. After they left here, we never heard of them again." With that final comment, Vincent donned his wet cap and slipped into the night.

Somehow his statement wasn't reassuring. I couldn't help wondering if anyone would hear from *me* again.

My stay with Jean-Marc lasted only a few days. However, I wasn't nearly as relaxed with this man as I had been in the Rousseau home or with Grand-père. Jean-Marc was a moody bachelor and not at all talkative. He also struck me as too nervous. I lost count of how many times he went to a window and, barely touching the curtains, peered left and right through a small gap between them.

In answer to my questions about where I was, he excavated a smudged and tattered map from a desk drawer and unfolded it.

"Denain," he said, pointing out the closest town with his index finger. North of Denain was Lille, a much larger French city, but still near the Belgian border. I could see that it was a long way from here to Paris, and much farther to the English Channel. When I asked Jean-Marc how I would be moved, he shrugged.

"Other people care for those details. I only provide food and a place to stay for a few days."

In addition to his nervous habits, Jean-Marc laid down an assortment of laws for my stay in his home: no going to the outhouse during daylight (he supplied a metal bucket for emergencies), no opening the curtains or standing near the windows, no firing up the wood-burning stove when he was at work, no talking above a quiet voice . . . I had joked about being under house arrest in the barber's home, but here the phrase struck closer to the bull's eye. By my second day there, I longed for a chance to go fishing again with Grand-père.

During the day Jean-Marc left me alone to go to his job. He said that he was a wood merchant, but I wasn't sure if that meant he worked at a sawmill, or at a lumberyard, or if he simply traded in firewood. I didn't ask though. Perhaps Jean-Marc used up his quota of daily words on the job. At home he clearly didn't care for conversation. I gave up trying to coax him.

The evening of my second day in Denain, a knock sounded at the door.

I fled to the bedroom and gripped my pistol while Jean-Marc peeked through the curtains once more.

My host opened the door and stood aside. *"Entrez."* Jean-Marc seemed to be expecting whoever it was.

"Gaston," he called. "Two friends have come to meet you."

I stepped into the room.

"Bonjour, Gaston," said the taller of the two men. "Welcome to Free France. We have come from Lille to make arrangements for you." He shook my hand warmly and with a sincere smile.

"Am I leaving tonight?" I didn't want to sound too hopeful, but I couldn't wait to find a more talkative host than Jean-Marc.

The shorter man, who sported a dark walrus mustache, smiled at Jean-Marc. "You were right. His accent is excellent."

Privately I wondered how Jean-Marc had reached this conclusion. He conversed with me little enough.

"No, not yet," the taller fellow said in response to my question. "We must not be reckless. First, you need proper documents for traveling. That is why we are here."

From a canvas sack, the taller man extracted a camera. "Jean-Marc, we'll need to cover the windows to make sure no one outside sees the flash."

My host grunted, nodded, and retrieved blankets from his linen cupboard. These he draped over each window in the room.

"Are those your only clothes?" the shorter man with the mustache asked me.

"Yes. Why?"

"You will need something else for the photograph. Very rarely will you find a person on the street wearing the exact same clothing shown on his identity card." He glanced at Jean-Marc, who was much heavier than I and obviously didn't wear the same size.

"Oh, well, let us do it this way," the taller man continued, unbuttoning his own shirt. You can borrow mine for a minute."

I donned the borrowed shirt, and then stood against the wall where the short man indicated. When he lifted the camera, I smiled for the shot.

The camera went back down. "Non, non, Gaston. This is not the New York World's Fair. Your face must carry the expression of a man whose country has been overrun by butchers, assassins, and barbarians of the worst sort."

I stared into the lens with a straight face and clenched jaw.

"Much better!"

The flash bulb popped into brilliance. The cameraman inserted another bulb and took a second picture for good measure.

"That is all for now. We should be back tomorrow or the next day to take you away."

"Wait. You haven't even told me how you plan to get me home. Will I be rowed out to a submarine, or what?"

While the taller man buttoned his shirt, his shorter companion with the walrus mustache smiled and said, "If only it were that simple. But you see, the Resistance is very short on submarines at the moment. So far, our total is up to zero."

I felt foolish and tried to cover my goof. "Well, yes, but the Allies have submarines. I thought maybe—"

"The coast of France is very well defended, Gaston. Even if we could radio for a submarine to pick you up, you would find it impossible to sneak past the coastal patrols to row out to it. Most likely you will be taken south, over the Pyrenees Mountains into Spain. From Gibraltar, the British can get you aboard a ship or a submarine."

I was stunned. Climb over the mountains to Spain? That would be miles and miles to the south, plus more delays. Having grown up in northern Indiana—whose terrain is about as mountainous as a table top—I had never even been near a range of mountains, let alone climbed one. Could I do that?

The camera went back into the sack, and the two visitors turned to go.

"Wait," I said. "I don't even know your names."

The two exchanged knowing smiles.

"Can you keep a secret?" the tall one asked me.

"Of course."

"So can we!"

With that comment, the two chuckled and shook my hand. Then they were out the door.

Two days later, true to their word, the two Resistance men from Lille showed up late in the afternoon. Jean-Marc had returned from work just a short while earlier, and I was glad he was there when their knock sounded on the door. Even so, the sound made my heart leap.

The two unnamed men entered, greeted me warmly, and presented me with the fruits of their labor: A genuine-looking French *carte d'identité* that included a photo of a stern-looking mechanic by the name of Gaston Bosman.

"It says my place of birth is Brussels. Why not some city in France?"

The one who had taken the photo shrugged. "A minor point. Your French is good, but it has a touch of accent that sounds a little like you're from eastern Belgium. If you ever get stopped, we thought that would divert suspicion."

His remark struck me as funny. In Brussels I had been told that my French had a slight accent, which made it sound like I came from Paris. Personally I concluded that it was just my American accent they were detecting, but I didn't argue. By this stage I would let them claim I was Adolf Hitler's French-speaking nephew if it would speed up the voyage home.

They had asked me what my occupation should be. Aerial gunner wasn't an option, so I had said, "Mechanic." The document stated this as my job. It was a good choice too, as a mechanic might have to travel on a repair job, and I definitely planned to travel.

"Merci, Jean-Marc, for letting me stay with you. I appreciate the risk you took."

He accepted my hand and acknowledged the thanks with a courteous nod. "Bonne chance," he said.

Outside, my new friends opened the door of a dark green sedan and let me slide into the middle seat. A turn of the key, and we were off.

This was the life! No pedaling, no stowing away on train cars, and no tramping by foot under cover of darkness. Here I was, being chauffeured to Lille in style. At last I felt that I had come under the wing of real professionals in the Resistance business.

"Ah, I nearly forgot," said the short man in the passenger seat beside me. He reached into the back and retrieved a small packet bound with brown paper and string. "We brought a gift for you. It's for the holiday."

I unwrapped the package and found a brand-new beret of black wool. When I tried it on, the driver adjusted his rearview mirror so that I could admire myself. It was perfect! I looked like a typical Frenchman, at least in my own eyes.

"Merci beaucoup! But I'm not familiar with the holidays in France. What's the occasion?"

Both men chuckled, and the driver said, "Today is not a holiday in France. But it is a holiday in Amérique, is it not?"

My blank expression must have surprised them both. However, I hadn't looked at a calendar in ages and had no idea what he meant.

"Joyous Day of Independence to you, Gaston!" said the man with the walrus mustache.

Day of Independence?

It was the fourth of July, and I hadn't even realized it. Riding along in silence for a spell, I reflected on this day and what must be happening back in Indiana. Backyard barbecues. Picnics in High Dive Park. Trips to the beach on the shore of Lake Michigan. Friends and neighbors getting together . . .

Being away from America wasn't so bad when I was surrounded by a bunch of buddies at Station 115 in England. Suddenly, though, a wave of homesickness swept through me, making me feel very alone despite the two allies sitting on either side of me.

At that moment, a cloud of steam erupted from beneath the car's hood. The driver pulled to the roadside and, using a hand-kerchief to shield his hand, lifted the hood. The engine compartment was a watery, steamy mess.

Both of the Resistance men stared at the dripping engine, but neither made a move. Evidently, neither one understood engines.

"What do we do now?" the short fellow with the mustache murmured to his companion.

When the steam cleared, I saw that a radiator hose had ruptured. Fortunately, though, the hole was not large, and it was right beside the radiator clamp. All we had to do was remove the clamp, snip off a couple inches of hose, and then reclamp it. We should be on our way in no time.

I didn't have the vaguest idea of what the proper words were for hose or radiator, so I pointed out the hole. "This is not a big problem. I can repair it."

"You can?" the driver said with relief.

"Of course. You've seen my papers. I'm a mechanic, remember?" I laughed. "Now, where are your tools?"

The driver's countenance dropped. "My brother-in-law is borrowing them. We have no tools in the car."

My countenance must have dropped too. All I needed was a screwdriver to loosen the clamp and something sharp to trim the hose. But even easy jobs become difficult when all you have are fingers to work with.

"We don't have many choices, do we?" I said. "Maybe I should pray about it?"

My spontaneous suggestion astonished my companions. But without waiting to see if they would imitate my example, I dropped my head and began speaking.

"Dear God. As You can see, we have a problem here. We need some tools, but we don't have any. I'll do my best without them, but if You're not too busy with the war on and everything, could You send somebody to lend us what we need? We would sincerely appreciate it. Amen."

I opened my eyes in time to see my new friends quickly crossing themselves.

"Amen," they repeated.

Still, there was no traffic on the road and no homes in sight either. Nowhere to beg for a screwdriver. From my pocket I fished out the Belgian one-franc coin that Jacques had given me as a souvenir. The reverse side showed a lion rearing on its hind legs. I hated to scratch it up, but it was the only thin piece of metal I had. With the little coin I attacked the clamp. It was a crude way to work, and it hurt my fingertips, but I had no choice. Dusk would soon be setting in, and we didn't even have a flashlight.

As I sweated under the hood, I heard the sound of a car crunching to a stop in the gravel behind ours.

"Go see if they have any tools," I suggested.

Moments later, several footsteps approached on the roadside gravel. "It looks like you are in big trouble. That's very unfortunate."

The voice spoke French, but it was guttural and choppy, not the fluid speech of a native speaker. I glanced up and locked eyes with a man wearing the uniform of the Third Reich. Beside him stood my two companions, looking nervous but saying nothing. I didn't know if I should bolt for the hills or reach inside my shirt for my weapon.

The German major turned and called out something I couldn't understand. A second soldier soon appeared with a khaki canvas satchel.

"Will anything here help?" the major asked, flipping open the satchel.

"Oui," I said, spying a screwdriver. "Merci!"

In seconds I had removed the stubborn hose clamp. Now I just needed to trim the hose. But the satchel contained no scissors or metal snips.

"Would you have a knife?" I asked the enemy in my best French. I hoped he didn't notice the sweat beading my forehead or the tightness in my throat.

The major interpreted, and his aide returned—with a razor-sharp bayonet, of all things. I had hoped for a pocketknife, but this would do the trick. I sliced off three inches of hose, and then clamped it back into place. The job hadn't taken long, but the engine was filthy, and my fingers were black with oily grime.

No sooner had I finished the job than the major's assistant was at my side again with a large metal can. He motioned that I should step aside so he could top off the radiator.

In silence I obeyed.

The driver took his water can and tool satchel back to his vehicle.

As the major eyed us, he sported a curious smile. "You see, *messieurs*, no matter what you may have heard, we Germans are not uncivilized animals. Please share that with your friends and neighbors."

He was about to turn away, and then, as an afterthought added, "Forgive me, gentlemen, but as you know we are quite near the border, and we are living in perilous times. Would you be so good as to show me your papers?"

He extended his hand, palm up.

My short, mustached companion recovered first. "Of course." He pulled a booklet from an inside pocket of his suit jacket. He yawned unconcernedly while the major examined it. The yawn struck me as slightly too casual, a bit too forced as he tried to appear relaxed.

Meanwhile my mind was racing. Did my two friends carry weapons, or was I the only one? Should I pull my pistol and drop the major on the spot? And if I did, how fast would his assistant, who was now back at their car, react? What kind of weapon did that man carry? Or perhaps I should simply hand over my forged identity card and hope that it was good enough to pass inspection?

By now the major had finished examining both my companions' documents and handed them back. Lastly, he turned to me.

I hesitated there with my grimy hands in front of me, undecided whether to go for the gun or my false I.D.

"Ah, I see your dilemma," the major said, beckoning to my blackened fingers. "You cannot touch your papers without soiling your clothing." His eyes swept me from head to toe. "Well, do not trouble yourself. Perhaps next time, *ja*?"

He graced us with an imperious nod, uttered a "*Heil* Hitler," and strolled back to his vehicle without waiting for a response.

As the enemy car pulled away, we waved and called out our thanks. When the car was out of sight, though, my knees went weak. I sank to the ground and rested my forehead on our vehicle's front bumper.

"Thank You, God."

"Gaston," said the taller of my two companions, "we have never seen such an answer to a prayer. But please do us a favor. The next time you ask God to help us, could you urge the Almighty to send someone from our own nation? That would be much easier on our nerves!"

The next several days became a blur of activity, which was a welcome contrast to my long, boring days in the home of the wood merchant Jean-Marc. In Lille I became a guest in the apartment of Raymond, which is the name that my tall driver finally gave for himself. I'm not sure if that was a pseudonym or if he finally trusted me enough to reveal his real name. But it didn't matter—I didn't have a last name for him, and I didn't know the address of the apartment. If the Gestapo ever arrested me, I wouldn't be able to lead them to Raymond no matter how they tortured me.

Raymond also supplied several useful items to round out my disguise. A battered leather briefcase was my main prize. Downed airmen don't carry briefcases, and I assumed that escapees from prison camps didn't either. However, because I would be riding the train from Lille to Paris, I needed at least a small piece of luggage to blend in as a genuine traveler, and the briefcase would fit the bill superbly.

Into the briefcase went a change of underclothes and spare socks, plus an assortment of small wrenches, a hammer, and a couple of well-worn screwdrivers intended to make me look like a convincing mechanic. Of course, if I had been a true mechanic traveling to a job site, I would've wanted more than these bare essentials, but I didn't point that out to Raymond. All in all, I was pretty satisfied with my disguise. The addition of the beret and the fact that I had passed a German major's scrutiny had me feeling quite confident that I looked like one of the locals. The handful of French francs Raymond provided gave me a feeling of independence.

Also, I received my own map of France, which I studied diligently. During my flying career with the Flying Eightballs—the 44th Bomb Group—my main interests in Europe had been the locations of antiaircraft batteries and enemy aerodromes. Now I wanted to learn about local geography, railway lines, main roads, and rivers.

As much as I trusted the Resistance to do their best, I wanted to know what I was up against. I also wanted personal knowledge of the terrain in case anything should go wrong and I was forced to flee alone. The one feature on the map that particularly drew my attention was the southwestern border, where the Pyrenees Mountains divided France from the Iberian Peninsula. I didn't relish the idea of climbing that barrier and hoped it wouldn't be necessary. But were my hopes in vain?

When I asked for more specifics about my pending escape from France, Raymond lifted his hands in a gesture that indicated he didn't know anything either.

"One step at a time, Gaston. First we must get you to Paris. A man may plan a trip of a thousand miles, but he cannot foresee every bump and turn in the road. The journey becomes even more difficult in a land ruled by enemies."

"But surely someone is making plans for me, even if the plans are still vague?"

"True. But that someone does not live in Lille. News of your arrival has gone ahead to Paris. When you reach the capital, Philippe will tell you what comes next."

"Philippe?" This was the first time I'd heard the name. "Who is this Philippe?"

Again the helpless gesture with the empty hands. "I do not know who Philippe is. Nobody in Lille knows. For safety, each of us knows only two or three persons close to us in the escape line. But Philippe is a mastermind. When you reach Paris, you might not see Philippe personally, but you will be in Philippe's care."

To prepare me for the next leg of my journey, Raymond sketched in detail the layout of the train station in Lille, and then made me identify each point back to him from memory. He quizzed me until he was sure I knew the exact location of the ticket office, the restrooms, the waiting areas, and every other feature of the station. Each fact could be crucial to my goal of looking and acting natural. He also described typical passenger cars and when the conductor would ask to see my ticket so that I could know what to expect.

"It is so wonderful that you speak our language," Raymond commented. "Not just because I can talk to you freely, but because it simplifies your traveling preparations. The last British pilot who passed through our hands had a poor memory for foreign words. He could not remember how to say anything more difficult than Bonjour. We ended up coaching him to act deaf and dumb. We even had a teacher of the deaf instruct him in some sign language."

"What a clever idea!"

"Yes, we thought so. However, we cannot overuse that ruse. Someone might get suspicious if a steady trickle of deaf and dumb men of combat age begins using the Lille railway station!" He punctuated the remark with a chuckle. "Or perhaps a genuine deaf person might try to communicate and see through the disguise."

I believe that I was in Lille for three days. It may have been four, but my memory is fuzzy on that. Raymond and I discussed the war, his visits to England during happier times, and our plans for the future. The flow of conversation was a welcome change of pace from the silence of Jean-Marc's home. Whenever Raymond could not be with me, his short companion with the walrus mustache—who never did give me a name for himself—would drop by and chat. Most importantly, this man also taught me scores of useful words that I hadn't learned before.

Every language consists of thousands of words, and each word has its own little nuances. Even though I knew thousands of French words by this time, there were still huge gaps in my vocabulary, especially when conversation departed from day-to-day expressions and delved into the military, religion, business, or politics. More often than I can recall I would interrupt a speaker and ask what a word meant. Shorty—as I nicknamed him to myself—made it his personal duty to beef up my vocabulary. My impression was that he might be a school teacher in real life, for he slipped very naturally into the role of tutor.

At last, on a sunny Wednesday morning Raymond surprised me at breakfast by nonchalantly asking if I were ready for a trip to Paris that very day.

I stopped chewing my omelet and nearly dropped my fork. My eyes met Raymond's to see if he were joking. His eyes twinkled as he witnessed my reaction, but I saw no jesting in them.

"Of course I'm ready. Let's go!"

Sadly for me, Raymond explained that he couldn't travel with me. His presence was required in Lille. Instead, he said, a fellow member of the Resistance would purchase my train ticket and escort me there.

"But you must never speak to your guide nor let it be obvious that you are traveling together. Don't stay too near," Raymond cautioned. "The Boches will kill any citizen caught aiding an escaping flier. If you are detained for any reason, you are on your own and must not expect help."

I nodded.

He went on to outline the course of action for the day. "Do you know the song '*En Passant par la Lorraine*'?"

"No, I don't believe so."

Raymond began whistling, and instantly I recognized the tune as one that Madame Scoville used to hum while ironing.

"This morning I will lead you to a park. You must not walk beside me. Stay back forty or fifty feet. When I sit down to tie my shoe, that will be your signal. After I walk away, I want you to sit on the same bench and stay there. From that moment on, my job is completed. Open the newspaper I will give you and read until you hear a bypasser whistle or hum 'En Passant par la Lorraine.' That will be your next guide. Do you understand?"

I nodded. "Then what?"

"Follow her to the train station. She will buy two tickets—"

"She?" I blurted. "A woman is taking me to Paris?"

Raymond smiled. "Oui. The wife of one of our people. She will buy two tickets. When she sits down in the station, she will place one ticket on the seat beside her. Without saying a word, you will sit down for a moment too, and put that ticket in your pocket without speaking to her. Follow her onto the train at a discreet distance. Go where she goes, and do not lose sight of her. She will lead you to a safe place in Paris."

"I wish you were taking me, Raymond."

"So does the husband of your guide. I also wish the war were already over. But we cannot have all of our wishes. We simply do what must be done. I warn you again: if you run into trouble, you are on your own. I cannot overemphasize that. You must never let it be known that you are with the lady. Is that clear?"

"Perfectly."

Raymond proved to be a magnificent guide. Even though I knew he was on a covert assignment for the Resistance, no one else would suspect a thing. He was composed and behaved as any normal citizen on an errand. A couple times he would cross streets and pause to glance into shop windows. At first I assumed he did that merely to look casual. The second time, though, I realized he was using the window glass like a mirror to see if I were still behind him.

While trailing him, I found Lille to be a charming city. Not nearly as big as Brussels, but larger and much older than my hometown in the States. Soldiers of the Wehrmacht passed me on the sidewalk, but I paid no more heed than anyone else did. Once again I found myself hoping for a chance to visit Europe some day when the war was over.

Listen to yourself, Yoder. You're already assuming you'll survive this nutty war. Don't be too confident. It's still a long way to freedom.

Despite that reality, I was feeling fairly confident. Raymond and his colleagues acted with a balance of wisdom and caution, which I appreciated. From Raymond's conversation, I trusted that this underground mastermind named Philippe would likewise be a huge asset in my bid for freedom. As I strolled the streets of Lille, I compared my success thus far to a baseball player who has passed second base and is approaching third. In other words, I was nowhere near home plate, but I was getting closer, and now I had friends to cheer me on.

Suddenly a man stepped into my path and looked me in the eyes. This wasn't part of the game. Had there been a change of plan? Or worse, could this be a plainclothes German agent?

"*Excusez-moi.* Do you have a match?" the man said, brandishing an unlit cigarette.

"No. Sorry. I don't smoke."

I continued walking, relieved that this was just an innocent encounter. At least, I hoped it was. It was amazing, though, how such a little incident could instantly set my heart racing.

On the outskirts of a park I saw Raymond suddenly halt and tie his shoe at a bench. That was my cue. When he strolled away, I settled onto the same spot and withdrew the newspaper from my briefcase. I wished I could have said good-bye to Raymond and thank him again for all he had risked on my behalf, but it was impossible. I immersed myself in my paper.

For some reason I expected my next contact to arrive almost immediately. However, no one showed up. That is, people passed, and some occasionally shared my bench. But not one of them hummed, whistled, or sang "En Passant par la Lorraine." A half hour passed. Then forty-five minutes. Then an hour. By the time I finished my newspaper, I was growing uneasy. Had something gone wrong? Had the Gestapo apprehended my contact? Or perhaps she was waiting at the wrong bench? I wanted to stand up and meander around, but didn't dare leave my appointed spot. I felt conspicuous just sitting there with nothing to do, so I flipped my paper back to page one and started rereading the whole thing—or at least pretending to read it.

Come on; come on . . .

At long last, when I was truly growing restless, a dark-haired woman in a light-blue hat in her midthirties paused near me and blew her nose. As she tucked her lace hankie into her handbag, I distinctly heard her humming the tune I'd been waiting for.

Thank You, Lord. I was getting pretty nervous there.

Folding my paper, I stretched my legs and followed her at a discreet distance. I admired the woman for her appearance. She wore no make-up and her clothing was of nondescript drab colors that did nothing to flatter her. Her hair was pulled back in a tight bun, and she wore glasses perched halfway down her nose, contributing to the impression that she was older than she really was.

Good girl. The dowdier you look today, the less likely that anyone will pay attention to you. Or to me trailing you.

At the train station the plan went as smoothly as we had rehearsed it. In fact, the whole scenario reminded me of being in a school play. Each of us actors had been assigned a role, which we had studied individually. Now we were walking through the motions that had been blocked out by the director. Actually, this was even easier than being in a play, for I had no lines to memorize. I just had to follow "Blue Hat," pause on a bench long enough to pocket the ticket she left for me, mingle with the crowd for fifteen minutes or so, then follow my guide into a passenger car.

Inside the train car, I noted where she sat facing away from me, then chose a seat where I could keep the back of her blue hat in sight.

Again, I felt conspicuous sitting there among strangers. I didn't want to get sucked into a conversation if I could help it. When my fellow travelers smiled and waved good-bye to friends or family on the platform, I looked out the window and smiled and waved too. To be honest, I felt foolish grinning and waving good-bye to absolutely no one. But so many others were waving farewells that this seemed the proper way to act natural. Once the whistle blew and the train pulled away, out came my newspaper again.

As they often did, my thoughts drifted across the Atlantic. Despite frequent disagreements with Dad during my last couple years of school, I longed to let him and Margo know that I was free and okay rather than wasting away in a POW camp—or dead. I seriously didn't want Margo to think I was dead!

Even though I had no Bible, I felt that God was teaching me lessons, helping me to grow in my new-found faith. As a result of my new spiritual awareness, I understood perfectly that a wholesome, godly girl like Margo never would have gotten romantically entangled with the old Jim Yoder. Still, I sensed that she had felt something for me. I was convinced that I was more than just another friend, or a missionary project of hers. Otherwise, why would she have written to me at all?

I had no name for the emotion I sensed from Margo. Was it "pre-attraction?" Or perhaps "potential" attraction? Those are some of the cumbersome adjectives I invented as I tried to nail down Margo's attitude toward me. The bottom line was that she liked—and I think cared for—me, but would never open her heart to the word "love" unless I came to know God the same way she did.

However, even if Margo didn't conclude that Jim Yoder was dead, she could open her heart to some Christian man back home.

This was the fear that gripped my gut whenever I thought about her. Futile though it was, I sent mental messages to her, crying, "I'm alive, Margo! I'm coming. Just wait for me!"

Up ahead a high-pitched whistle blew, and the train clunked into motion, slowly at first, and then gathering speed.

Well, Lord, here we go again, rolling into the unknown. I'm sure glad You know what's going to happen, because I definitely don't.

That was the extent of my prayer as I pretended to read the news I had practically memorized by this time. However, if I had known then what kind of reception awaited me in Paris, I'm sure I would've prayed a whole lot harder.

The train ride to Paris was blessedly uneventful. After the conductor asked for tickets, I tilted my head toward the window and feigned sleep. Even then, however, I frequently peeked out one eye to ensure that Blue Hat was still in her seat.

On arrival at the station in Paris I behaved as though I had been there countless times before. Threading my way through the crowd, I refrained from gawking. My only desire was to keep my female guide in sight. I did note, though, that Wehrmacht uniforms were much more abundant here than anywhere I had yet been. A special kind of exhilaration welled inside me as I casually brushed the shoulders of soldiers who would have been shocked had they known that an escaped airman was slipping through their fingers.

Blue Hat politely declined the sidewalk vendors who hawked newspapers, flowers, trinkets, and similar wares. I likewise ignored them. Outside the station, taxi drivers offered her their services, but she ignored them. For a moment I thought she was going to board a bus as she walked straight toward one idling at the curb. She strolled past it, though, and rounded a corner.

I was relieved. Raymond had never told me how much it costs to ride a bus or streetcar, nor whether a person must buy a ticket at a sidewalk kiosk, hand over coins to the driver, or what the correct procedure would be. It was a petty, everyday detail, but it was the kind of transaction that would instantly brand you as out-of-place if you didn't know it.

Halfway down the next block, I saw the lady with the hat pause beside an automobile parked at the curb. The passenger window was rolled all the way down, and through it she spoke to a figure slouched behind the wheel. Without even a backward glance, she opened the door and slipped into the front seat.

Now what? I continued walking with my eyes riveted dead ahead. I didn't so much as look at the car. When I drew abreast of it, however, I heard a female voice call out in French, "Oh, Gaston? Is that you? What a coincidence. Can we give you a ride?"

The air of pleasant surprise with which she uttered her words was flawless. I decided on the spot that Blue Hat was a born actress. Well, I could act too.

"Why, yes. Merci! So good to see you again!"

Once I had slammed the rear door, the driver revved the engine and maneuvered into the flow of traffic. My guide pulled off her unneeded glasses and turned to me with a smile. "Well, done, monsieur aviateur. Welcome to the City of Light!" She offered her hand.

"Is there any chance we were followed?" I asked.

"I do not believe so," the driver remarked. "I have been watching. Only three people came around the corner behind you. Two girls of about fifteen and an elderly woman hobbling with a cane."

"Where are we going now?"

"I am taking you to Philippe," the driver said.

I was immediately curious. "What can you tell me about Philippe?"

"Absolutely nothing," the driver replied, "because I know nothing. My role is limited to courier. In the underground, too much knowledge can earn a bullet through the head."

It was late in the day. I leaned back and watched the streets and boulevards of Paris slide past.

"Would you like to see a little of the city?" my lady guide inquired.

"Yes, of course."

"Do we have time?" she asked the driver.

He shrugged. "Probably. I was not told what time to deliver the package. Only where to deliver him."

So, instead of taking the direct route to the mysterious Philippe, my new companions wove a circuitous course through the city. In this way I saw for the first time the *Arc de Triomphe*, the Cathedral of Notre Dame, the *Palais Royal*, and a lot of supposedly famous places that I'd never heard of before. Paris literally oozed with history. Within minutes my guides pointed out more Saint so-and-so churches and Place de such-and-suches than I could ever hope to recall.

When the driver launched into an explanation of how Paris is subdivided into a number of districts called *arrondisements*, I ceased trying to retain all the information. I just sat back and admired the city. Of course, we also saw the Eiffel Tower. For this last sight the driver stopped the car and permitted me to stare in wonder at the metal colossus.

"According to rumor, the Boches considered dismantling the Tower to melt it down for tanks and cannons," he commented. "Thankfully, they did not do it. We would have hated them all the worse."

Again I marveled at the intricacies of the structure. Never would I understand how anyone could seriously harbor the notion of reducing it to scrap metal.

"This is where I leave you," the lady told me. "My sister and brother-in-law live not far from here. They are expecting me this evening." She opened her door.

"Good-bye. Thank you very much for helping me."

"Non," she replied with a shake of her head. "Thank you and your countrymen and the British for helping *us*."

Now, with daylight fading, the driver set a course for the address he had previously been given. On the north side of the city, however, he waved a hand toward the left and said, "There is an airfield in that direction. It is called Bourget Field. That is where the first American flier came down."

I was immediately intrigued. "Really? Do you know what kind of plane he was flying when the Germans shot him down?" I assumed it was a fighter since he spoke of one man, and bombers carried many crewmen.

The driver laughed. "Non, non. You misunderstand. I am talking about the very first American flier to arrive in Paris. You know—1927. Years before the Boches invaded. All alone, he flew a little monoplane named *l'Esprit de Saint Louis* over the Atlantic Ocean from New York. Thousands of us Parisians crowded the field to watch him climb from his cockpit!"

Now I joined in laughing at my misunderstanding. "Charles Lindbergh!"

Lindbergh was one of my boyhood heroes. That first solo flight over the Atlantic had taken place sixteen years earlier, but somehow it comforted me to know that one of the most celebrated Americans of the day had descended the skies near this very spot. I marveled at how much the world—and aviation—had changed in the span of those sixteen brief years.

With daylight fading, we halted in front of a large building of venerable age. In the gathering gloom I could make out the words on the sign: "*Hospice d'aliénés.*"

"Philippe lives in an insane asylum?" I whispered as we approached the front door.

"I do not know. I have never been here before today. I just make deliveries wherever they tell me." Then, after a pause, he added with a grim grin, "Maybe Philippe does live here. Working in the underground, it might help to be a little bit crazy. You know what will happen if the Boches catch us." He drew a slicing motion across his throat.

In response to his knock, a woman in a white dress that looked like a nurse's uniform opened the door. She appeared to be in her forties. My driver spoke to her in an undertone. She nodded and motioned for me to cross the threshold.

"Good-bye, monsieur," the driver said. "Good luck!"

We shook hands, and he headed back to the car.

"This way," said the woman in white. From the foyer, she led me down a corridor of many doors, then up a flight of stairs to the second level. Somewhere in the distance I could hear muffled shouting. Through another door I heard hysterical laughter. I had never been in a hospital for mental patients before and didn't know if this was normal or not.

"The patients," the woman replied to my unspoken question. "Some of them never utter a sound. Others are rarely silent."

I nodded, not knowing what to say.

At the last door on the left, the woman leading me stopped and turned the knob. "A reception committee is waiting for you. You may step inside."

The door swung open, and a male voice called, "Entrez," followed by a translation in heavily accented English, "Enter, enter."

Inside were three men, all of them in their twenties, I guessed. Two of the men looked so similar that I concluded they had to be brothers, although not identical twins. Those two had dark hair and a slight gap between their two front teeth, evidently a hereditary trait. They all wore dark, nondescript clothing that wouldn't be particularly memorable.

"We have been waiting for you," said the oldest man, the same one who invited me inside. Judging by the haze of tobacco smoke hovering below the ceiling, I concluded they had been waiting quite a while.

Each man stood and shook my hand warmly.

The spokesman had blue-gray eyes, a gold-capped front tooth, and a face that hadn't felt a razor for a day or two. Perched on his head was a dark-blue beret similar to my black one.

The room was sparsely furnished with an iron-frame bed, painted white; a nightstand; a small, round table; and two chairs. I saw no closet, wardrobe, or even a hook for hanging up a jacket. Two empty wine bottles on the table, plus three empty glasses, provided a clue as to the source of the men's cheerfulness.

"You must be Philippe," I said to the speaker of the group.

They laughed uproariously.

"Non, non. I am not Philippe. I am André. But Philippe should arrive soon."

They offered me one of the chairs, and André settled himself on the other. His companions, the two brothers, sat on the bed.

The three chatted amicably and described life in Paris under the Nazi yoke. I nodded sympathetically as they complained about how few grams of bread and meat were permitted at current ration levels. To be honest, though, I couldn't translate the grams and kilograms they spoke of into pounds and ounces, so I couldn't really picture the dismal scenario they were painting for me.

Before long, the door opened and in stepped an attractive brunette. She, too, wore a white dress, which I understood was the uniform of the establishment. I guessed her to be about forty. Although she was attractive, the set of her jaw and the serious look in her eyes communicated that here was a no-nonsense woman. I assumed she was a head nurse or some similar attendant until all the men hastily stood and showed her the utmost respect.

The woman made no move to approach me nor to shake my hand. Instead she regarded me with an air of aloofness. "You must be Jim Yoder."

"Yes, I am." I flashed my friendliest smile. Although I had no idea who she was, I wanted to see if friendliness could thaw the ice in this lady's gaze. "And I'm very happy to be here at last."

She didn't smile back. Maintaining her distance, she said, "The message said you are American, although you do not sound like one."

Before I could absorb that statement, she continued. "Allow me to introduce myself. In the Resistance I am known as Philippe."

The confusion I felt must have registered on my face. The men laughed heartily at my astonishment, and the woman showed the first thin trace of a smile. Evidently she found my reaction rewarding.

"You are Philippe? But I thought . . . I mean, I assumed—"

"You thought Philippe must be a man? That is why I chose the name. The fewer people who know that Philippe is a woman, the better chance I will have of surviving this war. You now know a secret shared by very few people in France, and by no one outside the country."

"I'm honored by your confidence."

"Do not be honored too quickly, Mister Yoder. I have revealed my secret for a reason."

Still standing well away from me, she addressed her three colleagues. "The Boches have been up to their devilish tricks again. Members of the Resistance in both France and Belgium have recently been arrested by the Gestapo. The enemy is infiltrating our escape lines by training special agents who speak English. They dress those agents in American and British uniforms and let them masquerade as downed Allied airmen. Sometimes these Boches agents even parachute to earth after bombing raids in order to appear more convincing."

"Are you serious?" I blurted. It sounded like the plot from a cheap novel.

"Quite serious, Mister Yoder—or whatever your name is." Then, addressing her colleagues, she added, "This man is a German spy. He must be executed immediately!"

The three Frenchmen leaped to their feet, their earlier smiles abruptly replaced by expressions of bewilderment.

I was on my feet just as quickly. "Wait! You're making a huge mistake. I'm not Boche!" I maneuvered to keep the table between the three men and me.

The three spread out, preparing to tackle me.

"I say you're making a terrible mistake. I'm American, not Boche! Look at my identification tags. I've fired my machine gun at more German fighter planes than you can count!"

Closing in, they didn't reply. Clearly, they were in no mood for negotiating.

"Listen to me!"

Realizing that I might have only seconds left to make my case—and to live—I whipped out the pistol that I wore under my shirt and pointed it at the female Philippe.

"Stop! Listen to me!"

Everyone froze, fear and indecision etched on each face, including the lady's. Obviously, despite all the other details they knew about me, no one had informed them that I was armed.

"Why do you believe I'm a German agent?" I demanded of Philippe.

"Because every circumstance points to it. After our man in Brussels led you to the border, he was picked up by the Gestapo.

Also, you stayed in the home of a barber named Rousseau. Both he and his wife were arrested too."

The news struck me like a kick to the face. "Jacques and the Rousseaus were arrested?" All along I had dreaded that my presence would endanger someone, and now it had happened. My stomach felt sick. "What about Brigitte? Did they get her too?"

The lady was studying me intently. "I received no information about anyone named Brigitte. But if you hope to convince us that you are not Boche, you will have to explain the string of arrests you left behind you."

"I can't explain it. I have no way of knowing what happened. But Jacques himself told me that he witnessed the arrest of a Resistance friend. That's why it was he who bicycled to the border with me instead of his friend driving me, as they planned. Or maybe someone in Brussels really is a collaborator. I don't know. But I'm innocent."

Lady Philippe hesitated. At least she was thinking through what I was saying.

"Radio London. Send my name and serial number to the 44th Bombardment Group. Col. Johnson is our Commander. He can vouch for me."

The men had lowered their hands. For the moment they wavered, not knowing what to do. But I wanted to remain in the land of the living and wasn't about to let my guard down, at least not yet. The pistol remained pointed at the lady.

At last she spoke. "Radioing London and receiving information back is not so simple. It takes time. Many days. We cannot stand here with your weapon aimed at me all week. Besides, no one in England can prove that you are who you claim to be. King George himself could not guarantee it. The Boches could have stolen the name badges from a dead airman and hung them around the neck of a similar-looking agent."

"Then interrogate me about America. Or about Indiana, the state where I live. Or question me about basketball. Ask whatever you want. But I'm telling you, if you kill me, you kill an ally. Even the Boches are not so barbaric. Do you want that on your conscience for the rest of your life?"

I lowered the pistol, but kept it ready.

Philippe crossed her arms and leaned back against the door. For the first time, a genuine smile of bemusement graced her lips. "What an interesting predicament we have here. I do not know enough about Indiana or basketball to ask you any questions. But you are the one holding the weapon. So, monsieur, how do you propose that we solve our little stalemate?"

"You're right. I do have the weapon. Jacques gave this to me. And I haven't shot any of you. If a real Nazi spy had his identity discovered, would he hesitate for one instant to murder you in order to save his own life? I don't think so. A real spy would have shot the great Philippe and her companions without mercy and then fled back to his precious Fatherland to gloat about it. Wouldn't he?"

I let that thought sink in. "And would a real German spy give you this?"

Doing the last thing they expected, I flipped the pistol around and held it out, handle first, to the lady. Surprised, she uncrossed her arms but made no other move. I stepped toward her, the gun's barrel still pointed backward toward me, and pressed its handle into her palm.

"We are allies, not enemies. I couldn't shoot you even if you weren't a woman. I will trust you with my pistol—and with my life."

The amazed woman regarded her cohorts and then said, "Please, everyone sit down. Perhaps he is not lying. I might be wrong, but he is entrusting his life to us. Now I will entrust my life to him."

She placed the pistol on the table. Then to me she added, "Jim Yoder, let us talk."

Talk we did. Philippe asked me to recount my entire story, going all the way back to the mission over Kiel and my fateful accident. André and his buddies lit fresh cigarettes and listened in rapt attention. Most people enjoy hearing a good yarn, and these patriots were no exceptions. I also explained about Madame Scoville talking to me throughout my childhood and about how I had been improving my grasp of the language ever since I encountered the thief Henri on the train in Cologne. From time to time one of my listeners would slip in a question to clarify a detail, but mostly they just let me ramble.

When I finished my saga, André exhaled a long stream of bluish smoke toward the single light bulb in the ceiling. "Philippe, if he is a Boche liar, then he is the cream of the cream. I have known many liars in my life, and none of them could weave such a smooth tale as that one."

"I agree," the lady said. "But from now on we will have to be especially careful. I believe Mister Yoder is a real American, but other so-called fliers are not. Too many of our people have been arrested."

During the conversation that followed, none of these locals shared details about themselves, and I didn't expect them to. But they did share a little about the asylum. Although suspicious of everyone, the Germans evidently had little time to worry about those they considered mentally impaired. As a result, the establishment had become an ideal sanctuary for hiding airmen as they made their way south toward Spain.

"So, is that the direction I'm headed? Toward the Pyrenees Mountains?"

"Probably," Philippe replied. "For us, it is the simplest. Of course, there are risks no matter which direction you go. I will inquire about finding a companion to travel with you."

My days at the asylum proved to be some of the most unusual of all my time on the run. Philippe gave me a choice: I could hide out in my room and fake insanity if the Germans pulled a surprise inspection, or I could don the white shirt and trousers of an asylum attendant and help out around the facility. I chose the latter. I had no desire to remain cooped up like a prisoner. That possibility still lay in my future. I much preferred to stroll the grounds openly, even if it meant sweeping, mopping, or peeling potatoes in the kitchen. In addition, I could see that the current staff was way too small for the number of patients. Philippe— who turned out to be the director of the asylum—needed help, and I was happy to earn my keep.

"Maybe I'm working too hard," I joked to my lady protector a week later. "I thought I would be on my way to Spain by now. I'm afraid I've become such a valuable employee that you'll never let me go."

"It is not that," she said seriously. "Our ranks are down in the escape lines. The Germans have arrested many of us, and some who used to volunteer are now too intimidated to continue. But do not worry. We will find a guide to take you south."

"Hopefully, that will happen before Père Noël comes to visit."

She laughed at my use of the name for Santa Claus. "Have no fear. You will be long gone before Père Noël arrives—if he can afford to come this year. There are shortages everywhere, you know."

Each day Philippe, whose real name was Jeanette, would sit and talk to me for a while. Sometimes she would ask me to recount more about my life in the United States and about our base at Shipdham, B-24s, the fellows in my crew, and what it was like to experience a bombing raid over Nazi Germany. If she had had any lingering doubts about me, I think our conversations put them to rest.

One time, though, I was sweeping the floor in her office when I noticed a framed photograph of a man in uniform.

"Who is this?" I asked, not realizing the depth of the well that I was uncapping. "He has the kind of face you see on Hollywood screen stars."

Immediately Jeanette's countenance changed. Her cordial expression disappeared, and her eyes dropped to the dark, hardwood floor.

"That is my husband. His name was Antoine."

Her use of the past tense, plus the look on her face, revealed that I had just reopened a wound.

She told me about Antoine, who had risen to the rank of captain in the French army. About how she had met him at a party and had instantly fallen under the spell of this unique man who exhibited all the charm and chivalry of a modern-day knight. About their courtship and their wedding.

When Jeanette spoke about Antoine, she could have been speaking to me alone or to an audience of hundreds. Instead of looking at me, she gazed toward the yellowed wallpaper, whose main recurring pattern reminded me of the Chevrolet symbol so common on automobiles in America. She told how Antoine had been stationed for a time on the Maginot Line, the series of connected fortresses that guarded France's eastern flank from her traditional enemy, Germany. She told how, when orders came for

Antoine to transfer from the Line to another unit in the north of France, she had rejoiced, thinking that if war ever broke out, he would be safer in the north than in a Maginot garrison. Then came May 10, 1940.

"The German panzer units bypassed the Maginot Line," she recounted. "They burst through the Ardennes and raced across the north. Instead of being far from the battle, my Antoine was caught in the thick of it, pressed back, back, along with the British Expeditionary Force."

Had I arrived a couple years earlier, I'm sure Jeanette would have watered her tale with many tears. But now she had no more tears to shed—just the lingering memories and the ache in her heart. Still gazing toward the wall, she ended by telling me how her beloved husband had fallen in battle near Dunkirk.

"For weeks after Dunkirk I received no word about him. Just silence. I clung to the thin hope that Antoine might be one of the soldiers who evacuated across the Channel by boat with the British. Later, after General Weygand signed an armistice, I even hoped that Antoine might soon return home to me."

However, that dream evaporated when a soldier friend sought her out and told how he had stood near Antoine when a machine-gun bullet thudded into the captain's chest.

"In his dying moment, even with destruction and carnage roaring all around him, he was still thinking of me. Our friend said that, as Antoine sucked air through his chest wound, he uttered, 'Tell Jeanette I love her.' And then—he was gone."

Her head sagged forward, as if relating all this had drained part of her being.

I didn't know what to say or to do. Here was I, the nineteen-year-old son of a mailman from a little town in the Midwest, and I felt that I should offer some solace to this woman who was twice my age and had seen more of life than I had. But what do you say to a lady who has just described her husband's death? Sure, I had seen bloodied airmen pulled from bombers after missions. I had witnessed corpses lined up on the tarmac under the bellies of B-24s. I had watched whole planes explode into balls of orange and black fire that snuffed out the lives of ten crewmen at once. But never had I sat near a woman whose husband was killed by an army of invaders and shared her grief. How could I begin to comfort her? What do you say?

I could have mumbled that Antoine "was in a better place now" the way others had repeated those words. But that expression rang hollow. After all, the only two destinations in the next life are Heaven or hell. How could I, who had never even met her gallant captain, guarantee that he was in Heaven with the Lord? I had no idea if the man even believed in God.

Or I could have mentioned what a great patriot he must have been, but that would sound flat. She already knew he was a hero. After all, he had been a career soldier. He had laid down his life defending his nation.

After an awkward silence I said the only thing that seemed suitable in that moment: "Sometimes in this world we meet people who are so special that no language has enough good words to describe them."

She nodded. "Oui. That is the way it is with Antoine. When I heard of his death, it was as if an iron claw reached inside my chest and ripped out my heart. Now I continue Antoine's fight by aiding fliers like you."

The two brothers who were in my room that first night at the asylum occasionally dropped by to visit me. I never saw their leader André again, but these two, whose names were Alain and Édouard Rostand, frequently came to see me after dark, always slipping over the rear wall of the asylum grounds to do so. My impression was that Alain and Édouard were caught up in the mystique of cloak-and-dagger warfare. For them, just talking with me, a downed airman, must have made them feel closer to the Allies across the English Channel. Being ages twenty-three and twenty-two, both were older than my nineteen years. But because of my airborne battle experiences, they accepted me without question as a comrade in arms. In a way, I suppose all my training and fighting really had aged me. I didn't feel nineteen anymore.

One evening, in response to their requests, I had recounted some of the aerial battles I'd been through. I certainly hadn't been trying to paint myself as a hero. In fact, I bluntly told them how scared to death I had been on that mission when a Messerschmitt had blasted a hole in the fuselage not six feet from my right-waist position. But that fear didn't diminish their respect for me. To the contrary, they seemed to admire me all the more for mentioning it.

"No matter how great the danger, and no matter how great the fear," said Édouard, the younger of the two, "you did not quit. You climbed back into your Liberateur for every mission, until you ended up here."

"There is no shame in being afraid," Alain added. "Only a fool would not be afraid in a moment like that."

"You are an inspiration to us," Édouard continued, smiling enough to show the little gap between his front teeth. "You have flown among the clouds and fought the Boches in ways we never will."

I was humbled by their respect. "And you in the Resistance are an inspiration to me, and to many like me," I replied. "In the air, I was able to return to a free land every evening. But you stay on the ground among the enemy and must be ready to fight day or night. You never know when the Gestapo will step out from the shadows to arrest you."

My words weren't just a courteous gesture. Following my ill-fated fall into the Fatherland, much of my time and resources had been focused on getting just one person—Jim Yoder—out of Fortress Europe in one piece. Not counting my longing to get back to Margo, my own survival had always been uppermost in my mind. But Jeanette, André, and the Rostand brothers were just the most recent links in a chain of freedom fighters that I had encountered. They could be jailed or executed for their activities. Yet, they persevered.

Sometimes Alain and Édouard brought along a small radio on which we tuned in to the BBC and heard the war reports first-hand. We would listen to the news, and then speculate on how it might affect the war.

The more I got to know them, the more I warmed to the Rostands. I came to think of them as older brothers. Despite the seriousness of the war, they both retained an infectious sense of humor that I thoroughly enjoyed. Like me, they had been raised in a small town, an obscure place called Salbris, which lay some-where south of Paris, beyond the Loire River. It wasn't until shortly before the war that they and their parents had moved to the capital in search of better work.

In those closing days of July 1943 I listened to radio broadcasts for news of any bombings that I could attribute to our Liberator Bomb Groups. Bombings were still taking place, yes, but the carefully selected details that the military censors permitted always seemed to point toward Bomb Groups comprised of B-17s. Where in the world were our Liberator squadrons? Surely not all shot down? I wondered in vain, not guessing at the time that the High Command had other plans in store for our B-24s.

When my two companions had gone and I was left alone in my room, I would agonize over the fates of Jacques and of Monsieur and Madame Rousseau. Obviously, they had been picked up because of me, even though I could not imagine how that might have happened. After all, if the Gestapo were on my trail, wouldn't they have arrested me at the same time? I couldn't understand it, and yet it made me nervous, as if unseen enemies might even now be preparing a noose for my neck.

And what of Brigitte? Was she, too, languishing in some German prison cell?

"Lord," I would pray aloud on my squeaky iron bed, "please protect those good people from harm."

My concern for my friends was so great that, for a time, I forgot to pray for my own safety. Perhaps I was finally absorbing the Bible's principle of loving others as myself?

During those final days at the asylum, a struggle emerged deep down inside me. On the one hand, I desperately wanted to get back to England. I kept telling myself that it was my duty to escape if at all possible, and that was true. But at least part of me was anxious to get away because, when this war was finally over, I wanted to be one of those left among the living. Everyone wants to live, to have a chance to love and to be loved, to raise a family . . . As far as I knew, this war might stretch to the end of the decade, and my odds of outlasting it would be much better if I could get out of Hitler's backyard.

On the other hand, my frequent chats with the Rostands ignited within me a smoldering desire to do more than sit on the sidelines. When I asked about their recent activities in the Resistance, Alain said they could not provide any details. However, he and Édouard exchanged winks and hinted that some Boches who had patrolled the city mere days before were now warming hospital beds.

"But I can tell you this," Édouard added mischievously. "Being a waiter at the Café Rouge has certain advantages. The Boche officers do not discuss secrets while I am pouring their wine or standing nearby. But they are too dull-witted to guess there is a hole in the wall right beside them. The moment I am out of sight, my ear is against that hole. What the swine discuss in private, I pass to the Resistance the moment they are down the avenue!"

The Rostands laughed heartily, and I joined in the merriment. In my mind I could picture my friend Édouard, his ear pressed to a knothole and grinning fiendishly while jotting notes on a loaf of French bread.

But even this simple conversation reminded me that, while others were taking considerable risks for a worthy goal, I was merely hiding. I wanted to do more than just go on existing. I wanted to pull my own weight in this war, to join Alain and Édouard on one of their nighttime raids, or whatever they did to frustrate the enemy.

When I voiced this wish to the Rostands, however, they immediately grew dead serious.

"Jim, you cannot do this," said Alain. "This work is not for you. *C'est trop dangereux.*"

"Too dangerous? Don't forget that I have fought German fighter planes with my *mitrailleusse* above the clouds. I have helped to drop bombs on Germany while the enemy shot at our airplane with antiaircraft guns. That was dangerous too."

"Oui, oui. Of course," Édouard said quickly. "We do not doubt your courage. And we would enjoy a chance to fight alongside you, even for a short time. But that is not what Alain meant. If the enemy catches you, they will not merely shoot you as a spy. You have seen too many of our workers. You know too much. If the Germans get hold of you, they will wring you like an old rag to squeeze information out of you. That would be very bad for us, for Philippe, and for others as well."

"Agreed," Alain chimed in. "We admire your spirit, mon ami, but this is our work. Be patient. You will get to fight again."

"Maybe I should talk to Philippe about it. She might . . ."

The brothers' shaking heads silenced me.

They were right. I did know too much. I could describe people in the escape line that even these two didn't know. Jeanette was responsible for too many lives to approve any scheme that unnecessarily risked my arrest. Whether foolish or patriotic, my sudden impulse to do more than mop asylum floors would have to go unfulfilled. Part of me was disappointed, but another part of me—the part that yearned to see Margo again on this side of eternity—was willing to bide my time.

Alain placed a hand on my shoulder. "Do not be down-hearted."

I nodded. Still, as I gazed at the faded, peach-colored wallpaper of my room, my emotions remained confused.

"Now for the big news," Édouard said. He straightened himself on his chair and cleared his throat as if he were about to make a speech. "André asked us to tell you—he has found a traveling companion to lead you to Spain."

I was on my feet before I realized it. "Are you serious?"

They laughed.

"Very serious," Alain replied. "We have not met this traveling companion, but André has. He says your guide comes highly recommended. You leave by train on Saturday."

Excitement raced through me like electricity. Saturday! And today was Wednesday. I wanted to shout, to run up and down the corridor screaming "Hallelujah!" until my throat went hoarse. Instead I leaped on the bed and danced a jig while repeating, "Thank You, God!" over and over in English. Now that my departure was imminent, all notions about remaining in Paris or helping the Resistance vanished.

Once again, the Rostands laughed and clapped.

"You say you do not drink wine, Jim, but this news affects you more than many bottles!"

I hopped to the floor. "Why didn't Jeanette—I mean Philippe—tell me earlier today? I stopped and chatted with her at lunch."

"She did not know," Alain stated. "The details were not confirmed until late this afternoon. We told her just this evening, before coming to your room. She sends her congratulations to you."

I could hardly believe it. Saturday! Freedom was so close I could smell it, but far enough away that the next two days would be slow torture. I would have left that very night, that very minute, if it were possible.

"Also, we have a going-away gift for you," Édouard announced. He handed me something I had never expected to see before the war was over—a photograph of the three of us. After much debate over the idea, we had posed together in the foyer just three nights earlier while one of the nurses snapped this shot of us. I marveled that they had it developed so quickly.

"In memory of friendship," Alain said. "May we meet again in happier times."

"But I thought we agreed—you were supposed to mail this to me after the war."

Édouard smiled sheepishly. "We did. But Alain and I are tired of doing every little action in fear of the invaders. For once we want to do a normal action and give this to you now as a souvenir."

"What is the harm?" Alain asked. "After all, we could carry this photograph to the city center and paste it on any wall. Nothing would happen. No one in France knows your face. Neither of us is famous either."

"Thank you. I'll keep it hidden for now. But when I get home, this picture will hang proudly on my wall for everyone to see."

Later, when I was alone in the darkness and stretched prone on my bed, I was too jubilant to sleep. Of course, Spain was not England, and I would still have to cross the mountains to get there. Nevertheless, Spain was still a significant milestone on my passage to England. Once in Spain, I could travel to Gibraltar and board a British ship or submarine.

"Thanks, God, for this answer to prayer. Thanks for providing a guide. I know there's still a long way to go, but I know You'll be with me every step of the way."

By mid-morning on Saturday I had said all my good-byes to Jeanette and to the nurses and male attendants of the asylum. Once again I was strolling down a busy boulevard, battered briefcase in hand, and relishing the opportunity to live like a normal human being. Fifty feet ahead, Alain walked briskly, leading me to the railroad station called Gare d'Austerlitz, which had a train departing for the southwest within the hour.

As I walked, I couldn't help but praise God for friends who were steering me to the correct station for the direction I needed to go. My hometown of Elkhart had a grand total of one small train depot, whereas Paris has several, and some of those large stations have more than one wing. Left on my own, I might have risked discovery by asking questions about the various stations and destinations that would have seemed extremely suspicious to genuine Europeans.

According to plan, Alain would leave me inside the Gare d'Austerlitz, near a particular newspaper vendor. I was to stand there reading until my next contact approached and commented, "What a wonderful day for a trip to the South!" He would then slip me a ticket, and I would follow him aboard a train car.

When I entered the building, the enormity of it amazed me. Our modest station back home was basically a little ticket office with an indoor seating area of dark wooden benches and the cement platform between the building and the rails. These European stations, however, featured soaring arched roofs of glass and steel with open ends through which entire trains passed. Pigeons and other birds fluttered about, looking for dropped crumbs among the trampled cigarette butts. At this time of summer, the air under the glass roof was muggy and stifling, without so much as a breath of wind stirring to cool it.

Alain sauntered past a newspaper vendor, turned long enough to catch my eye, then glanced at the ground, as if to say, "This is your spot." He ambled away, and I pulled out my paper and began reading.

I stood there for about fifteen minutes, pretending to be engrossed in the news, when I felt someone behind me place a hand on my shoulder.

"What a wonderful day for a trip to the South!" said a male voice that sounded familiar. "But what a shame that you are not going there, Jim. Instead, I have some new friends at Gestapo headquarters who would be very pleased to make your acquaintance."

My blood went cold. I turned and looked into the beady black eyes of a face I had never expected to see again—Henri, the Belgian outlaw who had planned to murder me and turn my corpse over to the Nazis in Brussels for a reward.

"You . . . ," I finally stammered. "But how . . . ?"

Henri beamed. With washed hair, a decent shave, a gray suit and navy necktie, he looked fairly civilized. Unlike the crowds milling about the Gare d'Austerlitz, however, I knew what foulness lurked in this man's soul.

"I see you were not expecting me. What a nice surprise, oui? It is a surprise for me as well. You see, when I—shall we say, replaced—the man who was supposed to be your guide for this excursion, I had no idea that you would be the escaped airman I was to pick up. Imagine my delight when I walked around the corner and found my old American friend and traveling companion standing here!"

I would have dropped my briefcase and bolted for the nearest exit if Henri hadn't been pointing a concealed object at me from his right jacket pocket. Even through the fabric, the rounded bulge was clearly the muzzle of a firearm.

"So, you're working for the Gestapo now?"

"Correct. When you and Brigitte deserted us, I decided it was time to find a new home and new line of work. After all, I had no idea whether Brigitte would mention my previous activities to the ruling authorities. It seemed fitting to get on their good side as soon as possible."

"You're a traitor, Henri."

He put on a wounded air. "Oh, those are such harsh words, Jim. They sting me so badly. But these are difficult days. A man must do what he can to earn a living. Can you not understand that, Jim? Or perhaps you are traveling under a new name now? After all, that is the usual procedure, *n'est-ce pas?*"

I didn't reply. I just glared.

"I'm curious," Henri continued casually, "where exactly did you go when you left the barber's home? We eventually caught up with your comrade Jacques, but so far he has been surprisingly resistant to conversation. The barber and his wife truly did not seem to know."

Finally the truth dawned on me. "It was you! You were the one who got them arrested!"

He chuckled. "Yes, I received the credit for those successes. Such a wonderful prize made the Gestapo very glad indeed to have me in their employ. But the barber really should have been more careful, you know. He should have thrown away those German boots and the American flying clothes that we found hidden in his attic. Of course, it took a while to figure out who might shelter Brigitte, but in time her half-brother Marc helped to solve that riddle. She did not have many friends, you know."

"What's happened to her?" I hissed.

Henri's eyebrows rose in surprise, and for the first time in this encounter it was he who was taken by surprise. "Are you trying to deceive me or really asking? No, I see it in your eyes; you do not know. Well, that makes two of us. When my colleagues raided the barber's house, she was not there. To tell the truth, when I walked up behind you just now, I was hoping that you could shine some light on that mystery. You see, I have a debt to repay Brigitte and would sincerely like to locate her."

Although Henri's hair was combed and his face had been scrubbed, words still slid from his mouth with an unpleasant greasiness to them. Just talking to this creature in man's clothing made me feel dirty.

He motioned toward the nearest exit with his left hand, the one not holding the firearm in his pocket. "Come. Let us go before we attract a crowd. As a result of my past—let us say, occupations—I never have enjoyed being the center of attention."

As we trudged toward the exit, I considered making a move for my own weapon. As usual, though, I carried it tucked into my belt beneath my shirt. It would be impossible to retrieve it before Henri plugged me with a couple rounds of his own. Instead I sent up a quick, silent prayer for help.

Once we were outdoors, Henri parted his lips in a smug smile. "You know, after I bring you in single-handedly, the Gestapo's opinion of me will rise even higher. I will be rewarded quite handsomely."

"The war won't last forever," I growled. "Some day you will pay for being a collaborator."

"Possibly, mon ami. But they will have to catch me first!"

Another question was nagging at my mind, but I chose my words extremely carefully so as not to reveal anything accidentally.

"So Henri, how much do you and your German friends know about my time in France? Where I've been and what I've been doing?"

"Nothing yet. But that situation will soon be remedied. Unfortunately, the courier I replaced was to be a new addition to the local cell group of Resistance, and he knew only how to contact one fellow by the name of André. The Gestapo has already picked up the courier's old contacts, and when we arrest André, he will lead us to the local group."

He chuckled, and even his laughter seemed greasy. "You know, for once in my life I am working on the side of the law, and I am rather enjoying it!"

With all my heart, I wanted to punch that weasel's face.

Then Henri caught me off guard by asking, "By the way, have you met Philippe yet?"

"Who?" I fumbled.

He laughed wickedly. "Ah, Jim Yoder, you should never be a thief or a politician—you do not know how to lie. I see it in your eyes; you *do* know who Philippe is. Très bien. Soon we will all know!"

Outraged, I stopped walking and clenched my fingers into a fist.

Evidently Henri expected this very reaction. He swiftly side-stepped away and pressed the concealed weapon even farther in my direction. "Do not even think about it!"

Spotting a taxi at the curb, he cocked his head toward it. "Let's ride to the Gestapo building. Paris in July can be so stifling for walking. But I warn you—I have a very nervous finger. Do not try to be a hero."

Henri opened the taxi's rear door and stood just inside it. With a sweeping gesture of his left hand, he said, "After you, monsieur."

Suddenly a blur of motion caught my eye. From out of nowhere, Alain Rostand hurtled across the sidewalk and rammed the taxi's door with all the force of a football linebacker. The door, in turn, slammed into Henri hard enough to crush him between itself and the taxi. He collapsed to the ground, and I saw his weapon—a snub-nosed pistol—clatter to the cobblestone street.

"Follow me! Vite!" Alain exclaimed.

I didn't wait for a second invitation. We sprinted from the scene, and for good measure I kicked Henri's pistol across the street as I ran.

In our wake came a shrill, angry outburst from Henri. "Stop! Stop them!"

Far from stopping us, however, the confused throng on the sidewalk parted before Alain and me faster than the Red Sea in front of Moses.

"Stop!" came an even shriller scream behind us.

Suddenly I heard a cacophony of screeching automobile tires and blaring horns. The next sound was a solid *thump*, accompanied by a woman's scream. Daring to glance back, I took in a sight that emblazoned itself in my memory—sprawled in front of a gray delivery truck was a crumbled figure in a gray suit. He was face up, but from that distance I couldn't tell if the eyes were open or closed. Vehicles were stopping, and pedestrians were quickly converging on the scene, which was now drawing a crowd. Like it or not, what was left of Henri had abruptly become the center of attention.

Alain tugged at my elbow. "Come. Let us be away from here."

That's when I realized I had stopped running and stood transfixed, gazing at the pitiful sight. Just seconds ago I had wanted to sweep the sidewalk with Henri's face. Now I had every reason to believe he was dead, but that thought sparked no joy in me. I knew that this weasel had no hope of entering Heaven, and there was only one other destination.

At a trot, Alain led me down Boulevard de l'Hôpital and around the corner to Rue Poliveau, then through a twisting maze of back alleys and side lanes. The commotion left far behind, we slowed our pace and mopped the sweat from our brows with handkerchiefs. We needed to appear as calm and normal as possible, not like two crooks on the loose. I also remember crossing the Seine River by one of the bridges, but I couldn't have retraced my route for all the Crown Jewels of England.

A sudden thought brought me to a standstill. "Alain, I just realized—I lost my briefcase. I must have dropped it in surprise when you rammed that man."

"Was there anything dangerous in the briefcase?" he asked in sudden concern. "Documents? Identification? Personal notes? A diary?"

I mentally pictured the case open on the bed, as I had packed it that morning. "No, no documents. Just some underclothes and a few tools to make me look like a mechanic if I was stopped."

Relief swept over his face. "That is good. If no one steals the briefcase, the police might assume it belonged to that rat-faced *collaborateur*."

"Wait! I just remembered. There was one other thing—the photograph of you and Édouard and me. I put it in the inside pocket of the case to protect it. I didn't write anything on the back, but our faces show clearly."

His brow furrowed, Alain pondered this new revelation. At last he shrugged. "There's nothing we can do about it now. It's too late to go back for the case. Probably the photograph is harmless, especially since no one in Paris but us knows your face."

I nearly mentioned that Henri had known my face, but I figured the miserable wretch was already facing the judgment of God and had no way of threatening me again. Still, I couldn't help wondering where the rest of his gang was. Had they split up? Or had some of them followed his example and joined ranks with the enemy?

Alain and I made our way to the Café Rouge, where a surprised Édouard met us and led us to an inconspicuous alcove where we could catch our breath and plan our next move.

Borrowing the café telephone, Alain made a couple brief calls. Thirty minutes later the same driver who had picked up Blue Hat and me on my arrival in Paris halted his vehicle down the lane from the café. He raised his eyebrows when he saw me slide into his rear seat for a second time, but he asked no questions.

Back at the asylum, Jeanette was genuinely alarmed when she heard of my encounter with Henri. She asked me to repeat every word that the man had said.

"It sounds like we are safe for the moment. But we must warn André immediately," she said when I finished.

"I already have," Alain assured her. "I telephoned his cousin and mentioned that a fox got into my chicken coop. That is the secret phrase we agreed on. André will not return home, and he will contact us when he can."

"I can't stay here any longer," I said. "You all are in too great of danger because of me."

Jeanette raked her fingers through her black hair. I noticed many strands of gray and wondered if they were the natural result of age or from the constant tension of covert warfare.

"Of course you can stay here. We were in danger long before you arrived. But now we have another complication. I received a cryptic message that a British agent has been wounded. He escaped his pursuers, but he cannot go to a regular hospital. That is the first place the Boches will look."

"So they're bringing him here?"

She nodded. "I do not know when. The message was brief and vague. I believe the agent's condition is serious. If so, he will not be able to walk far. In that case, they will need to bring him by automobile. All we can do is wait."

Alain surprised me by quoting a British expression: "In for a penny, in for a pound." Then, continuing in French, he translated the implication to his countrymen, "If they're going to hang us for hiding one Ally, they might as well hang us for hiding two of them!"

I returned to my old room for the night. However, my body was too tense to sleep. I kept reliving the incident with Henri. From everything the thief said, it appeared the Gestapo knew few concrete details about this cell group of Resistance. But they were definitely searching for Philippe. Wisely, each underground worker knew the identities of only a few close Resistance members. That way, if one were arrested, he could not be tortured into revealing a whole string of names. A turncoat or an imposter must have infiltrated one of the nearby cell groups. That's how Henri learned André's name.

"Lord, keep André safe, wherever he is," I prayed. "Blind the eyes of the Germans. Don't let them discover the asylum or Jeanette's role as Philippe."

During breakfast the next morning, a nurse named Marguerite hurried into the dining room looking greatly distressed. "The new arrival is here," she said anxiously. "He does not look good. We're putting him in the rear wing, room 17."

Immediately Jeanette and Alain—who had spent the night in the asylum for the first time—and I hurried to room 17, which had been vacant my whole time there. A graying attendant named Maurice was removing the shoes of a man who lay stretched out on the bed's coverlet.

The face of the wounded man was the color of an old newspaper. He looked pathetically weak. Eyes closed, he quietly moaned.

Another man I didn't recognize stood nearby. I guessed him to be about forty-five, with receding brown hair, which was graying around the temples. Jeanette apparently knew him, as she asked for no introduction.

"How bad is it?" she asked.

"Very grave," said the stranger, speaking in a deep, grating voice. "The Boches shot him in the back. He is lucky to be alive. The butcher gave him wine and pulled one bullet out of him. There is another bullet inside, but it is too deep to remove without a real surgeon. We did our best to bandage him, but he has lost much blood. We do not know if he will live."

"I will live," murmured the man on the bed. He spoke with determination, but his feeble voice did little to inspire confidence. Merely uttering those three syllables seemed to drain valuable energy he couldn't afford to lose.

"We are not prepared to handle a case like this," said Jeanette. "We have no surgeons. We are not a medical facility."

"I know," replied the man with the gravelly voice. "But we have nowhere else to take him. We have sent an urgent message to England. Perhaps they can make emergency arrangements."

"Did your message go by radio or by carrier pigeon?" Jeanette wanted to know.

The stranger looked embarrassed. "A tube has burned out in the transmitter. We had no choice. . . ."

Jeanette nodded, staring glumly at the forlorn agent on the bed. "Another life teeters on the brink, and his best hope is a handful of feathers."

"The pigeons have been reliable," the man defended, sounding offended. "True, they are not as fast as radio waves, but they get to London all the same."

"Is there anything I can do to help?" I asked.

Noticing me for the first time, the deep-voiced newcomer looked me up and down, then at Jeanette. "Who is this?"

"Our most recent package to deliver."

"French or British?" he asked.

She shook her head. "Américain. He was supposed to leave yesterday. In fact, he did leave, but he was nearly captured at the train station. His guide turned out to be a collaborator. Only Alain's quick thinking rescued us all from disaster."

The stranger winced. "They are closing their nets around us. Sometimes I fear it is only a matter of time . . ."

"It is only a matter of time before Hitler and his demons are put on trial for their crimes against humanity," I said. "Allied forces are growing stronger, and the Wehrmacht is stretched thin. The Third Reich will not last the thousand years that the pompous little Führer claims it will."

"No doubt," the stranger agreed. "The question is, will any of us be alive to see that day?"

The question hung in the air. My own nearly disastrous brush with a Nazi collaborator had me feeling very vulnerable. It was like balancing on the edge of a cliff on a windy day—one unforeseen gust, and over the brink you go. Which of us could say with conviction that he would not be arrested within the week, or within the hour?

In fact, the stranger's statement dredged up an issue I had been wrestling with. Back in Germany I had put my trust in God. Since then I had remembered a lot of verses from bygone Sunday school days about God and prayer. What bothered me, though, was that not every devout person in the Bible died of old age. Some were stoned to death by irate mobs. John the Baptist even got his head lopped off by King Herod.

So how does God determine which people to protect, and which ones to let die? Just because I trust in God now, does that automatically provide me with a heavenly flak vest?

This was a question I couldn't answer. Of course, I assumed all those Bible-time characters had been willing to lay down their lives for God, if that was what He wanted. Who was to say that getting off earth and going to the bliss of Heaven early wasn't actually a reward? Still, if I had any choice in the matter, I preferred to enter eternity on my own, without the assistance of some goose-stepping Nazis.

When the British agent on the bed muttered something in English, I pushed aside my own ominous thoughts.

"Let me sit with him," I volunteered. "He's not in his right head. If he says anything in English, I'll be able to understand him."

Jeanette turned to Maurice. "Bring him food and something for him to drink. He has lost much blood; we need to get fluids into him."

Maurice nodded and headed for the kitchen.

"There is something else I should mention," the stranger said. "This man is the last surviving member of a small network that was gathering intelligence on the Wehrmacht. The bullet holes in his back indicate that he has information that the enemy wants to keep from the Allies. If he should talk in his sleep, take notes. It may be our final opportunity to make his mission a success."

During the following days, the British agent did regain some of his strength. But the bullet still lodged in his abdomen was obviously causing considerable pain. We had no idea what organs it may have damaged. But it clearly had to come out. Unfortunately, the only surgeon Jeanette trusted for such an operation had been a member of the group Henri had penetrated. He was gone, arrested, and we had no one else with sufficient medical skill to help.

Our main hope now lay with London. Although little was said to me directly, the man who had brought in the British agent—I nicknamed him Gravel Voice since I didn't know his name—had implied that in some cases London would arrange for emergency evacuations. I understood Allied agents sometimes parachuted into France for espionage or to help coordinate Resistance operations. But how such agents were extracted from the field was mere speculation. Would it be possible to send our wounded man directly back to London?

Each evening Jeanette, Alain, Édouard, and I would huddle around the Rostands' radio set, listening to BBC dispatches and hoping for a covert message about our predicament. We enjoyed thumbing our noses at the will of the occupiers by tuning in to those forbidden words, "This is London. . . ." We also appreciated the four musical notes that preceded the war news. Those notes—*da, da, da, dum*—were not just the opening strains of Beethoven's Fifth Symphony. They were also Morse Code for the letter V, which stood for *Victory*. Living in the shadow of the swastika, we needed encouragement that victory would ultimately be ours.

Just before the news came a special portion of the broadcasts in which clandestine messages were delivered to people on the Continent. Of course, the messages were heavily veiled, and we could only wonder at what they might mean. For instance, the announcer would slowly read a string of statements such as, "My aunt has stored her potatoes in the cellar," or "In springtime the tulips will be yellow," pausing just long enough to repeat each signal before continuing on to the next one.

Jeanette would strain to hear a particular phrase, which she would not share. All she would say was that we should help her to listen for the word *cigar*. So we listened. My own imagination would run wild trying to decipher phrases such as, "Little sister has a new birthday dress," or "The cat has seven kittens," or even "Baby likes to play in the sand." At last, on the third day after the wounded agent arrived, we heard the sentence, "Uncle Anton wants his cigar back."

We three men looked immediately at Jeanette, who alone could unlock the phrase. She cocked her head and listened to the words the second time, and then smiled widely.

"Do you hear that?" she asked, triumphant. "Uncle Anton wants his cigar back!" She hugged me and blurted, "And he can have you at the same time, Jim!"

"But what's it all mean?"

"The cigar is the British agent. The 'A' in the name 'Anton' stands for *avion*. They will send an airplane to pick our man up tomorrow night. As long as they are picking up one man, the airplane can take you at the same time, Jim. This is the best possible outcome!"

Édouard and Alain were beaming, the little gaps in their front teeth showing clearly.

"The Englishman must be valuable indeed," Édouard commented. "It is not for just anyone that London will send an airplane."

"Whatever he knows," Alain surmised, "must be worth the trouble. They don't want him to die before he can report."

Thank You, I was silently praying. *I don't rejoice at our wounded ally's condition, but thank You for letting me be here to take advantage of this unexpected opportunity.*

I could hardly believe my escape from occupied Europe would be so quick and simple—by air, the same way I had arrived. Even my near capture by Henri would be worth the stress if this really worked out so smoothly.

Margo, I'm on my way now! Do I have a long story to tell you!

Despite the high spirits, though, I couldn't quite forget my mother's oft-repeated advice not to count chickens before they're hatched.

But what could go wrong now? I asked myself.

The answer, of course, could be summed up in one word. Plenty.

The next evening found our group in a modest little farmhouse northeast of Paris. Alain, Édouard, Jeannette, and Gravel
Voice had driven the wounded British agent and me here in the
afternoon to await nightfall. Gravel Voice informed us that "others" would rendezvous with us around dusk. I had no idea who
these others might be, but I didn't want to pry into Resistance
affairs. As long as they could arrange safe passage to England for
me, they could guard all the precious secrets they wanted. The
middle-aged couple that owned the house did likewise, offering
cheese, bread, and fresh well water, but remaining in the background and bridling their curiosity.

As the orange disk of the sun sank into a bank of clouds on
the horizon, two knocks sounded at the front door, and a man
entered without waiting for a response. With only a glance and a
nod at Gravel Voice, this newcomer settled onto a wooden chair
and waited. Every few minutes, this scene repeated itself until
four men I had never seen before had joined us.

"The signalers," Jeanette finally whispered to me. "The airplane will not come until after dark. These friends will stand at
the four corners of the clearing with flashlights so the pilot knows
where to land in the dark."

I nodded. Although conversation in the room remained strained, I was impressed with this organization. They seemed to have covered all the bases.

As for me, I felt coiled tighter than a clock spring. Like the feeling I used to get before a bombing raid. Once you're actually in the air with the enemy in sight, you have something to do and can react without thinking. But just sitting and waiting . . . I wasn't even sure what exactly we were waiting for.

The lady of the house fussed over the wounded agent. He had regained some strength and no longer moaned. Sometimes he spoke enough to request a drink and seemed to comprehend what was going on. But he still could not walk without help, and sweat constantly beaded his forehead. So the lady of the house made it her mission to make cold compresses and replaced them every few minutes.

Silence fell over the assembly, and everyone occupied himself with his own thoughts. The only sound in the room was the ticking pendulum of the wall clock.

When the clock's cuckoo bird popped out his door and signaled ten o'clock, I stiffened and caught my breath. The others laughed, and I felt my face glow with warmth. I felt foolish, especially since I had been hearing that cuckoo sound the time for the past several hours. But at least laughter helped to lighten the tension we all felt.

We rested. We closed our eyes, though I suspect none of us dozed. Finally, when the clock indicated a quarter to midnight, Gravel Voice broke the silence. "It is time to go."

As one, we stood.

Gravel Voice placed his hand on Jeanette's shoulder. "You do not need to come. You have done too much already, coming this far."

She shook her head. "I will not live in fear. I want to see this operation finished."

The man of the house turned off the table lamp, and we bumped and fumbled our way to the front door in darkness. We filed out of the house, whispering our thanks and farewells to our hosts as we did.

Édouard and I supported the British agent between us, but a homemade stretcher was fetched from somewhere, and Édouard and Alain and Gravel Voice and I carried him by the light of a finger-clipping of moon.

Around the house we went, and down a footpath bordering a field of what I thought might be wheat. By moonlight, however, things are not always what they appear, and by this time I had been living normal daylight hours long enough that I had lost most of the night senses I had developed earlier.

Trekking to the far rear of the property, we crossed a wooden footbridge over a drainage ditch and entered a forested area. The group padded along silently, not uttering a word. Eventually we exited the trees and found ourselves in a large clearing. The dim silhouettes of treetops all around us revealed that here we had a protective shield from prying eyes.

"Ici," Édouard whispered to me, and I knew this was the place we were to meet the airplane. "There was once a farm here, long ago. Now only flat ground remains."

Like phantoms, the four unknown men fanned out in different directions, quickly merging with the gloom of midnight.

"Now we wait," said Gravel Voice.

However, we hadn't waited more than forty-five minutes before we heard heavy droning growing louder overhead. It was the unmistakable sound of bombers flying in formation.

About that moment a large dark mass whooshed overhead so close that it startled me out of several years of life. I very nearly threw myself to the ground before realizing what the mysterious shadow had been.

The sound of curses and oaths being muttered drew my attention to the ground, where I saw that Gravel Voice, Jeanette, Alain, and Édouard had, indeed, hit the deck beside the wounded agent's stretcher.

"What was *that*?" hissed one of the Rostand brothers. In the darkness, I wasn't sure which one.

"An owl," I replied. "He's searching for breakfast. One of his American cousins once did the same thing to me when I was hunting in my country."

More muttered oaths followed as my companions rose to their feet. I didn't recognize these words, but judging from the tone, I assumed it was just as well.

The bombers were now passing directly overhead. They had to be British, I knew, because our American bombers made only daylight missions. The British, on the other hand, preferred to fly under the cover of darkness. I didn't understand how their pilots could remain in formation without colliding in the dark, but that's how they operated. We in the Eighth Army Air Force thought the English fliers were nuts, of course, but they thought the same about us. In a pub, one British gunner had once predicted, "The Jerries will shoot down every last one of you in the daylight, and that's no error."

In each corner of the clearing, a flashlight popped on, their beams pointed skyward. With the entire countryside blacked out, I imagine that those lowly flashlights were as visible as spotlights to the friends passing overhead.

When the bulk of the armada had passed, the droning of one lone aircraft grew increasingly louder. As the plane approached, the sound of an engine coughing and hesitating could distinctively be heard. I couldn't see the plane, though, until it crested the trees right behind us and roared overhead. Instinctively, all of us ducked our heads, even though the craft was still a hundred feet off the ground.

It was an Avro Lancaster bomber! Like our American Liberators, the RAF's Lancasters sport two vertical tailfins instead of one central tailfin. The familiar-looking silhouette of this craft made me want to shout for joy. But then I noticed something odd.

Is one of the propellers not turning?

In the darkness I couldn't be sure, but it sure seemed that the number four prop was motionless, possibly feathered to reduce drag.

Like a pro, the pilot of the Lanc' swooped to the ground and rolled across the clearing. Reaching the far corner near one of the flashlights, he braked one side and swung the bomber in a tight circle before cutting power and silencing the engines. Now I understood the strategy: the drone of the bomber formation covered the sound of one lone aircraft descending to earth. Very clever.

"Did someone telephone for a taxi?" Alain asked.

Then Édouard quoted an unexpected line in English: "Jim, give my regards to Broadway!"

I laughed. I didn't know where these two picked up this stuff. Both the Rostands liked to surprise me with little snippets of English they kept tucked away for just the right second.

My elation was off the scale. Finally, after weeks of running, dodging, and hiding, I was on my way home—or least back to England, which was the next best thing for a downed airman. The four of us picked up the stretcher and hauled our human cargo across the field.

At the Lancaster, a figure loomed out of the darkness.

"I stand in Piccadilly Circus," pronounced Gravel Voice in English, but with a thick accent.

"And Nelson stands in Trafalgar Square," replied the new figure, completing the code phrase. "I'm the pilot. Do you speak English?"

"He doesn't, but I do," answered a feminine voice.

I literally stepped backward in shock when I realized it was Jeanette. "You speak English? You haven't uttered one English word the whole time I've known you. Why didn't you tell me?"

"You never asked," she replied flawlessly. "I studied for two years in Cambridge. But you were doing fabulously in French, so I decided to let you keep practicing."

The pilot interrupted. "It's certainly nice to know you're all getting on so famously, but I have a job to do. The quicker we can be about it, the better. Let's get this chap on the stretcher aboard."

"Can you carry an extra passenger?" Jeanette asked. "This man is an American flier off one of their bombers. He has been on the run for months."

The pilot paused. "That wasn't part of my instructions. Are you sure you're a Yank and not a Nazi in disguise?"

Indignation got the better of me. "I wouldn't be caught dead being a Nazi!"

"Yes, well, if you're not on the up and up, that's exactly how you'll be caught." He turned to Jeanette and Gravel Voice. "Anyway, you two know the passwords. If you say he's all right, then yes, we can give him a hop over the Channel."

Another man in flying garb joined our group. "I'm afraid we've got a bit of bad luck," he said to the pilot. "That Jerry night fighter did more than knock out number four. He got number one engine as well. It was gasping its last breath just as we touched down."

"Can number one be repaired?" asked the pilot.

"Hard to say, sir." He paused. "Hastings bought the farm on this trip. Took a shell in the throat. Bled to death before we realized he was hit. Foley caught it too. No tail gun for the trip home."

Even in the wan moonlight, I saw the pilot's head slump slightly. No matter what anyone says about the British "stiff upper lip," they feel hurts the same way we do. He had just lost two of his seven-man crew.

"Hastings was our flight engineer. If any of us could have fixed an engine in the field, he was the man. I'm afraid we might be here to stay."

"But sir," said the other Britisher, "a Lanc' can fly on two engines. Without a load of bombs to weigh us down, we can—"

"Look at that tree line," the pilot interrupted. He pointed. "Yes, we could wing home quite happily on two engines if we had more runway. But without at least three engines in this postage-stamp clearing, we'd run straight into the woods and kill the whole lot of us!"

"Oh. Right."

My heart sank to my toes. Here was an Allied aircraft not forty feet away and a pilot willing to fly me back to friendly soil. Now all that stood between England and me was a damaged engine. Was God deliberately trying to frustrate me?

"I'm a mechanic," I piped up. "At least, I can repair automobile motors. Let me borrow your flashlight—I mean your electric torch—and I'll have a look at that coughing number one engine."

"We have nothing to lose," the pilot said skeptically. "Go ahead and have a look if you want. But a Rolls Royce Merlin engine won't be like any automobile engine you've ever tinkered with."

Laboring under flight jackets to contain the gleam from our flashlights, the copilot and I began removing the cowling around the number one engine. While on pass in London, I had heard much bragging about the Rolls Royce Merlin engines that powered the RAF's Lancasters, Spitfires, and Mosquitoes, but this would be my first time to see one up close, and I wasn't sure what to expect. The metal cowling was pretty chewed up from gunfire. It wasn't an encouraging sight.

"Couple of Jerry night fighters jumped us from behind near Amiens," the copilot explained as we worked. "Because we were the last plane, they hit us first. One of them raked us over several times before we could shake him."

"Probably the Abbeville boys again," I replied. "They keep things hot for us in the daytime too."

Enjoying the chance to converse in English, I said, "You want to hear something funny? When I was crossing Belgium, one of the locals tried to tell me that an RAF outfit dropped 'bouncing bombs' on Germany and smashed a dam. Have you ever heard of anything so crazy?"

"It's no joke, Yank. That's the 617 Squadron you're talking about. Happened back in May. Nineteen or twenty of our Lancasters flew over and dropped secret, barrel-shaped bombs right above the water. They skipped along like rubber balls and blew great, gaping holes in three dams. Flooded a good bit of the Ruhr Valley, where the Jerries built a lot of their heavy industry."

I was dumbfounded. What I had dismissed as a wishful blend of rumor and fairy tale turned out to be true. Sometimes truth really is stranger than fiction.

"Just why did Bomber Command send such a big aircraft for this pickup?" I wanted to know. "You were expecting to pick up only one man, right? Wouldn't a smaller plane have been more sensible for this size of a clearing?"

"I don't have the answer to that one," the copilot replied. "I believe one of the Mosquitos of Pathfinder Force was meant to handle this one. Us, we were loaded with bombs and ready to go when orders came down to remove the bombs. Some kind of last-minute change of plans. All I know is, here we are."

Much to my surprise, once the cowling was off I discovered that the Merlin engine wasn't the obliterated hunk of junk I had expected to find. In fact, it appeared that the engine itself had sustained only minor damage.

"Gloire à Dieu!"

"What's that, Yank?"

"Sorry. I'm still not used to having people around who speak English. I was praising God. Look! Here's the problem. Part of your fuel line has been shot away. I bet this engine will work good as new once we repair the line!"

"Righto," said the copilot, catching my enthusiasm. "Will that take long?"

It was an excellent question. Kneeling on a wing under a flight jacket with a screwdriver in my hand and figuring out the problem was one thing. Scrounging a spare length of fuel line out of the woods to repair the damage was another matter.

I snapped off a two-inch section that hung by a sliver. "I don't suppose you would have anything like that aboard?"

He shook his head. "I'm afraid not. So that's it, then?"

Unwilling to admit defeat, I jumped to the soft earth below and gathered my companions and the remaining members of the Lancaster crew around me. Speaking in English, I let Jeanette interpret for the others.

"Here's the situation. I can't promise, but I believe this engine will run if we can replace this fuel line. We need a section about two feet long." I held up my hands in the moonlight to show the length in case the Parisians didn't understand feet and inches. "Would there be anything like that back at the farmhouse?"

Gravel Voice shook his head. "No. And we cannot expect such a large group to hide there with an RAF bomber in this clearing. It would be asking too much of them."

"I can find what you need in Paris," Édouard declared. "And if I cannot find the exact size of tubing, I will get something close. With rubber from the inner tube of a tire, and with some clamps, you could make it work long enough to reach London, non?"

"Édouard, just find me those parts, and we'll be out of here in no time!"

Because of curfew, no one could drive back to Paris that night. So we borrowed a couple handsaws from the farmer who had sheltered us and spent the next several hours cutting branches and trying to camouflage the bomber. An airplane is a pretty distinctive shape, and once the sun rose a German pilot would need only one good pass to recognize an Avro Lancaster standing in a clearing. At last we had accomplished the job as best we could and settled down to rest under a wing.

At dawn, Édouard, Jeanette, and Gravel Voice made the return drive to the capital. There was no need for such vital figures to risk capture along with the rest of us, and so, after hearty handshakes and farewells, I urged them not to accompany Édouard when he returned with the parts I needed.

That day dragged on with agonizing slowness. Flies buzzed about us in the shade of the Lanc's wing, where Alain and I hid with the trapped British aircrew and the wounded agent. The Frenchmen who had manned the signal lights the evening before took up positions around the perimeter to stand guard in case anyone approached.

In hushed tones, my fellow airmen and I shared insulting stories about Hitler and his so-called master race. Alain had a few disparaging jokes of his own to share, and so I interpreted them for the fliers, who got a good chuckle out of them. Even the wounded agent roused enough to share a brief anecdote at the Führer's expense. By noon, though, the conversation petered out, and each of us occupied himself with his own thoughts.

Won't the guys from *American Pride* drop their jaws when they see me come waltzing into the hut? I'd give anything to have a photograph of that moment.

Of course, for me to see the expressions on those faces, I still had to get back to Shipdham. As the day grew longer and hotter, I kept worrying about Édouard.

Could anything have gone wrong? What's taking so long?

I saw the same questions in Alain's eyes, and I knew he was concerned about his younger brother. But after all, why should anyone question Édouard? Sure, he was in the Resistance, but he had never been caught or photographed or anything.

The photograph. It suddenly sprang back into my mind. In my briefcase there had been the photograph of Alain, Édouard, and me. No one who had never been in the asylum would recognize the establishment's foyer where we had posed and grinned defiantly into the camera lens. But the three of us were definitely together in the picture.

Was that a foolish thing to do? I swept the thought from my mind. *No, it was just a harmless photograph, a souvenir. Nothing in it could trace us to this clearing. All I have to do is wait a little longer, and then I'm home—or at least as close to home as I can get until shipped stateside again.*

Trying to pass the time, I shifted my thoughts to my favorite subject—Margo. I pictured her as she looked the last time I saw her. It was a Sunday afternoon, and she still had on the off-white dress with the lace-trimmed neck that she reserved for Sundays. A wind was blowing, tugging at her chestnut-colored locks. Add a pair of wings, and she would have looked like an angel.

I wished I could have stood there all day, just drinking in her beauty. But this girl was more than attractive. How to describe her? Even if she had been plain-faced, she would have glowed with the radiance of her personality. She was simply a beautiful person, regardless of looks.

Ah, Margo, I can't wait to be with you again.

Out of nowhere, a thought shattered my reverie faster than a Focke-Wulf diving out of the sun: *She's probably dating somebody else by now.*

Angrily, I picked up an oval piece of sandstone and hurled it into the clearing as hard as I could. The stone vanished into the grass, but the thought remained with me like a bad aftertaste. I made up my mind right on the spot: As soon as I got back to London I would telegram Margo and let her know I was alive. I would tell her I had put my trust in God too. And I would ask her to wait for me.

Is that being too pushy? After all, we haven't really spent that much time together . . .

Well, pushy or not, I would send that telegram the first chance I got. But one thing at a time. First I had to fix this confounded airplane.

Around 5:00 p.m., long past the time I had expected Édouard to return, a whistle came from one of our vigilant Frenchmen. The car that had brought us from Paris the previous afternoon now appeared in a gap at the far end of the clearing and slowly approached our position.

The airmen were immediately on their feet and held handguns at the ready.

"Put your guns down!" I hissed. "It's Édouard."

Grinning his widest grin, Édouard practically leaped from the car and triumphantly held up a slender object about two feet in length. "Voilà! An imitation fuel line for an aeroplane! I promised to find what you needed. But what a shame that my parents no longer have running water in the kitchen."

"Édouard, I could kiss you!"

Still grinning, he said, "Non, non. Save your kisses for the beautiful mademoiselle in America that you told us about."

"You can get those branches off the plane and your wounded man aboard," I said to the pilot. "In less than five minutes I'll have this bird ready to fly."

The two Rostand brothers had boosted me up to the wing before Édouard said the words that made my blood turn icy. "Alain, we will have to go into hiding after today. The Boches are looking for us."

Standing on the Lanc's wing, I whirled around and stared down at him. "What do you mean?" I asked, fear beginning its familiar squeeze on my stomach.

"On the way back, I stopped at the Café Rouge to tell the owner I would not be in to work today. While we talked, he whispered a warning to me. He said that two men had been to the café looking for Alain and me. One was a German. In fact, he said they had showed him a photograph and asked where they could find me and the other man who resembles me. Of course—"

"Did Monsieur Bouchard describe these men?" Alain interrupted.

"Yes, he said they were very arrogant. Both in civilian clothes. One of them, however, had his left arm in a sling, and bandages wrapped all around his head. Monsieur Bouchard told me that the one with the bandages had a face that did not seem right for a man. With his close-set black eyes, he said it was more like the face of a mouse, or a rat."

Alarm bells clanged in my mind. "Or the face of a weasel. It's Henri! The one who tried to capture me at the train station! He's alive!"

With a speed born out of gut-wrenching horror, I feverishly began attaching the replacement tubing.

"But Jim," Édouard called up from the ground. "Do not worry. Just in case anyone was watching, I had the driver take a very long, indirect route back here. I do not believe anyone could have followed us."

I didn't reply. My fingers were working as rapidly as possible. I had already met Henri's sinister face twice, and I didn't want a third opportunity, no matter how twisty the road Édouard had taken back.

Praise God I left the tools up here on the wing!

I was just beginning to tighten the second clamp around the fuel line when I heard an urgent double whistle from one of the perimeter guards. Then an engine roared. Sparing a split second to glace up, I saw my worst nightmare coming true—not one, but two black Citroen automobiles appeared in the same opening in the trees through which Édouard and our driver had arrived just minutes before.

A hand thrust a pistol out the passenger side of the lead vehicle. Did I just imagine that the passenger had his head wrapped in white?

Crack! Unseen, a lead slug bit into the Lancaster's fuselage.

Crack! Crack!

Suddenly gunfire erupted all around over the clearing. Near the plane, the British aircrew flung themselves into the grass and returned fire with hand weapons. Our French friends likewise began a crossfire at the approaching vehicles.

"Faster, Yank, faster!" urged the pilot.

My fingers were already working as fast as I could make them. An eternity was packed into that last sixty seconds, but at last the connection was tight. I threw away the screwdriver and kicked the toolbox off the wing. At this point replacing the cowling was unthinkable. Our time was up. It was now or never.

"Let's go!" I shouted over the din of gunfire.

Just before I leaped from the wing, I saw the driver who had chauffeured Édouard ram his car into the lead Citroen. Their second car, however, swerved around the collision and was bearing down on us. From it, too, weapons were spitting bullets in our direction. There was no time for prayers, but my soul was hoping for a miracle.

The Lancaster's engines sputtered to life, and one at a time the British fliers climbed aboard while the others returned fire at the approaching enemies.

"Ahh!"

It was Édouard. He collapsed backward onto the grass. A wet, crimson stain was blossoming from my friend's shoulder.

"Come on, Yank! You're the last one!" shouted an airman from the door.

I looked at that open portal to freedom, then back at my friend Édouard.

Alain had dropped his weapon and was pressing a hand to the younger brother's wound.

Crack! Crack! Bullets whizzed past my ears.

"Yank! Now!"

Édouard opened his eyes and parted his lips in a feeble smile. The little gap between his front teeth barely showed. "Give my regards to Broadway." His eyes closed.

In that instant, something inside me broke. I was outraged. These barbarians had just shot my friend. Jerking the pistol from my belt, I gritted my teeth and faced the attackers.

Good-bye, Margo. I can't leave my friends like this. But I'll still see you in Heaven . . .

30

What followed next remains a jumble of impressions in my memory. If I had been smart, I would have at least dropped to one knee to offer a smaller target. But I didn't. It wasn't courage. It wasn't strategy. Blind anger had seized me, and I stood there with bullets pinging into the Lancaster as I raised my pistol.

Sighting carefully along the barrel, I squeezed off a round at the nearest German soldier. Nothing. I squeezed off another round and saw the man topple. Clutching his thigh, he lay writhing in pain.

The next thing I knew, the pistol flew from my grasp even before I felt searing pain in my right bicep.

Shrill laughter pierced the tumult, and then I saw its source. Henri, crouched behind the hood of the disabled car, twisted his mouth into a hideous expression of glee. His head was wound about with bandages, and his left arm was in a sling, but his right hand wielded a pistol. He clearly considered the bullet that gashed my arm one of his own.

From various points in the clearing, the valiant men of the Resistance were still plugging away at the Germans, who were caught in the middle. Some of the enemy returned fire at them. Others, though, were more intent on stopping the Lancaster and were pressing closer.

Weaponless, now, I turned back to Édouard. His eyes had opened again, and Alain seemed to be saying something to him. The bomber's three good engines were now revving faster. My repair had been successful!

"Alain!" I shouted to be heard. "Let's get him on the airplane!"

He couldn't hear me above the roar of the powerful Merlins. Without waiting to explain, I grabbed Édouard and hauled him to a seated position. Alain quickly took him by the other arm, and together we lugged Édouard to the hatch. An airman's hand reached down, grasped our comrade by the back of the trousers, and just that fast, Édouard was aboard.

With gunshots still cracking all around, I pushed Alain toward the hatch, and the same airman pulled him up.

The plane was beginning to roll across the grass as I leaped for the opening. I stumbled and nearly fell to the ground, but once again a friendly hand appeared, and suddenly I, too, was aboard, though the wound in my right arm felt like the sting of a hundred hornets.

With agonizing slowness, the craft lumbered across the uneven terrain. Noises like hammer blows raining along the fuselage told us the German agents were still firing at us. Bright spots of sunlight were suddenly appearing where the enemy's rounds struck home.

Flannery, the top gunner who had helped to pull us inside, dropped to his knees. A round had caught him in the stomach.

In one of those moments that seem so detached from reality, I suddenly wondered what was the odd-feeling mass my two elbows were digging into behind me. I turned and found myself face to face with the corpse of Foley, the dead tail gunner. Hastily I pulled my elbows off his chest and stomach.

Crack! Crack! Crack! More rounds thudded into the Lancaster.

Faster! Get off the ground! I willed the plane.

I glanced again at Foley, and then inspiration struck me: Foley was the tail gunner. The tail gun was unmanned. But I was a gunner!

With the Lanc' bouncing over the turf at a faster clip now, I half crawled and half stumbled aft. Reaching the rear, I squeezed into the cramped tail position. Through the shattered Plexiglas I saw a black Citroen giving chase and closing the distance.

They're trying to ram the plane's tail!

Then I spotted the white cloths atop the driver's head.

Blood was running down my right arm, and the fingers on that side were feeling numb, but I grasped the handles of the machine gun. The twin Browning .303 wasn't the fifty-caliber weapon I was used to, but it would do.

Sighting the gun on the front grill of the Citroen, I opened fire. No short burst for me this time. I no longer cared about overheating the barrels. A river of hot lead poured from the muzzle and straight into the pursuer's engine. The front of the car exploded into bits of flying metal, smoke, and steam.

As the Lanc' lifted from the earth, I saw orange flames engulf the vehicle. I had no idea whether anyone escaped alive from it. If they did, the men of the Resistance would take care of them before making their own escape.

Suddenly feeling exhausted, I took a deep breath and closed my eyes. I imagined the next letter I would write home: *Well, Dad, you'll never believe this, but your son has become the first gunner in the USAAF to shoot down a Nazi automobile!*

I could also imagine a miniature picture of a black Citroen painted on a bomber's fuselage to record the kill.

Opening my eyes again, I saw the French countryside dropping away, receding behind us.

At last! Now, if only we can make it home without the Abbeville boys noticing us.

The next day, August 1, when the train pulled into Shipdham, I was painfully aware of the fact that I looked nothing at all like a member of the Eighth Army Air Force. I was dressed in civilian clothes, a black beret adorned my head, and my right arm was in the linen sling that a clucking Red Cross nurse in London had rigged for me. Under the circumstances, I could have stayed in London for a few days before reporting back, but as soon as I made sure Édouard was well cared for at the hospital and that Alain had a place to sleep, I was eager to send a telegram home and then to catch the next train out to Shipdham.

All the way from London, I had rehearsed just how I wanted to do this. Without stopping at my hut or seeing any of the guys from *American Pride* first, I would strut straight to the office of Col. Johnson, Commander of the 44th.

After the colonel's aide admitted me to the office, I would snap to attention and say, "Sir, Staff Sergeant James Yoder of the 506th squadron reporting for duty. I have just completed an escape from the Third Reich and request permission to rejoin my crew."

In my mind's eye I could already picture Col. Johnson's flabbergasted expression. Perhaps his eyebrows would shoot up. Perhaps his jaw would drop open before he recovered himself. Or perhaps he would lean back in amazement, stroking his mustache while looking me over with incredulous eyes. Then he might finally say something like, "Would you repeat that one more time?" Very possibly he would invite all of his staff into the office to listen while I retold the highlights of my adventure.

However, none of these imaginings panned out. When I got to Station 115, where the 44th Bomb Group was posted, even as I approached the front gate, I could tell that something had changed. Before, Station 115 had been a bustling, active base. Now I saw almost no signs of activity. Out on the hardstands, no Liberators were in sight. At least, none that looked airworthy. The few that I could see remaining had been cannibalized for spare parts.

The sentry on gate duty had a Brooklyn accent, and I'd never seen him before. At first he didn't want to admit me in my civilian clothes. Finally, by dangling my dog tags in front of him and talking my head off and naming just about every officer I could recall ever having seen on station, I finally convinced him that, uniform or no uniform, I really was S.Sgt. Jim Yoder, and that I truly did belong on this base.

"So you're back from France, huh?" he said, as if not knowing whether I was pulling his leg or not. "Okay, Sgt. Yoder, what exactly do you plan on doing here?"

"What kind of question is that? I plan to rejoin my crew. I'm a gunner. But first I'm going over to Col. Johnson's to report in."

"Yeah? Well, that ain't gonna be so easy. Col. Johnson ain't here."

This was the first kink in my plan to dumbfound a commanding officer for once in my life.

"He's not? Well, where is he? When will he be back?"

"Sorry, I couldn't tell you that."

"You don't know, or you aren't allowed to say?"

"What's the difference? Either way, I can't tell you."

"Okay, then, I'll go to my hut and talk to some of the guys while I wait for Col. Johnson to get back."

"Sorry, Sergeant. If you're a gunner, you ain't gonna find any buddies in your hut."

This peculiar conversation was going nowhere. "Well, at least tell me one thing," I said. "Where are all the Libs? Out on a raid? Don't tell me every one of them got shot down?"

"Oh, no. They ain't shot down. But they're not coming back from a raid today either. As far as where they are . . ."

"I know—you can't tell me."

"Bingo."

"Well, I need to report to somebody. Who is on station that I can talk to?"

"Go ahead to Col. Johnson's office. I think some major from intelligence is holding down the fort."

As I trudged my way to the office, I couldn't help but notice how little activity there was. Even during raids there were ground personnel patching shot-up planes back together. By comparison, the base was practically a ghost town.

Just as the sentry had predicted, at the office I found a Maj. Waverly shuffling through stacks of files when I entered. After all my mental rehearsing, I decided to go ahead with my line. I snapped to attention.

"Sir, Staff Sergeant James Yoder of the 506th squadron reporting for duty. I have just completed an escape from the Third Reich and request permission to rejoin my crew."

The major squinted at me, took a slow sip from his coffee cup and then said, "What is this, some kind of gag?"

It wasn't the reaction I was hoping for, but at least I got his attention. I briefly recounted some highlights from my last ten weeks. At first I think Maj. Waverly really did think that someone had put me up to this to pull his leg. But when he saw my dog tags and the very real wound under my bandage, he was convinced.

The major went to a file cabinet and pulled out a manila folder. Leafing through it, he paused and said, "So, you're S.Sgt. James Robert Yoder, right-waist gunner on Lt. Conover's crew?"

"That's right. I'm Jim Yoder, and I'd like to rejoin my old crew. I realize they'll have replaced me with another gunner by now, but if it's at all possible—"

"Sgt. Yoder, there is a strict policy against escaped Allied airmen resuming duties over enemy territory. That's not my decision, and it's not Col. Johnson's either. That's the order handed down to us, and we have to live with it. If you want to stick with the 44th, we can find a ground position for you, but . . ."

"But what?" I asked.

He hesitated. "Hasn't anyone told you?"

"Told me what, sir?"

"Lt. Conover's plane never came back from the raid on Kiel. According to eyewitnesses, shortly after releasing her bombs, the plane went down, and the rest of the crew was eventually reported as captured. You were the only one left unaccounted for, so we have you listed as missing in action. Sergeant, if you hadn't fallen out that bomb-bay door when you did, you would be cooling your heels in a German POW camp this very minute."

Suddenly I realized that my mouth was hanging open.

Even before I turned to God, He was looking out for me. Right from the beginning, the accident that I figured was so terrible was really the best blessing that could have happened.

"Well, I'll be," I said at last. "Well, I'll be."

EPILOGUE

War has a way of changing people, and so it was in the Yoder family. My father—the same postman from a Mennonite background who had vehemently opposed my enlisting—proudly took me around and showed me off to everyone at Jordan Memorial Tabernacle on my first Sunday back in Elkhart. With a smile that outshined the sun, he told everyone who would listen that "the Germans should have known better than to tangle with a Yoder when he's angry!" In 1946, I began receiving letters bearing foreign stamps and return addresses bearing the name "Rostand." Dad would spot these in his mailbag and proudly tell people, "Today Jim received another letter from his European war buddies!"

Of course, I had changed too, even more than my father. I had left Indiana with a chip on my shoulder and a grudge against God. By the time I got back, I was reading every day from the Bible I had bought in a London bookshop. A few Sundays after my return, Pastor invited me to preach a short sermon. I had never liked public speaking, so that first try was clumsy. But this time I had something worth sharing and didn't mind speaking up. Little did I realize that in time I would be doing this weekly as the Sunday school teacher for the sixth-grade boys' class. In the neighboring classroom Margo taught sixth-grade girls.

One thing Dad realized during the war was that he didn't like living alone. With mom gone and me in Europe, our rambling place on Beardsley Avenue made him feel "like a little marble rolling around in a coal scuttle," as he put it. So it was only natural that he should invite Margo and me to come and live with him after the wedding. Since I was only starting out as a mechanic, I wasn't bringing home much money in those early years, and this way Margo and I reaped the benefit of a much better house than we could have afforded on our own.

When little Jimmy Junior was born eighteen months later, it was hard to tell which of the Yoder men was more excited, my father or me. Every time Dad got the chance, he would stop along his mail route and brag about how big his grandson was growing, or what new word Jimmy had learned to say. The morning Jimmy Junior conquered the word "Grandpa" at breakfast, I bet half the population of Elkhart heard about it before nightfall.

While Jimmy was little, Margo stayed home and took care of him herself. On some occasions, though, we asked kindly old Mrs. Scoville next door if she would babysit while Margo and I attended revival meetings at church or went for rides in the country on my motorcycle. While she was babysitting, just as I knew she would, Mrs. Scoville would cuddle our son, talk to him in her native French, and sing him lullabies from the old country.

"Marie," my dad said the first time he heard her doing this, "why are you talking to that child in French? He's never going to use that."

"Don't stop her, Dad," I said. "Maybe he will, and maybe he won't. But you just never know when a foreign language might come in handy!"

I taught Jimmy a few French songs myself, including "En Passant par la Lorraine," which had been my secret signal in the city of Lille.

Not until 1949 did I learn the answer to a question that had bothered me for a long time. One chilly Monday evening in October I came home from Yoder's Car Repair, and Margo met me at the door.

"Do you know somebody named Pierre de la Tour?" she asked.

"Pierre de la Tour?" I shook my head. "Never heard of him. Why?"

"Because you got a letter from him today." She fished the envelope from her apron pocket and handed it to me.

I was baffled until I slit open the envelope and began to read. "It's from Jacques! You know—the one who bicycled with me to the border of Belgium. Jacques was only his cover name in the Resistance. His real name is Pierre."

Jacques—or now, Pierre—had tracked me down with the help of a friend he had made in the Red Cross. In his letter, he recounted how the Germans had arrested him outside the barber's home in Brussels. But not before he relocated Brigitte to his parents' apartment so she could be closer to her new job at the tailor shop. That move was just in time, for she escaped arrest and lived with his parents for the duration of the war. When Jacques finally returned from prison, Brigitte was still there. Romance bloomed, and in 1947 Brigitte became Pierre's bride. I was ecstatic for both of them. Sadly, though, neither Monsieur Rousseau nor his wife survived prison. They had paid the largest possible price for sheltering me. For years afterward I would get a lump in my throat every time I sat in a barber's chair.

When little Jimmy was about four, he began a new game. He would find my black beret—the only one like it in town—and parade around the house with it perched on his head. "Look at me!" he would say, "I'm Papa!" Of course, the beret was too large for him, and it usually slid down over one eye. But Jimmy didn't care. He still liked wearing his father's beret.

One night when Margo and I were tucking Jimmy into bed, he suddenly asked, "Papa, where did you get your special hat?"

Before I could reply, Margo said, "Why, Jimmy, didn't you know? Papa got that hat when he was away at his war."

My war? Millions of people worldwide had taken part in the war, and my role was just a minor one. But that didn't matter to Margo. For Jimmy she always referred to my string of experiences as "Papa's war," and to friends and neighbors she would call it "Jim's war."

At first our acquaintances would chuckle at Margo and her little habit. In time, though, whenever friends recalled something from the war years, they would at first call it "World War II," and then say with a wink, "Oops. I mean 'Jim Yoder's War.'"

That's how it turned out that, for most of the globe, the world's largest conflict is known as World War II, but for one family and some special friends in north central Indiana, it became known as "Yoder's War."

But whatever people called the war, this gunner's run for freedom was over. How I thanked God for bringing me all the way to the place I most wanted to be—*home*.

AUTHOR'S NOTE

The 44th Bombardment Group of the United States Eighth Army Air Force was fondly nicknamed the "Flying Eightballs." This was also the first Bomb Group to receive B-24 Liberators. According to veterans and historians who maintain the Internet website for the 44th, this unit operated from England for a longer period than any other B-24 group, sustained the highest number of aircraft missing in action of 8th Air Force B-24 groups, and claimed more enemy fighters shot down than any other 8th Air Force B-24 group.

During the period when Leon Johnson served as Commanding Officer of the 44th (January 4–September 2, 1943), the unit participated in two missions for which it received Distinguished Unit Citations. The first of those was the mission over Kiel on May 14, 1943, mentioned in this novel. The second was the low-level bombing of the oil refineries in Ploesti, Romania. For the Ploesti mission, the 44th first redeployed to North Africa, and from there it flew with other formations 1,200 miles over the Mediterranean to Ploesti on August 1, 1943—the same day that the fictitious Jim Yoder returned to Shipdham and found Station 115 practically deserted. In Shipdham a monument to the 44th stands in memory of these men and their deeds. For his role in leading one of the formations on the Ploesti raid, Col. Leon Johnson was subsequently promoted to general.

Two incidents mentioned by the barber in Brussels are historical facts. In January 1943 Belgian-born Jean-Michel de Selys Longchamp of the Royal Air Force completed his assigned mission and then proceeded with a personal exploit—an attack on Gestapo headquarters in Brussels. With machine gun and cannon fire from his Typhoon fighter, Selys Longchamp killed four Germans, wounded a dozen others, and shattered glass and bricks across the building's exterior. Because his action was unauthorized, he was demoted in rank—but also received the Distinguished Flying Cross for his gallantry. It is said that his attack lifted the spirits of the entire nation. To this day, the former Gestapo building stands at 453 Avenue Louise, and a plaque on it commemorates the incident, as does a nearby monument. Sadly, Selys Longchamp perished while attempting to land his fighter at the conclusion of a mission in August 1943. The cause of the crash was never determined.

The "bouncing bombs" that breached dams in the Ruhr Valley were also real. Specifically designed by the British for a low-level (60 feet) release over water, these barrel-shaped, spinning bombs skipped along the surface until stopped by the dams on the Moehne and Eder Rivers. The bombs then sank alongside the dams and exploded beneath the surface, thus blowing holes in the dams and flooding the valley.

Closer to home, the Jordan Memorial Tabernacle was an actual church on Second Street in Elkhart, Indiana, for many years. During the 1960s the congregation moved to a larger property on the north side of town and built a new facility renamed Grace Bible Church, which remains an active church. Over the years, various families named Yoder have attended, but to the best of my knowledge, none of them has ever had to evade Nazis by hiding in a pickle barrel.

If any serious errors have crept into the final editing of this book, the author takes full responsibility. I unearthed many interesting facts during my research, but I didn't find answers for every question that arose. Because not all historical details get recorded, they sometimes slip from memories. Where necessary, I filled in the blanks with fiction.

In closing, I would add that I had the option of creating a totally fictitious bomb group and squadron for Jim Yoder, but it was much more satisfying to assign him and the fictional *American Pride* to an actual unit. I admire the men who flew and maintained the bombers of the 44th and other B-24 groups. During a time when the swastika dominated so much of Europe, they did all they could to be the name given to their aircraft—Liberators.

—r.b.